A Tale of Two Sisters

A Tale of Two Sisters

a novel by Adeena Leiber

SAPIR PRESS

JERUSALEM / NEW YORK

Paperback Edition
ISBN 978-1-68025-460-0

Typeset by Eden Chachamtzedek

FELDHEIM PUBLISHERS
POB 43163 / Jerusalem, Israel

208 Airport Executive Park
Nanuet, NY 10954
www.feldheim.com

Distributed in Europe by:
LEHMANNS
+44-0-191-430-0333
info@lehmanns.co.uk
www.lehmanns.co.uk

Distributed in Australia by:
GOLDS WORLD OF JUDAICA
+613 95278775
info@golds.com.au
www.golds.com.au

Printed in USA

For Baba with love

With thanks...

First and foremost, to Hashem, Who has granted me untold *berachah* — including the fulfillment of my dream to publish this book.

To the wonderful people at Feldheim: Deena Nataf for her beautiful acceptance email; Shuli Kabalkin for her copyediting; Eden Chachamtzedek for typesetting; for the graphics, Michael Silverstein; and to Rabbi David Kahn for pulling it all together.

To my office at EUF, for giving me no choice but to write this book: Esther G., who liked every scene except one (I took it out), and Rachel L., my fashion consultant, who took the risk of not reading the book until it was printed.

To my sisters, sisters-in-law, and aunt, whose insightful comments helped fine-tune the characters and plot. To my brothers, who cheered me on and obliged me by fighting over the manuscript. And to Elaina Goldstein, who will mention me in her book one day.

To Zaidy and Baba, Grandpa and Grandma, and Aunt Phyllis who are, and always have been, my biggest fan club. To my husband's grandparents — Zaidy and Bubby, and Zaidy and Grandma — for joining the club later in life.

To my parents, who gave me their writing genes and taught me that I can do anything I put my mind to — thanks for helping perfect the writing in this book.

To my in-laws, who support whatever I do — thanks for staying up until 3:00 AM to finish reading.

To my husband (and children), who graciously lived in my imagination during the course of writing — thanks for listening to me hash out the scenes at every opportunity.

And once again, to my grandmother, without whom this book would truly never have come into being. Baba edited and re-edited and edited again. But most of all, Baba believed in me and never let me give up. Hence, *A Tale of Two Sisters.*

Thank you!
Adeena

Prologue

 "OH, HOW BEAUTIFUL!" MARY cooed. She had been a delivery room nurse for almost fifteen years and still got misty-eyed at the sight of each brand new miracle. "Two little girls... how sweet!"

"I don't want to see them!" cried the mother. "They're not mine! I've given them away — they're up for adoption." She broke down, sobbing.

"Oh! How sad! Are you sure you don't want to see them? Give them a kiss before they go?" Mary bit her lip after she spoke and hoped no one heard her. The adoption regulations were strict, and she did not want to lose her job over a careless sentence.

"No! I never wanted them! Take them away!" She turned her head away. She did *not* want to see them, these babies who were hers and not hers.

Melissa, the nurse from the adoption agency, was there, filling out the necessary paperwork, taking down measurements, assuring that everything would run smoothly. There were couples waiting anxiously for these little girls, and every minute was precious.

As she came to the side of the bed for the signatures, the new mother sat up suddenly. "They're Jewish. Make sure to write that down. Make sure to send them to a Jewish family."

Melissa nodded soothingly. "Of course, that's in your file."

"Show me!" she demanded.

"Right here, hon, there's nothing to worry about," Melissa assured the distraught young woman — *really not much older than a baby herself.* "Just sign here and we'll be good to go."

The new mother sighed. She turned her head as her babies were taken away, and once again burst into tears.

She had never wanted these babies! She was all alone; how could she keep these — *her!* — babies? How could she take care of them? She was too young to have kids weighing her down, stepping on her skirt. She had a whole life to live.

So why did she feel as though she had signed her life away when she affixed her signature on the documents that would take her daughters from her, forever?

*   *   *

Dovid Steinhardt had just shaken hands with the seller and his lawyer when he felt his belt vibrating. He glanced down at his pager and saw that his wife was trying to reach him. They'd set up a system that would let him know if her call was merely routine or an emergency. The number on the screen told him it was an emergency.

Dovid felt himself sweating. Rivky knew where he was and she knew how important this meeting was for him and for Steinhardt Design. It was unlike her to interrupt. But then, it was an emergency. Had something happened to her? Maybe it was about his father. Could he have taken a turn for the worse?

The men who were gathered around the conference table were busy men, impatient to get started. Dovid was buying the property his business was presently occupying, and he needed these men to finalize the deal. They all seemed to be waiting for him to sit down so they could begin.

"Uh, I…" Dovid, usually self-confident and in control, found himself at a loss for words. "May I have a moment to speak to my attorney?" he asked. Michel Keller rose with a question in his eyes and the two walked out of the room. Sruly Morgenstern, Dovid's broker, followed in short order. "What's up?" Keller asked. He did not try to hide his annoyance.

"This is a bit embarrassing, I know, but…" his pager vibrated a second time, "My wife is trying to get through to me," he explained. "It's an emergency. I'm not sure about what. I hope nothing happened to my father."

"What would you like to do?" Sruly wanted to know.

"I guess I'd like to call her and make sure everything's okay…" his voice trailed off in embarrassment.

Sruly looked at him, imploring him not to make them all look like fools. When Dovid did not respond to his silent inquiry, he went back to the conference room. Dovid was shown to a desk and a phone where he could make his call in relative privacy.

"What's up, Rivky? We just sat down."

"Oh, Dovid! The agency just called! They have a baby for us in Chicago if we're there in twenty-four hours."

"Are you serious?" Dovid was breathless. All thoughts of closings, of buildings, of furniture and business left him as he demanded his wife repeat the conversation she had had with the agency — word for word.

"Just come home, Dovid. You can, can't you? I'll call Menachem at the travel agency and he'll put us on a flight. We need to call and confirm, and if we're not there the agency will move on to the next person. It won't take you more than an hour to get home, will it? It's not rush hour. Or should we meet at the airport? At least it's in Chicago. We can get food and stuff there." Rivky was babbling; it was only the second time in the fifteen years of their marriage that Dovid heard his practical wife lose her cool. The first time was when the doctors had told them they should give up trying to have a baby on their own.

"I'll get out of here somehow," he told his wife. "I'll be home in an hour and a half. Call Menachem and we'll go to the airport together." He ended the call and got up to find Sruly. "Sruly, I'm sorry to do this to you, and I hope it won't reflect badly on you. But I can't go ahead with the deal right now. I need to be in Chicago tonight, and my wife is arranging tickets. We just got a call that there is a baby ready for us to adopt!"

It took a second for Sruly to process the news, and then his face widened in a happy grin. "*Mazal Tov*, my friend," he said, pumping Dovid's hand warmly. "*Hatzlachah rabbah*. I'm so happy to be able to share this with you. We'll work it out. Go get your stuff and get outta here."

Dovid flew back to the conference room and met Michel standing outside. "What's going on?" Michel asked, irritated. "You have many impatient people waiting for you in there. Let's hope everything goes smoothly."

"Michel, I can't close now," Dovid said, his eyes shining. "I must run." He told the attorney his news. "I must go. I'll tell them and you'll smooth it over, won't you?" he asked.

"Go, go, we'll take care of it," both Michel and Sruly were urging him onward.

"Gentlemen," Sruly addressed the assembled men. "I'm sorry. I know this is a tremendous inconvenience for you all, but something has just come up, and Mr. Steinhardt has to leave. It's an emergency…"

"A wonderful emergency," Dovid broke in. He wanted to share his *simchah* with the whole world. He had waited so long for this day! "My wife just received a call that there is a baby ready for us to adopt. We have been married for fifteen years and have not been blessed with children. I'm sorry to have dragged you all out here for nothing, but I have less than a day to show up or they'll give the baby to the next person on the list." He turned to Michel, "Michel, Sruly, you'll take care of things, won't you? I know I'm in good hands." He looked back to the group, "Thank you for understanding."

Briefcase in hand, Dovid turned to go but was stopped by the lineup of men who vied to shake his hand and offer congratulations. His obvious happiness had transformed the sharp businessmen of just a few minutes ago into a genial group of proud fathers and grandfathers who were happy to welcome Steinhardt into their club. For the moment, business took second place and as Dovid left the room they were swapping tales of their own children and grandchildren, bragging about their precocity and the joy they brought to their lives. How wonderful, they all agreed, that Steinhardt should now also know that joy.

And three weeks later, when Dovid met with them to finally complete the transaction, he was gratified to be able to join in the conversation. He regaled them with stories of his own, about how cute his baby daughter was and how tired he was from being kept up all night.

*   *   *

They named their little girl Ahuva and, true to her name, she was loved by everyone. Her parents were overwhelmed with joy. She was a princess, of course, and was raised with an abundance of love, but also with carefully set boundaries. This upbringing, together with her naturally sweet nature, ensured that she grew up unaffected rather than spoiled.

She knew she had been long anticipated; her father had even

left *kollel* to find work that would support their quest for children. He had known nothing about furniture when he found a job working for a manufacturer. Dovid had put in long hours, not only doing his job but learning all he could about the furniture business, until he felt confident enough to venture out on his own. He had worked hard; it was necessary that he be successful in order to pay the many debts incurred in their fruitless efforts to have children of their own and to enable them to move towards adoption in the hope of becoming a family.

When she was five years old, Ahuva asked her mother for a new baby. Her mother told her to *daven* to Hashem. At seven, she got tired of waiting and complained that she had *davened* so hard and Hashem wasn't listening. That night her parents sat down with her to explain that she was adopted. She had nightmares of abandonment for about a month afterward, but the unconditional love and warmth she received from her parents meant more to her than the vague pictures of an unknown mother conjured up by her imagination.

When she turned eighteen, Dovid and Rivky Steinhardt made it clear to their daughter that if she would be interested in finding her birth parents, they would stand behind her as they always had in every situation. Ahuva thought about it and reached the conclusion that she knew who she was.

She was Ahuva Steinhardt, the only child of Dovid and Rivky. She was tall and thin and had thick dark hair. Her eyes were bright blue, her cheeks rosy, her nose petite and her lips curved into a perpetual smile. She was a seminary graduate who was about to embark on a teaching career while at the same time taking courses towards her bachelor's degree. When she was finished with that, Ahuva planned to enroll in the local college towards a Master's in Special Education.

Music was Ahuva's love and she played the piano with skill and passion. She enjoyed cooking and baking as well and had an inborn sense of order and neatness. She also had great taste in fashion and in interior design, as befitted the daughter of the Steinhardts. At twenty-one years old, she was idealistic; she wanted to marry someone whose goal in life was to learn Torah and more Torah. She would go to the end of the earth to realize this aspiration. Money would never be her primary goal, but still she would work towards becoming a professional to enable her husband to *shteig* without the worry of *parnassah*. She would *not* rely on her father's success for the attainment of her dreams and the fulfillment of her goals.

Ahuva had the best parents in the world; they helped make her into who she was and stood behind her through every circumstance. What did the woman who had abandoned her have to do with her life?

*   *   *

Rachel Bergmann's parents, Marc and Linda, had waited ten years before acquiring their little princess. Marc had entered his family's real estate investment business immediately after college, and with his sharp mind and keen business sense had expanded Bergmann Holdings to become a premier real estate holder in the Northeast and Midwest.

Money has power, and in the Bergmanns' case the power was used to push their name up the list at the Jewish adoption agency. The result was Rachel.

Rachel was a JAP, but a cute one. She grew up knowing she was beautiful and was taught that there was nothing she couldn't do if she tried hard enough. Rachel was also shown that there was nothing her father's money and status couldn't buy, and hers was a pampered life. Although she was energetic, capable, and far from lazy, she lived for the summers spent at the Bergmanns' summer home on the Jersey Shore where all that was required of her was to have fun in the sun and practice piano at night. She loved music and was becoming an accomplished pianist.

Despite her wealth and status, Rachel matured into a sincere, genuine person — friendly with everyone, though friends with only a few.

The Bergmanns had a strong Jewish identity, and raised their only child in a life centered around the Temple. Marc Bergmann was president of Am Shalom, and Linda was active in the sisterhood. They were proud of their religion and culture and taught their daughter to be the same. Staunchly liberal, while at the same time active and vocal in their concern for the State of Israel, the Bergmanns were satisfied that they had given Rachel a well-rounded upbringing.

Rachel grew up knowing she was adopted, but it meant nothing to her. Once, in the fifth grade, a girl in her class taunted her, "Your mother doesn't love you! She gave you up and didn't care who took care of you!" Marc and Linda calmed their daughter and assured her not to give the girl another thought. "She wishes she could be you. She wishes she could be beautiful like you, and smart and kind. It's easier for her to put you down than to raise herself up." But what about her mother, who did give her up? "She didn't give you to just anyone, did she? She gave you to us. We waited ten years for you, honey."

And Rachel didn't give her tormentor another thought.

But at twenty-one years old, she suddenly became obsessed with finding the woman who had abandoned her.

Chapter 1

"AHUVA STEINHARDT? A GREAT girl. She's smart, pretty, quick, talented, kind, helpful — what more can I say? She's the type who will stop everything and run to help, but seriously. When I broke my foot a couple of years ago, she was here every night helping me with the kids. Her suppers were out of this world! And she entertained them… made bath time fun, you know… the kids just flocked to her… My house was never as spotless again. She's also extremely talented on the piano, and she gives lessons in the community, besides helping out with the Bais Yaakov production every year.

"She's… I guess creative, but practical. Seriously, a girl like Ahuva is one in a million. What I wouldn't do to have her as a daughter-in-law…"

"And her family?"

"The nicest. They raised her you know!" Bracha Schwartz spent the next few minutes extolling their virtues. But it was fun. She hardly ever got *shidduch* calls anymore. She had known the Steinhardts for over ten years, since she moved next door, and had watched Ahuva mature into a lovely young lady.

Miri Friedman hung up the phone and reviewed her notes.

Ahuva seemed to be everything she was looking for in a girl for her only son.

"Shmuely," Miri called her husband as she walked into his study. "I think I am ready to give a yes. Everyone I spoke to had only good things to say."

"And everything you were nervous about?"

"I thought we discussed it. I *was* nervous because Mr. Steinhardt is in business. But they say that he is a *talmid chacham* and very *makpid* on his *sedarim*."

"I wonder who told you *that*," Shmuely said, grinning. He was the one who had found out about the family and had pushed Miri to go ahead with her inquiries into the young lady, even though she was adopted.

"Anyway," Miri ignored the interruption, "her grandfather was Rabbi Miller. I told you, my friend Rivky was always *machshiv* Torah. Her father and brothers were always held in such high esteem in that house... You know why Steinhardt went to work. It's not his fault he was successful."

"Well, as long as he is in business, he might as well be successful. I'd rather he was successful in business than not, wouldn't you?"

"Stop!" But she smiled as she said it; she always enjoyed his teasing. "Everyone I spoke to had only the nicest things to say about her. Her *chesed* and her kindness and sensitivity." She ticked the girl's virtues off on her fingers. "And she sounds practical, and *geshikt*. But — I *am* nervous, because she is an only child. I don't want a spoiled brat for Moshe."

"That's not really fair, you know," Shmuely's tone was serious now. "Being an only child doesn't make one spoiled, and a brat, and insensitive and selfish..."

"True, but one needs to spend a lifetime working on *middos*. If sensitivity is not cultivated, it is easy to become selfish. Like that other girl that was *redt* to us… ugh." Miri shook her head. "I would not want *her* as a daughter-in-law. What awful *middos*! And *her* parents have no excuse for bringing her up so poorly. *They* didn't wait fifteen years for children and then adopt."

"So…"

But Miri wasn't finished. "The only thing I want to know is why she isn't married yet."

"What?"

"I mean, if she's as beautiful and wonderful as they say she is — and I'm not doubting it — and she has money, and her family is quite respectable, then why is she twenty-one years old and still around?"

"Miri, don't talk like that. Maybe she hasn't found the right one yet. How would you have felt if someone had said the same thing about Blimi? She didn't get married until she was twenty-three. And she is pretty and smart and quite successful herself, I might add."

"Yes, but we don't have the kind of money the Steinhardts have. Who am I kidding, Shmuely? We don't have any money period. It's no wonder *shidduchim* came harder for Blimi. A girl like this — only child, wealthy parents, and a father who knows how to learn — I would have expected her married at eighteen! Except she *is* adopted. That's probably the reason."

"Miri, we went through this a million times and we spoke to the Rav about it."

"I know, but still, it feels weird. I am *sure* that's what it is, and I wonder if perhaps we're making a mistake even considering it. I mean, if other people wouldn't take her…"

Shmuely did not like the tack the conversation was taking. "How do you know she didn't have boys knocking down the doors and just didn't want to marry any of them?" he countered. "Or maybe, in addition to everything you said about them, the Steinhardts are also sensible and didn't want their daughter married while she was still an infant?" Shmuely smiled. Miri had expressed her feelings on "girls who get married out of the nursery" often enough for him to know this statement would hit home. While Shmuely fully agreed with this sentiment and wanted his daughters to have earned some money before flying the nest, he had his suspicions about the origin of Miri's mind-set against early marriages and wasn't entirely sure she hadn't built it as a defense. The fact was that *shidduchim* had not come easily to the Friedman home, and none of the Friedman girls had even dated before their twentieth birthday.

Miri didn't respond to Shmuely's bait and continued as though he hadn't said anything. "Besides, I *know* Rivky Miller," she went back to the previous conversation. "I told you, she was always sensitive and kind." Miri stopped to take a breath, and then said, "I'd like to meet her."

Shmuely smiled to himself. Miri would never admit to being wrong, but he knew that she had gotten the message because she changed the subject.

"Who? The former Miss Miller or the current Miss Steinhardt?"

"Shmuely, will you quit it?"

"But she's Rivky Miller's daughter. And you know Rivky. You practically know the young lady in question already. Why do you need to meet her?"

"Shmuely, you are impossible!"

*   *   *

At twenty-one years old, Rachel Bergmann was in college

pursuing a degree in music therapy. Her dream was actually to be just like her mother and stay home with the kids. But twenty-one years old is too young to be married with children and so Rachel, by nature energetic and loving both children and music, channeled her talents in that direction. Already doing fieldwork, she had begun to earn a name for herself.

One day in mid-January of her senior year, as Rachel was sitting cross-legged on her bed studying, her friend, Beth Schwartz, walked into the room. "Rachel, check this out," she said as she thrust a paper into her hands. "You're coming with me."

"I'm what? What is this?" she scanned the flyer. *Finding the Real You,* the headlines blared, announcing an inaugural lecture given at the Hillel by Rabbi Hoffman of Journeys/Pathways to Judaism. "What in the world? I don't have time for lectures, I'm writing a term paper."

"Rach, listen. Daren got himself on this committee somehow, and I promised I'd help him find some people to attend this lecture. You have to come. I've already roped Susan Lankry into this, and I think she is going to bring Christina."

"Christina? But she isn't Jewish."

"I know. We told her to pick a new name." Beth giggled. "What am I supposed to do? You have to help me, Rachel. It's only one night. I promised Daren, and I… " she trailed off.

"Okay, I'll come. But I don't know where you picked Daren up. Or where he picked up these crazy ideas. I don't need Pathways to my Judaism. For goodness sake, my dad's the president of the Temple! And *Finding the Real You*? I'm right here, thanks."

"Come on, Rachel. If anyone needs to go to this lecture, it's you. You know you've been a mess since you broke off with Brad."

It was true. Rachel had taken Brad's goodbye very hard. Being the dumped instead of the dumper in a relationship was misery enough, but Rachel had been together with Brad for three years, and when he left her it awakened feelings of abandonment that she had not had since fifth grade.

Rachel did not tell anyone about her new obsession with finding her birth mother. She did not want to hurt the parents who loved her and raised her, and so she had not taken any steps to find the woman who had given her away. But that woman was constantly in her thoughts. In Rachel's mind every woman she met, from a college professor to a supermarket cashier, was potentially the woman who had given birth to her.

"I'll go, but only to be nice to you, Beth. This has nothing to do with Brad. But I'll come."

Beth smiled knowingly.

*   *   *

Tuesday at 8:00 PM found Rachel, Susan, Beth, and some other recruits sitting in the Hillel lecture hall. Daren thanked the group for taking time out of their busy schedules to come and assured them they wouldn't regret it. The door in the back of the room opened to let in a group of students in *kippot*, talking and laughing. As Daren went over to them, Rachel elbowed Beth. "He's certainly got a way about him… Reminds me of my dad… Assuring us we would be happy we came!" She laughed. "Only thing he is missing is that *kippah*. Think one of those guys in the back will lend him one?"

Beth beamed. Susan turned around to look and exclaimed, "Check out that guy who just walked in. Look," she gestured towards a tall boy who had just become Daren's next victim. "Beth, get me introduced to him!"

After the lecture Susan got her wish. The tall boy sauntered over. "Hi, I'm Ian." But Susan, never at her best with strangers, blushed pink and began to stammer her replies. It was Rachel who answered with her usual composure. "I'm Rachel Bergmann and this is Susan Lankry."

Ian Tawil was in his third year in medical school and had already starting sending his transcripts and resume to hospitals. Medicine was a tough field and left him little time for socializing, but his mother would have none of that. She wanted to know why he never talked about any nice Jewish girls, so Ian had come to the Hillel tonight in order to meet some. As he left with Rachel, he said grinning that now at least he could get his mom off his back.

Looking after them, Susan remarked to Beth, "Okay, that's a couple. Her dad will support them while he is finishing his internship and residency, and Rachel will live her dream life, dividing her time between her kids and her therapy." Her voice held a tinge of jealousy.

"She always lives her dream life," was Beth's flippant reply. "You don't know her as long as I do, but Rachel always gets what she wants sooner or later. And you don't know Mr. Bergmann either. He will cross-examine that boy a thousand times over to make sure he is right for his princess, that he'll be good to her and whatever." Her tone was light, matter-of-fact. She did not begrudge Rachel any happiness; her own father would do the same. "And don't think that he will support them without first being sure that his Rachel's future husband is very able to support his wife and children in style. Only then will he agree to give away his daughter, and when he does, it will also be in style."

Chapter 2

"SHE WANTS TO WHAT?" Ahuva looked up from her soup. "Abba, that is not normal. I mean, I've gone out with other boys, and the only mother I met was Kornbluth, and I met her when I met him. No. Mommy, help me," she turned to her mother, pleading. "I am so not meeting a mother. What does she want to see, that I don't have two heads? I mean, she just did two weeks of research. Doesn't she trust her son?"

"Ahuva…"

"Didn't you say he is the only boy in the family? He's probably still tied to Mommy's apron strings. Thanks, but no thanks."

"Ahuva, this is the Friedman boy," Dovid Steinhardt appealed to his daughter. "He's the top catch this *z'man*. We knew she would be picky; she may as well be. And you're right, he is their only boy."

"Right, but Abba, there is a limit. I mean, I will be marrying the boy, not his mother! And if they are committing to going out anyway, what in the world is the point of this meeting? I mean, just me and her, alone? Let mommy tag along with baby on the date."

Rivky Steinhardt smiled at her daughter's choice of words, cynical though they may have been. "Honey, you don't really mean that, but I'll tell you what. Why don't we agree to meet Mrs. Friedman on condition that we will be able to back out?" She looked at her husband for confirmation. "That way, if she really is this overbearing mother-in-law who can't bear to part with her son, you won't be forced into anything. But it's Miri Weiss. I remember her as being quite normal."

"What would you accomplish by making this condition? It would just give the impression that you want to have the upper hand." Dovid didn't like the idea. "What's the point?" He turned to Ahuva. "You'll meet the parents without any *tenai'im* and you'll go out with the young man. And if you can't stand his mother, you'll say no after the first date. I don't think it is right to play control games here. Okay, so the mother is asking something a bit ridiculous. So it's a boy's market out there. So what? What will you accomplish by giving yourself the chance to back out?"

"I won't have to get dressed twice. And I won't be out for two nights."

"Ahuva, please. One is supposed to do *hishtadlus* in *shidduchim*. So you'll get dressed twice in the name of *hishtadlus*. The Friedmans obviously feel that this is what they should be doing to ensure their son gets the right girl… So we don't agree. But guess what, Huvs? You'll never agree with everyone all the time in life. Maybe this is a good preparation for marriage. Learn to give in."

Privately, though, Dovid did think the request was unreasonable and was inclined to share his daughter's views about this Moshe Friedman being tied to Mommy's apron.

"Everyone I spoke to," he said to Rivky later that night, "including his Rosh Yeshiva, said that he is bright, articulate and, above all, mature. And Avromi Lichtenstein told me that it is a very normal family. He did a *shidduch* with them. But I don't know. I don't want Ahuva to have a controlling mother-in-law. Girls are supposed to consult with their mother, so that would not seem controlling. They say he is not the type to run into mama's arm every time someone looks at him the wrong way, but if she will stick her nose into the marriage and family..."

"Dovid, I think you are getting ahead of yourself." Rivky answered. "As you told Ahuva earlier, let's take it as it comes. They'll meet and we'll see what happens. We'll both be there at the meeting, and if the mother seems to be... whatever... we'll deal with it then."

*   *   *

"Shmuely, this is the address. Park here."

The Friedmans got out of the car and were immediately attacked by the cold. Miri shivered and pulled her coat tighter. Nice house, she noted. The Steinhardts lived in an impressive Victorian with no lack of property, it seemed. Even in the winter the landscaping was attractive and no doubt bloomed in full color come spring and summer. *Well,* Miri reasoned, *as Shmuely said, once you are successful, you may as well be successful.* She hoped the people inside were just as nice as the house. Shmuely's jokes aside, she hadn't really been in touch with Rivky Miller in almost forty years, and as she told her husband, many, many things can happen in forty years.

The Friedmans stopped halfway up the path. There was music breathing out of the house into the cold air. "I heard she is great at the piano," Miri murmured. They stood there mesmerized, until the music stopped abruptly.

*   *   *

Ahuva sat at the piano, filling the house with her music. She was waiting to meet the Friedmans — without the *bachur* — and was understandably a bit nervous. She peered out the window and noticed a car parked outside. "Mommy, I think they're here," she called as she got off the bench and went to sit on the couch. She was not interested in playing for *this* audience.

The doorbell rang and Rivky went to answer it. "Hello, come in," she said, her demeanor no more than polite. Though she had given in to Dovid, she still was miffed that they were coming to interview Ahuva. Moshe might be the Friedmans' only son, but Ahuva was her only child.

"Rivky!" Miri was enthusiastic in her greeting. "How are you? You have not changed a bit!"

Rivky smiled back and said, "I'll take that as a compliment." As they stood in the hall reminiscing, Dovid came to the door. "Let me take your coat," he said to Shmuely Friedman. "Thank you," Shmuely smiled, relieved. He had felt awkward, silently watching the two ladies converse.

Rivky stepped back. "Oh, I'm sorry! Here, Miri, give me your coat and come into the dining room. Can I get you something to drink?" she asked, addressing both of them. "Coffee? Or something cold?"

She went into the kitchen to fill the orders and beckoned to Ahuva to come help her. Miri Friedman's first glimpse of the young lady came as she brought a steaming cup of coffee to Rabbi Friedman, and she was immediately impressed. Ahuva stood poised and confident, her back straight. She handed the drinks to her guests, then made her way to the other side of the table and sat down.

There were pastries on the table, and a bowl of fruit in the center. It was ordinary winter fruit, Miri noted. She was disappointed there was nothing more exotic, fruit flown in from the tropics, perhaps. That would have been more in keeping with the soft undercurrents of wealth that permeated the home.

She turned her attention to the coffee in front of her and took a sip. "Perfect for a day like today. Thank you, Rivky. Tell me, what's going on? Are you in touch with any of the girls? You know that Chayala Rosen's oldest child just made a *chasunah*? The girl is not a day older than nineteen. Runs in the family, I guess. Chayala herself got married in twelfth grade, remember? And her daughter was also married young. I still keep up with her, you know." *As though,* Ahuva thought, *it was an accomplishment that she was still friends with girls from her high school class.*

As the former classmates talked, Ahuva berated herself. *For goodness sake, what else should they discuss? At least they have something in common to break the ice. I am sure she will show a different side when it is time to talk to me.* She sat at the table with her hands in her lap. No napkin-shredding display of nerves for Ahuva, Miri noted with satisfaction. She deftly turned the conversation to the girl across from her.

"So, what subjects do you teach?"

"I teach tenth grade *Chumash* in Bais Yaakov." The answer came swiftly, no stammering or fumbling. The voice was sweet and clear and, above all, confident.

"Do they usually give *Chumash* to such a young woman?"

"No. I started out teaching on the remedial level, but the tenth grade teacher became sick and the administration was stuck. So I filled in, and they hired me." Ahuva maintained eye contact with both Mrs. and Rabbi Friedman. The latter had been speaking quietly with Dovid Steinhardt, and their conversation ended as the discussion turned towards Ahuva.

"How many periods a day is that?"

"I teach twelve periods a week so each day is different. But my school day is over at 12:30." Ahuva went on to describe her week.

She was in school working towards a Master's degree in special-ed. "I'm doing fieldwork now, in a special school in the afternoon, and I have night school twice a week this semester." Ahuva explained, "My real love is teaching *Chumash*. But I am under no illusions, and I know that it is very hard to get a job. If I have a degree, it will be easier for me to look outside the box."

Ahuva did not speak like someone who was the only child of a wealthy businessman, and Miri could not help but be impressed. She proudly interjected that both she and her children understood what it meant to work hard to support Torah. All of the Friedman girls were supporting husbands in *kollel* or *chinuch* and none worked harder, Miri said, than her daughter Avigail. Ahuva smiled politely, uncertain of what was meant by the interjection and unsure of how to proceed. Was Mrs. Friedman simply showing off or was she trying to tell Ahuva something?

Rivky noted her daughter's hesitation — indeed, she herself was not sure what Miri wanted — and veered the conversation back on track. "Yes, and on those nights when Ahuva doesn't have school, she gives piano lessons. She also volunteers for Bikur Cholim when she has time."

Dovid laughed. "When she has time. Ahuva has no time. But she still is there at least one night a week and delivers suppers for Chai Lifeline every Sunday." There was pride in his voice, and rightfully so. Rivky beamed.

"You sound very busy," Rabbi Friedman noted.

"I like to keep busy. And I have the time now; I want to get it all in. I may as well do what I can now, before I have a husband and children to take care of. Right now my time is my own, and I want to use it wisely."

The visit lasted another twenty minutes. Ahuva maintained her calm throughout. She was composed and spoke with dignity. She did not turn towards her parents for confirmation of each thing she said, which Miri had seen other girls do, and at the same time, she did not dominate the conversation but let her parents take over where appropriate.

*   *   *

"That wasn't so bad, was it, Ahuva?" Dovid asked after the Friedmans had left. There was concern in his face.

"No, I had fun actually," Ahuva said. "You could see the mother's brain churning. Too bad she had already agreed to the date when she asked to meet me. If he is anything like her, I'd stop right now."

The *shadchan* called that night. "They were very impressed, Mrs. Steinhardt. Ahuva made a really nice impression. They would like to schedule. How does Wednesday night sound to you?"

"Tomorrow?"

"No, next week. The 'freezer' doesn't officially open until then — you know, when the *yeshiva* will let him begin to go out on dates — so the *bachur* wants to wait."

"Sounds good, thank you."

"Great, we'll be in touch."

Chapter 3

"BARUCH?"

Startled, Baruch looked up and absently nodded his thanks for the tea and cookies his wife placed at his elbow. "Baruch?" Avigail asked again, hesitant. "Can we talk for a few minutes?"

"Uh, now? I'm in the middle of something here…" He looked at his wife's face and broke off. "Of course." His finger held the place in his *gemara,* and he turned his attention to Avigail.

Still hesitant, Avigail motioned to her husband to eat a cookie. "Your tea will be cold." The words sounded stilted, and Baruch, anticipating Avigail's next words, sighed inwardly as he prepared his usual response. He closed his *sefer* and bit into a cookie. "Thank you," he said, and looked encouragingly at his wife. "What's the matter?"

"I can't do it anymore, Baruch. I really can't."

There was no need to explain; they had had this conversation many times in the past. Avigail valued the *zechus* she merited as the *ezer kenegdo* enabling her husband to become a true *talmid chacham,* but sometimes the difficulties she had to deal with overwhelmed her. Baruch would give his wife *chizuk,* reminding her that her hard work was building a beautiful palace for her in *Gan Eden*. Avigail always came through in the end; it was her dream to allow her husband to learn, and she would do whatever was necessary to make the dream come true.

Twice in the past fifteen years of their marriage, Avigail had brought up the issue in a manner that was more than a grumble. Both times, Baruch had asked a *she'eilah* of his Rosh Yeshiva. Five years ago, the issue had been money. Money was always tight, but wasn't that a natural part of *kollel* life? It helped that neither he nor Avigail came from affluent homes and that both of them were used to living with less. But Avigail was concerned that the children were feeling deprived.

The Rosh Yeshiva had given them a *berachah* for *hatzlachah* with the children, and reinforced the idea that there was nothing comparable to being *mistapek b'muat*.

Three years ago, Avigail had told Baruch that it was just too hard; the children were not only being deprived of *things,* but of *her.* She was missing too many *siddur* plays and *Chumash* parties. At that time the Rosh Yeshiva had asked to speak to Avigail herself. The meeting had been private, and Baruch never knew what had been discussed. But nothing changed, as far as he could see. He still went everyday to the *beis midrash,* and she to the office.

Baruch knew that Avigail had a hard schedule. She left the house before 9:00 AM and worked an eight-hour day. When she came home, she dealt with their children. She served them supper, did homework with them, and got them ready for bed. The house always sparkled by the time Baruch came home from second *seder.* The younger children were sleeping, his supper was hot, and Avigail was smiling. Afterwards she would be up all night preparing lunches, doing laundry and whatever else it is that women do. Baruch felt he valued every bit of it. He encouraged her and bought her small gifts to show his appreciation. He helped out with the children when he was home and did the weekly grocery shopping.

Money was still tight, but they had made peace with that, hadn't they? And in the past three years the children had grown up and were able to help Avigail, especially Malka. What had happened?

"I — I..." Baruch stopped, unsure of how to go on. Suddenly the words he had used in the past seemed so tactless: telling her that she was a wonder woman, that he understood how hard it was for her, that he appreciated all she did, that she not be so hard on herself, that she take a break. What kind of break? Don't make supper? What would they eat? Let the laundry pile up? What would they wear? Have Malka help more? She already helped more — more than any child her age could be expected to help. This very question had been the topic of many a discussion between Baruch and Avigail. They believed that children should be taught to help, but they didn't want Malka to feel as though her parents placed their burdens on her shoulders.

"It's different now, Baruch," Avigail said. She did not look at her husband. Instead she stared at a corner of the room, apparently fascinated, and Baruch recognized the signs. She was trying not to cry. "I'm becoming a bad mother. No, let me finish.

"It was different when the kids were young. But now Malka is becoming a teenager and I'm thrusting more and more responsibility on her. It's just not right. She's not the mother. Why should she be the one to pick the children up from the babysitter? And help with homework? And with baths and bed? And supper? As the children get older, yes they can help, but everything becomes so much more of a deal. I can't rely on just serving scrambled eggs anymore when I'm too tired to make supper. The kids' homework only gets harder, and Malka has her own homework to do. She hates doing laundry, and really, I don't blame her. My mother never asked me to wash dirty socks. That's what *mothers* do.

"I feel like I am not allowing her to be a child, Baruch. There's so much she has to do at home she never has time to play. When was the last time she went to a friend?"

Avigail took a deep breath, and swiped at her eyes with an angry motion. "I feel that because I work I'm not allowing her any normal fun. And I don't want her to resent it. I got a note from her teacher, and I spoke to her earlier on the phone. Malka has been neglecting homework and her excuse is always that she's helping at home. The teacher said she'll accept that every once in a while. She understands that mothers need help at home and sometimes it has to take precedence over homework. But she said Malka uses that excuse constantly and she feels enough is enough. She told Malka she would have to penalize her for any more missed work. I told the teacher it wasn't an excuse. It was true. I work hard and Malka is my right hand. I told her I'll make sure she does her schoolwork but that she really shouldn't punish her. It's not her fault." A tear escaped Avigail's eye, and made its unseemly way down her left cheek. Avigail swiped again with the back of her hand, and it came away black with running mascara.

"Homework is a separate issue, and whether or not we agree with it, it's here to stay. I… I don't want…" she stopped, unable to continue, and Baruch knew that finally they were coming to the crux of the matter. He took a long gulp of the tea, fortifying himself for what was coming, and looked at his wife.

"You know it was always my dream to have a Torah home. And I wanted my husband to sit and learn forever. I still do." The tears tumbled down, falling over each other in a race down her cheeks. "But I don't want our children to come to resent it, Baruch. I don't want Malka to react to the way we live by deciding that when she gets married *she* won't work and burden her children with responsibilities that are not theirs. I overheard her talking yesterday to a friend, and while she didn't say exactly that…" Avigail broke off again. She put her head down between her hands on the table. Her voice, when she spoke between her tears, was muffled. "She was explaining to her friend that she couldn't come over because she needs to watch the kids and make sure they don't turn the house upside down before her mother comes home. And after, she helps with supper, and…" She sat up suddenly, "You get the point."

Baruch sighed. "I'll talk to Reb Shua."

Chapter 4

"HEY, BETH, CHECK THIS out!" It was after another of the Pathways lectures that Beth had persuaded Rachel to attend. She didn't attend them all — that would be a bit too much for the daughter of the president of Am Shalom. "A Presidents' Day Weekend Retreat. Let's go."

Beth scanned the flyer. Journeys was hosting a weekend retreat in Connecticut which offered a variety of lectures and afforded participants the opportunity to learn more about Judaism. "Rachel, you're joking."

"No, I'm not. Look at the hotel it's being hosted in. We'll have a blast!"

Rabbi Hoffman of Pathways joined them. "There is a student discount, you know. You can join the seminar for a third off the listed price. It really is enjoyable and informative." Rabbi Hoffman went on to explain the program. "Journeys' top speakers will be there. They speak on a variety of topics ranging from proving the validity of the Torah to raising a Jewish family in today's times. The catering is superb. They've booked a recently renovated DoubleTree, so you'll be staying in beautiful accommodations."

"Will you be there?"

"No, I am afraid not. I do go to some of them, but this time it won't work out."

"What's involved? Do they make sure you are at every lecture?" Rachel wanted to know.

"Of course not. Journeys never takes attendance. You can come to every lecture or none at all. The hotel is situated on beautiful grounds; if a lecture topic doesn't appeal to you, you are free to explore or do anything you'd like." He stopped short of telling them to bring along their swim suits. Although Journeys would not stop a participant from using the hotel's pool, he was certainly not going to recommend it.

"But if I were you," he told them, "I would not want to miss anything. I have been to many seminars, and I am amazed anew each time I attend. The topics get better and better, and the speakers are truly incredible. Think about it and let me know. They need a count by the end of next week."

*   *   *

"Faigy?" As all good teachers do, Ahuva called on the student who had slept through half the lesson, and waited with ill-concealed impatience as her student lifted her head.

"Can you repeat the question?"

She could not. "Will you see me after class?" Some of the girls in the class tittered, and Ahuva shook her head. She felt torn; she had always hated when teachers picked on students and made them look like fools. On the other hand, Faigy's first few months in school had shown her to be a promising student, and she had been on her way to becoming Ahuva's prize pupil. However, over the past two weeks, Ahuva had seen first subtle, and then drastic, changes in Faigy's school work and class participation. She had tried to speak with her student but received a cold shoulder. She hoped today's talk would end differently.

In her effort to shake off the sense of guilt she felt at her treatment of Faigy, Ahuva threw herself into the lesson and kept the class on its toes as they navigated a difficult *Rashi*.

After the bell rang and the class filed out for lunch, Ahuva walked over to Faigy's desk.

"What's up?" she asked conversationally. Faigy stared straight ahead.

"Come on, Faigy. What happened in the past month that turned you from a such peppy teen into a morose adolescent?" No answer.

Ahuva took a deep breath. Obviously, she was not to be the confidante in this interplay. "Okay," she said briskly. "You don't want to tell me, and I understand that and respect your desire for privacy. In that case, though, I cannot make any allowances for you, and I expect you to perform at the same level you used to. I want class participation; I want homework done; I want 100 on tests. Got it?"

"What will you do to me if I don't participate?" Faigy asked derisively.

Whew! Finally! Faigy's response opened the way for Ahuva to connect with her student.

"That is a good question, you know, and hopefully we will never need to know the answer. Faigy, I care about you and I'm here to help you. If you'd rather speak to someone else, that's fine. I can put you in touch with the guidance counselor if you want. Would you rather I spoke to your parents?"

"As though my parents care!" Faigy burst out, and then, as if realizing that she had broken her vow of silence, she put her hand to her mouth, stricken.

"Faigy, what's the matter?" Ahuva's heart went out to the younger girl. She could never imagine a situation where she would entertain thoughts of her parents not caring.

"Nothing."

"Faigy, you can't say something like that and then say it's nothing. What's the matter? Is everyone okay in your family?" Ahuva thought desperately back to the students' synopses she received at the beginning of the year. Under each girl's name there was some family background and any special conditions the teachers needed to know: Was a parent or sibling sick? Was the student on the remedial track? Was she new to the school? She could not remember anything out of the ordinary on Faigy's report.

"Everything's fine," Faigy answered shortly. "Just dandy." She burst into tears as she said it but resisted all Ahuva's efforts to draw her back out of her shell.

Ahuva finally admitted defeat, but she promised herself that she would see this through. Yet how would she go about that? On the one hand, she did respect Faigy's need for privacy; on the other hand, Faigy was such a promising student, and it hurt Ahuva to see her break down like this.

And if she was to be completely honest with herself, Ahuva *was* a bit curious about what was going on.

*   *   *

"Shmuely, Rabbi Lazarus called earlier. He wanted to confirm that you're speaking at the Journeys Seminar next week." At the question on Shmuely's face, Miri continued, "Apparently you told him to get back to you."

"What did you say?"

"I said yes, why not? We were planning to go, weren't we?"

"What about Moshe?"

"What about him?"

"What about him? Miri, have you forgotten about a certain young lady named Miss Steinhardt? And a Wednesday night meeting between your son and said girl?"

"Shmuely, I wish you would be serious! I am not sure what Moshe's date has to do with the Journeys Shabbos."

"Only that I wasn't sure if you'd want him home for Shabbos. You know, to talk it over… I thought we'd probably invite all the girls so you can discuss the color scheme of the wedding."

"Shmuely Friedman, you are the most impossible man I have ever met, do you know that?"

"Well, I seem to recall your mentioning it once or twice in the past thirty-five years."

"Shmuely, be serious! He'll come home next week, after they've been out two or three times. Planning the color scheme is a bit premature after one date…"

"True, and you know, I just thought of something. Who will get to choose this time? I mean, I can't see Moshe really caring too much if you wear pink or yellow."

Miri threw her husband a dirty look, but there was laughter in her eyes. "He'll come the week after. You have not spoken at Journeys in a while, and especially now, if we're planning a wedding, I think it is a good idea. We could use the extra…"

"Okay, okay. Does he want me to call back or are we set?"

*   *   *

It didn't take Rachel long to have Beth convinced. Susan Lankry and another girl, Sarah Kessler, decided to join. "Why not, it's a weekend off, and the price is good for the DoubleTree. I checked out the hotel online yesterday; it is stunning. And the pools! Indoor *and* outdoor! Do you think we should wait till the summer?" Rachel said.

"Nope, I can't wait that long," Susan responded. "I need a vacation now."

Rabbi Hoffman was delighted to have four students to send to the seminar. "I'm sure you will learn a lot and have a great time," he told them. "Let me know how it goes."

"Just don't tell my parents!" Rachel laughed. "My dad would shoot me if he knew I was going to an Orthodox seminar."

"What's the big deal," Susan wanted to know. "It's not like you are going to turn Orthodox from one weekend."

"Certainly not, but you don't know my dad. He is irrational about the Orthodox sometimes."

"You know anyone Orthodox?" Susan asked.

"No."

"Well, my cousins are religious. Like Rabbi Hoffman. And they are very nice. Not that I plan on turning Orthodox or anything," Susan was quick to disclaim, "but…"

"But what will you tell your mom?" Beth wanted to know. No one knew as well as she that Rachel and her mother kept no secrets.

"Oh, anything. I'm twenty-one years old. If I want to go to a hotel for the weekend, I can."

"With daddy's piece of plastic," Sarah Kessler opened her mouth for the first time.

Rachel smiled. "My dad's very generous. And he would never shoot me, you know; he loves me too much. I think I *will* come home Orthodox just to see what would happen." Her tone was light and she spoke simply, confident in what she was saying, secure in her parents' love and the fact that they would stand behind whatever she did.

Whatever she did. That is what was keeping her from trying to find her birth mother. She had never kept a secret from her mother, but she could not tell her parents about her yearning to meet this unknown woman who had given birth to her and then given her away. It would be like slapping them in the face. Even her budding relationship with Ian could not suppress her thoughts of the woman who abandoned her.

Chapter 5

MIRI STEPPED OUT OF the elevator into the lobby of the DoubleTree. She was on her way to the tea room to pick up some pastries for her room. "Moshe," she said into her cell phone, "I just spoke to the *shadchan*. The girl had a nice time, too… She said 7:30 on Sunday night, okay… Have a good Shabbos. I have to run."

Miri looked up and was surprised to see Ahuva Steinhardt signing in at the front desk. *That's cute,* Miri thought. She decided to use the other entrance to the tea room. No doubt Ahuva would be embarrassed to see the parents of the boy she was dating at the seminar. Miri wondered what she was doing there. She thought back to their meeting. Did Ahuva say anything about Journeys? Was she involved in Pathway Partners? Although registration was usually restricted to secular Americans, sometimes the *frum* partners were invited to the seminars to meet their non-religious partner.

She turned to catch a better glimpse of the girl and almost cried aloud in shock. Forgetting the pastries, Miri turned on her heel and ran back up to her room. She bypassed the elevator which was too slow for a crisis like this.

Shmuely," she said as she burst into their hotel room. "You'll never believe who I just saw."

Shmuely waited patiently for the name of the person his wife had seen. He was sure that sooner or later, it would be revealed. It was not long in coming.

"Ahuva Steinhardt." The name came out in a shudder. "She is downstairs in the lobby."

Shmuely laughed, having completely missed the significance of the shudder. "Miri, this is even better than spending Shabbos with Moshe! Now you can hear from both sides! Maybe ask *her* what color she wants the dresses to be? I mean, it's now after the first date, not before it, and we know that the young couple had a nice time, so…"

"Shmuely, this is not a time for jokes. If you would have seen her, you would not talk like that. She is downstairs in the lobby with a group of girls who I would not have thought…" She broke off, unable to continue.

"Miri, calm down. Maybe the estimable Miss Steinhardt is a volunteer for Journeys in addition to her other worthy accomplishments."

"She is no volunteer."

"Okay, maybe she works for them. That can't be so bad seeing that I do so myself."

"Shmuely, if you would stop interrupting and listen to me for a minute…" Miri shuddered again.

"Sounds drastic." After thirty-five years, Shmuely was immune to his wife's dramatics.

"Shmuely! Go down and check it out for yourself. I am calling the *shadchan* right now. She was there with a group of girls — college kids! Dressed in jeans and a sweatshirt. She is not the girl we want for our son." Miri ended on a definitive note. "We were told such nice things about her. And she seemed so fine when we met her… I can't believe it."

"I can't believe it either. There must be some mistake. Do not call the *shadchan*." Miri put the phone down at her husband's words. "There is no reason to call now; we'll call after Shabbos if this girl is really Miss Steinhardt."

"You don't believe me?"

"I believe that you saw someone who looks like her, but I can't believe it really is her. I'd like to see for myself. The whole thing just does not make sense. Look, Shabbos is in about an hour. I'd like to have a chance to learn a bit. Why don't you get ready now, and we'll deal with this later. There is nothing to do now anyway. I don't want to disturb anyone an hour before Shabbos, and I want to see for myself."

Shmuely turned around suddenly and asked, "What did she do when you saw her?"

"Nothing. She didn't see me." Miri sounded defeated. "I was walking into the tea room and she was standing across the lobby." She saw Shmuely looking at her out of the corner of his eye, grinning. "I am able to see perfectly well, thank you. I need glasses for reading, not seeing distances," she said defensively.

Shmuely said nothing, but the smirk did not leave his face.

*   *   *

Friday night offered Shmuely no glimpse of the girl in question. Miri saw her briefly during the *seuda*, but the Friedmans were sitting at a table with other guests and Miri was not able to speak privately with her husband. After the meal, Shmuely got up to give his first class and Miri, good wife that she was, went to sit in on the lecture. Ahuva did not come.

*   *   *

"Hey, Rachel, this *is* a nice place. Did you see the gym?" Beth asked. They were in their hotel room getting ready for the Friday night services which would begin in a little less than an hour.

Beth, chic in a pink woolen dress, was at the mirror putting the finishing touches on her makeup. Rachel's dress was a light blue Oscar de la Renta cashmere-knit that ended about one inch above her knee. She pulled a black belt around her waist and completed the outfit with opaque tights and patent pumps.

"I keep gravitating toward that pool. Let's go swimming tonight."

"What about…" Beth gestured with her hair brush toward the Journeys pamphlet on her bed.

"We'll go swimming after the meal tonight. Seems to me that there are plenty of lectures tomorrow and Saturday night; I'm sure nothing will happen if we skip tonight's program."

"Well, I think I'd like to go. There is one speech that sounds interesting. It's called 'Age-old Judaism in a New-Fangled Generation.' Someone named Rabbi Morgenstern is speaking."

"Well, if you'd rather hear a speech than swim. Do what you want, of course. But I'd rather go to the pool tonight. Tomorrow's lectures sounded more appealing to me. I'm going to go to the one about healthy relationships or whatever they called it."

"'Long Term Commitments in a Healthy Relationship.' It's for women only," Beth told her after looking it up in the program. "Yeah, it does sound nice. You go swimming. Maybe Susan or Sarah will want to come to tonight's lecture with me. The way I look at it, as long as I'm here at the seminar, I may as well make the most of it. I can go swimming anytime."

Rachel laughed. "Well, enjoy yourself. I didn't come for the lectures, you know. I came to relax. And you are welcome to ask Sarah to go with you, but I'll bet she'll say no."

"Well of course, she'll do whatever you do."

"Yeah, and it works to my advantage sometimes. Like now, I need a swimming partner. But you know," Rachel suddenly became serious, "she's not as dumb as you make her out to be. She had a very hard life, and she never really had anything stable in her life past age twelve or so."

"So how did she get to Brown?" Beth asked, referring to the expensive Ivy League university they attended.

"Oh, her dad has money, and it sounds as though he is generous enough. But money is all she has. You've just met her, but I remember her from East Hanover, before she moved to the city, before you came to town. You know, I had a long conversation with her once."

"When?"

"I don't know... she once came in to my room to visit. I guess she's comfortable with me because I knew her when we were kids. She doesn't really have many friends, you know. But I never really was particularly friendly with her. She was very shy, and when she *did* hang out, it was with Laurie and Elizabeth and that crowd," she said, referring to some of the girls they had gone to elementary school with. "Anyway, we started talking about the old days, and... and she was sort of baring her soul, whatever. I don't know. But I really shouldn't be telling you this; it's sort of confidential." She stopped and then started up again.

"I really shouldn't have said anything. Sarah really is a nice person, and she is good to have around... I don't want you to look at her any differently... I just told you all that so you shouldn't think she is a wimp who can't think for herself... She had a hard life, that's all."

"Okay," Beth knew that once Rachel decided something, she would not change her mind. "You have fun with Sarah in the pool, and Susan and I will attend the lecture."

But they were wrong, because Sarah did not want to go swimming and opted to go to the lecture given by Rabbi Friedman on 'Validity of Torah — Security in an Insecure World.' Susan went with Sarah leaving Beth and Rachel at it again.

"Now, you're the one who will have to choose. I am going to the lecture. Are you going to do laps or come with me?"

Rachel smiled sheepishly and went with Beth to the lecture. Swimming alone was really no fun. She had been certain that Sarah would follow her lead and go to the pool but couldn't deny a sense of pride in her friend's independence.

The lecture was interesting, but Rachel did not stay for the question-and-answer period. Instead, she went upstairs and began flipping through the channels of the television in her room.

She missed Mrs. Friedman.

*　　　*　　　*

Sarah Kessler really enjoyed Rabbi Friedman's lecture. If there was anything missing in her world, it was, as she had once told Rachel Bergmann, security.

Sarah's mother fell ill and died when Sarah was only seven years old. She left behind a distraught husband and three small children, the oldest of whom was Sarah. From the outset, it became clear that Mr. Kessler was not able to handle his grief, and the children went to live with their maternal grandmother.

Slowly, with the help of family and close friends, David Kessler pulled himself together. By the time Sarah was nine years old, and her younger brothers, Sammy and Benny, were seven and five, David had resumed his old job and worked his way up within his company. He became a manager of private client banking with JP Morgan Chase.

He frequently visited his children at the home of his late wife's parents and took them on trips. He made life thrilling; he gave them the feeling that not only did they have a father, they had an exciting one.

When she was twelve years old, Sarah opted to move in with her father. She craved normalcy and did not want to be known as "the girl who lives with her grandparents." Her brothers followed her, and Sarah understood that she would be the surrogate mother in this household of men and boys.

Sarah's grandmother threw the children a lavish party the day before the big move. It was early September, just before the start of school. They would have less than a week before school started to get settled in Manhattan, and that is exactly how Grandma wanted it. She didn't want Sarah or her brothers to have too much time to worry about the new turn their life was taking.

It was with this in mind that she arranged the party. The afternoon brought friends to Grandma's pool and at night, aunts and uncles — from both sides of the family — came to a barbeque to wish the children luck in their new home and school. David was there, too, and accepted with good humor the tips he was given on child-rearing, especially raising a girl on the brink of her teenage years.

Sarah was a thinking person and she silently thanked her grandmother in the ensuing years as she came to an understanding of the motive behind the party.

When she left East Hanover, Sarah knew that she would always be welcome in Grandma's home. "If it is too hard for you, honey, or if you want your old school and your old friends, or if you just don't want to be the only girl in the house, you know you can come back, right?"

"But it will be fine, right Grandma? It will be fun to live with

Daddy. I have everything I need in his apartment already, and I know how to take care of the boys."

"Just remember that Manhattan is very different than East Hanover, sweetie, and if for any reason it doesn't work out, you come right back home."

Grandpa, too, reassured Sarah that she had a home in East Hanover, NJ. "We're going to miss you. All of a sudden we'll become old," he said. "We'll be able to go out to eat without finding a babysitter."

The move was indeed a tough one. Sarah was starting middle school and found the city public school a huge and terrifying place. In middle school she was more on her own than she had ever been in a school setting, and it seemed that everyone else had friends from their old elementary schools and didn't need to look twice in her direction.

At home, too, things were different. Her father was not the fun man he had been when they only saw him on weekends and holidays and he took them on trips and made life exciting for them by letting them stay up late and eat ice cream. Instead, he was a working man. He had a high-powered job, and was already in the office before the children left for school at 8:00 AM; he didn't come home until 7:30 PM or even later most nights. He hired a sitter to tend to the children while he was at work, and Sarah resented her because she was there and not her father. The sitter prepared supper and was responsible for giving the boys baths and doing homework with them, and Sarah was offended that her father did not think she was capable of those tasks. She therefore made life as unbearable as she could for the sitter — which of course meant making life miserable for herself as well. When spring came around and they were already on their third round of hired help, David Kessler admitted defeat and sent his sons back to his mother-in-law.

He wanted Sarah to go as well, but she refused. As much as she understood that Dad's place was only her house and Grandma's was home, Sarah had made her bed and was determined to lie in it. She understood that her father needed to work and promised she wouldn't be a burden. She would take care of herself.

Too old for a sitter, she grew up without any adult and, more important, without any woman to talk to and share her feelings. She had no friends because she was too shy and reserved to reach out to anyone. Grandma tried to keep up the relationship, but Sarah, in her desperate attempt to prove herself, shrank from her grandmother's advances; the fact that she still had a relationship with Grandma was due only to the older woman's love and understanding.

That she had not fallen in with a bad crowd was due to Sarah's integrity and the fact that she was too shy to be sought out by gangs. By nature one who shunned the spotlight, she made only halfhearted attempts to gain some popularity and went through her teenage years working hard in school and writing in her diary. She had no mother and essentially no father and brothers. David made a point of going back to East Hanover to see his boys every weekend, but Sarah came along only on rare occasions. David understood that he had failed in his daughter's eyes and had no idea how to regain her respect. Instead, he lavished his oldest child with everything money can buy; but all she wanted were the things that cannot be bought — stability and happiness.

*   *   *

Sarah had not attended the Journeys bimonthly lectures, but she was glad she had come along to this seminar. She was quiet as they went back up to their rooms after the lecture. Rabbi Friedman had spoken about the Torah, and the fact that it had not changed in the three thousand years since it was given. If a practicing Jew were to meet another anywhere in the world each would immediately feel a kinship with the other, because they would both be following the same laws and they would know that they both were connected to the same Source. There might be some minor cultural differences, but it would be the same Torah.

The Rabbi's words affected Sarah deeply and she wanted to learn more. She had been yearning to find some meaning to her life. If his words were true, the Torah would provide her with something solid to hold onto and a link to the past. Rabbi Friedman had mentioned the Afterlife and Sarah desperately wanted to believe in the truth of that; she wanted to know that her mother was somewhere looking after her, loving her. She wanted to be sure that life had a purpose and a meaning beyond what she could see.

Chapter 6

SHABBOS DAY, SHMUELY FRIEDMAN caught a glimpse of Ahuva Steinhardt as he walked into the dining room for the *seudah*. She was walking with two girls who had attended his lecture the night before and he was as horrified as his wife.

Miri had to admit that she was dressed tastefully… for a college student. She wore a grey cardigan with a pencil skirt in dark pewter. The problem was that the skirt ended above her knees. The cardigan had an open V-neck and underneath she wore a scoop-neck ruffled blouse. Her hair, which had been worn down the night before, was now pulled into a loose braid and her makeup was fresh. She definitely had a sense of style, but it was *not tzniusdig*. She wore chunky jewelry and she held herself in a manner quite unbecoming a Bais Yaakov girl.

The rest of Shabbos passed too slowly for the distressed Miri Friedman. "It doesn't make sense. It just makes no sense," Shmuely kept repeating.

*　　　*　　　*

The matter was clinched on *Motza'ei Shabbos* when Rachel Bergmann spied a baby-grand piano in the lobby of the hotel.

"I didn't see this before!" she exclaimed and made a beeline for the bench. As her friends clustered around the piano she started playing one of her favorite Chopin pieces. Suddenly, Beth narrowed her eyes and lowered her voice.

"Who is that woman? Every time I turn around, she's staring at us." She pointed with her chin at Miri Friedman who was staring in the direction of the piano, a look of revulsion on her face.

"She was at the lecture yesterday," Sarah said slowly. "I think she might be the rabbi's wife. But why is she looking at you like that?"

"Oh," Rachel snickered, "she probably never heard classical music before. Wave at her. It's the quickest way to get someone to stop staring." She lifted her hand from the keys in a salute.

Miri turned away in disgust and left to find her husband.

"I don't care if it makes sense or not. You saw her and I saw her. And she's in the lobby playing the piano. Remember how we heard her playing when we went to meet her? I saw her playing — and she waved at me! Waved at me!" Miri seemed perilously close to tears. "Listen, we know she attends college in the afternoon. She obviously made friends in school. I don't care why she is here with them. I don't care if she has all the right intentions. She waved at me!

"She's not the girl I want for Moshe. And you don't want her either." Miri concluded definitively.

Shmuely couldn't argue with her and said nothing as Miri called the *shadchan*.

"I'm sorry; I'd rather not go into it… She's just really not for us… Yes, I know, she made a very nice impression… Something came up; I really don't feel comfortable… I'm really really sorry… Till tomorrow night? You mean go out as scheduled? No. No, that will not work out, I'm sorry. I hate to do this…"

*   *   *

"Rebbe," Baruch cleared his throat and looked at his Rosh Yeshiva. He should have spoken to the Rosh Yeshiva a long time ago but had procrastinated until he could not delay any longer. He knew Reb Shua would hear him out, would understand the situation, and that his *eitzah* would be well thought out and compassionate. But he was afraid of the *eitzah;* he understood that this time... He didn't even want to finish the thought. Avigail was right; kids need to be kids, and both Avigail and he knew that bringing the children up with the right *chinuch* was their most important job as parents. They wanted their children to feel the way they both did and choose to live a *kollel* life. Perhaps they were giving their children the wrong message, and were actually failing in *chinuch,* because they worked them too hard? Baruch wanted the Rosh Yeshiva to ask, with his trademark sense of humor: "So, you want to stop learning so your son-in-law can start? Worry about yourself, and let Hashem take care of him," but he knew that the conversation would probably not end like that, and he was apprehensive.

"It's like this," Baruch began, and updated the Rosh Yeshiva on the events of the past few weeks. "She's really right, I know. I mean she works so hard so that I should be able to stay in learning, but if my learning takes such a toll on the family that they may come to resent it, then I am doing something wrong. The only help she has is my Malka; my next daughter is only seven years old."

"And how does your wife feel in all this?"

Baruch looked nonplussed. "She's worried about my daughter," he repeated.

"No," Reb Shua said. "How does she, herself, feel?"

Baruch was quiet. In all honesty, he had not even thought to ask her. He took it for granted that she was happy to leave the house in the early morning and come home late at night. She was doing it for his Torah, and it afforded her the greatest pleasure. Being a mother? Getting the kids off to school? Being there for them? He had never thought along these lines before, and his response, when he answered, reflected that.

"She wants to do all she can so I can continue to learn, Rebbe. That is what she always wanted. Rebbe spoke to her three years ago," Baruch recalled the exact date and the amazement he had felt at being excluded from the meeting. "That hasn't changed. It's just that she is worried about the *chinuch* of our children."

The Rosh Yeshiva sat in front of Baruch, a faraway look in his eyes. Baruch could see him contemplating the *sugya* from every angle, but still was surprised to hear him say, "I'd like to talk to your *rebbetzin*, Baruch."

"Oh. Okay, I'll tell her. What time is good for Rebbe?" *What did I say that did not accurately convey Avigail's feelings on the subject? What would the Rosh Yeshiva gain by speaking to her directly? Hadn't he already done that, and hadn't the decision been that I stay right where I am? What had changed now?*

"Whenever it's good for her, Baruch'l. *Da'agah nisht.* It will be good." The Rosh Yeshiva smiled and the meeting was over.

*   *   *

Ahuva opened the door to her walk-in closet. What should she wear tomorrow night? The green jacket with the big black buttons was really pretty, but so was the navy jumper. Rivky came into the room to put something on Ahuva's desk and joined her in the closet.

"I think the navy is too much. It is only the second date, you know." She smiled broadly.

"I know, Ma, but this is different."

"You don't want to rush things."

"But, Ma, the navy looks so much better on me. The boy has no idea that I usually don't wear that on a second date."

"Try them both on, let's see." Rivky was getting into the spirit, and the two of them discussed fashion for the next hour as Ahuva tried on a few different outfits.

Suddenly, there was a knock on the door. "Can I come in?" Dovid called from behind the door.

"Sure," came the response.

"What's happening in here?" he asked as he eyed the bed and its contents.

"Ahuva is doing a little fashion show," Rivky answered. "Deciding what she should wear tomorrow night. What do you need? Are you ready for a *Melaveh Malkah?* We are just about done in here." She turned to her daughter, "You're right, it's the navy. Let's put everything back and go downstairs."

They started clearing away the clothes when Dovid's next words stopped them both. "I just got a call from the *shadchan.*"

Both mother and daughter turned around at the sound of his voice. "I am not really sure what happened, but they said no. I mean, they called to cancel." He looked miserably at the two women.

Chapter 7

MOTHER AND DAUGHTER STARED, uncomprehending. "You mean they want to change the day? It's okay, we're flexible…"

"No, it's not that. They changed their mind about the *shidduch*. They don't want to move forward."

There was a stunned silence.

"But — that's not possible! We had such a good time last week! I *know* he had a nice time. And they even told us he was happy…" Ahuva felt suddenly queasy. *She* had had a nice time. *She* had been happy. "But why?" she asked, trying to hold on to her composure. "Did they give a reason?"

"The *shadchan* didn't really say… She was very uncomfortable, and it sounded as though she herself didn't have the story straight. She kept apologizing, and she said this never happened before…" he trailed off, and turned away from his wife and daughter. Their shock and incomprehension mirrored his.

Rivky was the first to recover. She squared her shoulders and stood up. "If they don't want us, we don't need them," she said briskly. "Come, I'll help you clean up in here and then we'll go down to eat a *Melaveh Malkah*."

"You go, Ma. I'll clean up."

Rivky gave her daughter a quick hug before joining her husband at the doorway of the room and walking down the stairs with him. Ahuva turned back to her bed and picked up the remnants of the dreams she'd had the last few nights. "I don't care," she told herself fiercely. "I *don't* care. I don't *care*."

Later that night her parents heard the piano; the music came fast and furious. "It's not such a big deal," Dovid told his wife as he tried to make sense of what had happened. "This is not the first boy who has said no, and it's only been one date."

"But there was so much energy invested in this already. She had to meet the mother-in-law... And there's no explanation. That's what bothers me the most. Tell us what the problem is. She had been so excited... I should have seen this coming. I didn't like it from the beginning... Have you ever heard of parents making a separate meeting to see the girl? If they wanted to see her, let them spy at a wedding or something."

"Don't go there, Rivky, please," Dovid pleaded. "Don't lower yourself like that. You know that if we had to do it again, we would. And if they came back tomorrow and said it was a mistake and they wanted to continue, we'd jump, right? So don't say anything you'll regret."

Rivky kept silent in the face of her husband's wisdom. But before the week was up her freezer overflowed with cookies and miniatures; Rivky always baked when she was upset. She called up some organizations and *gemachs* and let them know she had a freezer full of food if they needed to make a *vort* or *Kiddush* for someone. Her good friend Leah, head of Tiferes L'Kallah asked, "Is everything okay?"

*   *   *

As a child, Avigail had always been bemused by the women

who came to speak to her father. Why would a *woman* talk to him? Whenever her own parents needed advice, it was always her father who called the *rav*. She wondered about them and about the conversations that went on behind the study doors. Her mother would walk in and out at various intervals to ensure that there was no problem of *yichud*. Did the conversation cease when she made her entrance? If not, why wouldn't the women feel more comfortable speaking to her?

As she grew older, her interest grew as well. Only now it was accompanied by a vow: *I'll never be one of* those!

And then she had gone with Baruch as a *kallah* to meet his Rosh Yeshiva, Reb Shua Kraus. Her shyness left her as she was greeted by the Rosh Yeshiva and his wife behind the closed doors of his study. His demeanor was more of a concerned father than a stern Rav, and Avigail could understand why a woman might confide in him about her husband, his *talmid*. Still, *she* would never do so. And yet, she had done so — first meeting him together with Baruch and then, three years ago, alone. The meetings had felt natural, not awkward or embarrassing. Now she found herself checking the calendar, eagerly anticipating the opportunity to pour out her concerns to her husband's kind and wise Rosh Yeshiva.

Of course, all she had told Baruch about her concerns for Malka were true, but there was much more... more that she had not told Baruch, that she could not tell him. She was afraid to voice the concerns, even to herself, as if voicing them gave them credibility. And giving them credibility meant giving up on her dreams.

But the truth was that she was *tired*, and she really could not handle it anymore. She was a perfectionist, and it did not matter how many times she was told by her mother, sister, friend, even Baruch himself, to leave the dishes for tomorrow. She couldn't do it.

But neither could she do it *all* anymore. She didn't have the strength to make supper and give baths and smile. She felt short-changed because she had missed so many important milestones in her children's lives. And the hours she put in! No mother of children should be allowed to work such hours. And she had done it for fifteen years! Wasn't she finally entitled to her *kesubah?* Her unvoiced complaints picked up steam, like a runaway train.

Avigail recoiled at her thoughts.

Do you think that's how the Chafetz Chaim's wife thought? If she had, he wouldn't have become the Chafetz Chaim! But the Chafetz Chaim's wife didn't live in this generation. She didn't have to prove herself to be a supermom. And although Avigail wouldn't want to live back in those days — no indoor plumbing! — life *was* simpler back then and it was understood that a woman's place was in the home.

There was also the money issue. Of course Avigail didn't expect to stop working once Baruch started bringing home a paycheck. She was realistic and knew that whatever salary he'd make, they'd still need her income. Baruch's working would bring its own set of money problems anyway. They would no longer be eligible for tuition breaks and scholarships. Besides, he had no practical training; he'd have to start at the bottom in any kind of job. It was highly doubtful he'd bring in enough money to enable her to stay home. But oh, how nice it would be not to have the responsibility of being the only breadwinner! And not to worry about the bills! To see the children off on the bus before heading out to work! And to watch them come home! That was also a dream she had, one she wished would come true.

She couldn't tell her husband; he wouldn't understand. He was so simplistic sometimes and it infuriated her. *Well, this is what you want. You've wanted it forever. We'll make it work.* Easy for him to say when his part in the whole thing was going to the *beis midrash!* Sure, he ferried the children to and from the babysitter and ran errands such as the weekly grocery shopping, and it was a big help, but still… Did it compare?

Avigail's thoughts moved to her children. Bless Malka for giving her an excuse which she could use while holding her head up high. Now she would not be suspected of less than complete fealty to the ideal of *mesirus nefesh* for Torah.

But the decision to leave *kollel* brought with it its own issue; the reason Baruch had not stepped out of the *koslei beis midrash* three years ago.

There was no way to say it nicely. Although Baruch would like to stay in the *yeshiva* world, he was not cut out to teach young children. And to dream of being a *maggid shiur* in a *beis midrash*, or even a *mesivta* — that would never be anything *but* a dream. In her daydreams she had toyed with the idea of Baruch starting his own *yeshiva,* but with no reputation at all as a *rebbe* and no financial backers, that option was completely unrealistic. If he did open a *yeshiva* and managed to find *bachurim,* Avigail would need to work doubly hard to support her family *and* the *mosad.* That would certainly defeat the purpose.

There was no other choice and it was time to face reality. Baruch needed a job. Avigail tried to reassure herself that she had spoken to Baruch because of her children's needs, not her own. It didn't work, and her feelings of guilt returned. *I guess I've failed.*

*   *   *

What bothered Ahuva most, as she told her grandmother a couple of days later, was that "the other side" had already agreed to a second date before backing out. "I mean, this is not the first boy who has said no," she said, echoing her father. "And it has only been one date, so as much as I may have enjoyed myself, there hasn't been too much emotional energy involved," she refuted her mother's statement unknowingly. "But why did they say yes and then change their mind? What happened over Shabbos that was so drastic that we can't even go out? Why couldn't they call up after the second date and say it's not for him, or we didn't click, or my dress was ugly, anything? Why not the courtesy of a date? What information about me did they hear that frightened them so much?"

"You never know, Ahuva. Maybe something happened on their end," Bubby answered.

"What do you mean?"

"I recently heard about a boy who started dating and then found out he was sick."

"Oh." Ahuva was silent for a moment. "But they could have said something to that effect, don't you think? The way it happened makes it seem as though they were too nervous to let their son go out again because they found out something about me."

"Maybe he broke it off?"

"Huh? What do you mean? We know they broke it."

"I mean maybe it was him, not his parents. Maybe he thought about it and broke it off himself?"

"Well that makes no sense because I *know* we had a good time, and I got very nice feedback from the *shadchan* originally. Maybe he's getting cold feet is what you mean, and in that case his parents should force him to go out again and see if his fears are rational. And if they baby him too much to make him do that, then I am happy not to marry him."

But Mrs. Miller had accomplished her goal, because now Ahuva viewed the situation differently and was not as upset as she had been. In fact, her attitude now sounded much like her mother's. With her head held high, she said, *if they don't want me, it's their loss. And I am better off without them.*

Almost.

Chapter 8

 "MOMMY, WHAT DO YOU mean, you don't want to tell me? It's my life and my wife. What did you hear that was so bad you won't even let me make my own decision? You liked her well enough originally."

"It's not what we heard, it's what we saw. I told you that at least a hundred times." They were sitting at the Shabbos table a week after the Journeys Seminar. Moshe had come home for Shabbos hoping that speaking to his mother face-to-face would make her see reason. If they were dead set against resuming the *shidduch* with Steinhardt, at least they should let him know why.

He turned to his father.

"Sorry, Moshe. Mommy's right. It was something that forced us to stop this cold turkey, and I'd rather not tell you what it was. There's no *toeles* in your knowing." Moshe opened his mouth to speak, but his father cut him off. "No, Moshe. This is not something that needs to be your decision. Trust us on this one. Have we ever let you down?"

"There are other fish in the sea, Moshe," Miri said brightly. "This one is not for you, but that doesn't mean anything. In fact I am looking into someone right now. I think Chani might know her from camp. Her name came up a few days ago, and I haven't had a chance to call Chani in sem to speak to her about it."

Moshe sighed, and gave up. "Where is Chani this week?"

"I think they went to Tzefas for Shabbos. Or Meron, maybe? Somewhere up north."

"They took the whole seminary?" Shmuely asked.

"No, I think just a couple of friends went with her. I am not sure exactly," Miri answered.

They spent the remainder of the *seudah* discussing the family and the antics of the grandchildren. Moshe saw his siblings in Lakewood more often than his parents did and had many stories to repeat that would bring them *nachas*.

The Steinhardt case was lost, he saw, and there was no reason to mull over his first date. There would be others.

*   *   *

Ahuva felt her mind wandering in class. She would ask a student to read a *pasuk* and then space out while it was being read. She shook her head to try to clear it. *Give it up,* she commanded herself. *This is not the first guy you ever dated. This is not the first guy you liked. This is not even the first guy who said no to you when you were excited. Get over him. There are many fish in the sea and you'll catch the next one. They don't deserve you anyway.* But these pep talks fell flat and she was annoyed. She found she couldn't concentrate on anything; nothing distracted her from her thoughts. Ahuva thought back to what Bubby had said. Could it be that he was sick? Maybe he really did not like her? But she found that hard to believe. *You don't want a mother-in-law like that, who babies her son and doesn't allow him to make his own decisions. Quit it.*

"Miss Steinhardt?" Ahuva was startled out of her reverie by the voice of a student.

"Yes, Mindy," she replied with a distracted smile. *Not now!* Ahuva groaned to herself.

"It's... It's... about..." Mindy Glassman was having trouble getting the words out. *Say it,* Ahuva commanded silently. *Spit it out!* She smiled again, an inviting smile that belied her impatience and Mindy, who had no idea of what was behind the smile, seemed encouraged. "It's about Faigy," she said, her voice barely audible.

Ahuva sat up straighter. Faigy had been relegated to the back of her mind in the recent weeks, and she had neglected to follow through on her promise to find out why the loquacious teenager had become so withdrawn. Thoughts of Moshe Friedman were banished and she turned her focus on her student.

"What's up?" Ahuva asked.

"Did you hear about Mr. and Mrs. Baum?"

"No."

"They're getting divorced." The words came out in a rush, as though Mindy was embarrassed to say anything. She took a deep breath, "Faigy told me I could tell you, because she likes..." Mindy broke off and colored slightly. She tried again, "She said you were the only one who noticed anything was wrong and that you tried to talk to her. She... she's going through a hard time right now, and she's the oldest so she feels like she needs to protect everyone. But if you ask me," Mindy assumed a knowing air, "it's about time, and I think everyone will be happier like this. *I* never went to Faigy's house because I couldn't handle the way her parents would fight, and *I'm* her best friend!"

Ahuva nodded slowly, trying to digest what Mindy was telling her. Divorced? That would explain it. Immediately, the image of Bracha Weinberg entered her head. Bracha was the only girl Ahuva had known whose parents had divorced. Bracha's parents divorced when she was in kindergarten, and Ahuva knew the trauma never left her. Mrs. Weinberg tried hard as a single mom to give Bracha and her brother a normal childhood, while Mr. Weinberg spewed hatred about their mother to the children whenever they visited.

Ahuva remembered Mrs. Weinberg's remarriage when Bracha was in eighth grade and how nervous Bracha had been about having a stepfather and two stepbrothers. Thankfully the marriage had worked out, and today Bracha herself was happily married.

Maybe I should put Faigy in touch with Bracha? Ahuva thought about doing so, but decided against it. There was something exhilarating about being able to deal with such an issue. Wasn't that what teaching was all about: helping students overcome challenges?

"Thank you for telling me, Mindy. Is there anything else you think I should know?"

Mindy was silent, contemplative. "I don't know. She could tell you the rest, I suppose. But that is why she's been — the way she's been. Her father moved out, and her mother needs her help to deal with everything… though she always had to deal with things, because her father never helped out anyway. But she said it's harder now, and her mother goes to rabbis all the time. And she is failing in school and she said no one cares except for you."

"Thank you, Mindy." Ahuva looked at her watch. "I need to run, but I'm glad you brought this to my attention, and don't worry. I'll take care of it."

Ahuva finished gathering her things and walked slowly out of the school building. In all honesty, she was not equipped to help someone deal with the trauma of going through a divorce, and she knew it. But Ahuva always enjoyed a challenge and was determined to see this one through. Faigy Baum would become a better, stronger person, and Ahuva Steinhardt would have a hand in it.

*　　　*　　　*

Now that it was a done deal, Avigail was plagued with doubt. Was this really the right thing? But the Rosh Yeshiva said it was! He had heard her out — all her concerns, from money to exhaustion to Malka — and he told Baruch it was time to get a job. But still, was it the best thing for her family? Did this mean she wasn't the idealistic young woman she thought she was? Did it mean that the past fifteen years weren't real? *But I worked hard! I made it happen for fifteen years! That's a long time! So why do I feel like… like a failure?*

Avigail was overwhelmed with guilt. She would never have believed that her husband would leave *kollel* because of her. Baruch had been on his way to becoming a *gadol baTorah,* and she squashed it. At least they had a *pesak.* That felt virtuous. "Our Rosh Yeshiva said this is the best for our family right now." But really, who wouldn't see behind it? The Rosh Yeshiva didn't just march over to people and tell them what to do. They had obviously asked him the *she'eilah,* and there could be no doubt who was behind that.

Well, we better get to work. They had to let people know Baruch was on the job market. He needed a resume. He needed to do some research into what type of job he wanted. *Don't be ridiculous, Avigail. He'll take whatever he gets.* Still, it would be nice for him to enjoy what he was doing. *What are his strengths? Come on, Avigail, this is going to be your headache until he actually gets the job.* She thought about it. He was good with numbers, even if she took care of the bills. But he was not an accountant type, so give that up. What else could he do?

Mortgages. But every guy and his brother-in-law was a mortgage broker. And mortgages are commission-based. How would it help their finances if they would have to wait for Baruch to close his first deal? Or solve any other problem, for that matter? Avigail would have to work just as hard until Baruch was actually bringing home a steady paycheck, and she couldn't stomach the roller coaster of sales. What else was there?

That was all she thought about. *What could Baruch do?* And, *we have to tell people.* The second part was harder. She woke up every day with a nagging feeling and made up her mind — again, that today would be the day she'd pick up the phone. Baruch refused to tell his parents until she had told hers, and although it exasperated Avigail, she understood.

*   *   *

It wasn't until a week after they had made the decision that she mustered the courage to call Shmuely and Miri Friedman. *I'll speak to Tatty,* she decided. *Why hadn't I thought of that?*

Avigail called her father's study line. She loved her mother, but Miri was not one with whom to discuss sensitive issues, and Avigail could imagine the way the conversation would unfold if her mother answered the phone.

"Can I talk to Tatty?"

"Is everything okay?"

"Yeah, I just have a question for him."

"Is it private?"

"No. Uh, yeah."

Mommy would be really upset and insulted when she found out why Avigail had called. And she would find out. *"What was wrong with talking to me? Am I so scary? You couldn't have told us both at the same time?"*

The study line was the way to go. It was Shmuely's private line and Miri never answered it. She wouldn't have to know Avigail had reached her father there; this way Miri might think she had not been home when Avigail called.

Chapter 9

 LIFE GOES ON, AND time passed. Ahuva went out with Chaim Baskin, but it was *no, no, no.*

"And it has nothing to do with the Friedman boy," she told her parents. "I *have* gotten over him. This guy was just not for me."

Ahuva forced herself to focus on helping Faigy Baum get through the trying time of her parents' separation and divorce, and she found it was helping herself as well. She had spoken with her cousin Michal after the conversation with Mindy Glassman and asked the former for advice. "What should I do? I'm sure the family isn't functioning normally, but I don't know them, so I can't assess what they would need."

"Do the other teachers and staff know about this?"

"I doubt it. I assume that we would have gotten a memo or something. That's what happened when Miriam Gross lost her mother last year. We got a memo that she was taking a turn for the worse and we should have extra *rachmanus.*"

"But this is a different kind of situation. Maybe they don't want people to know and start talking about them?"

"That makes no sense. It's hard to hide something like divorce.

They're not living together anymore!"

"True… I gotta admit, I'm happy I'm not a teacher. We certainly don't have these sorts of problems in the office!"

"Thanks," Ahuva responded sarcastically. "That is completely not helpful. What should I *do?*"

"Don't *do* anything," Michal suggested. "Just take her out and listen and show her you care. Let her lead the way and let her feel comfortable having someone to talk to. And if there is something concrete to do, you'll figure it out. Sometimes just showing someone you care goes a lot farther than supper and *chesed* for an hour a week."

Ahuva took the advice to heart. She contacted Faigy at home a couple of days later and let her know that she was concerned about her and wanted to be there for her. "If you don't want to talk at all, I understand, and if you want to, but not during school, I'm here whenever you need me."

And Faigy took her up on the offer. She spoke about how hard it had been for her growing up, because even though she never had another model for marriage, she knew her parents' marriage was wrong. The Baums were not especially close to their extended family because her father could not get along with her mother's family and vice versa, but Faigy craved a relationship with her family, especially her young aunt, Miriam. Faigy told her about the first time she spent Shabbos at a friend's house and she saw "what a real family" looks like. She told Ahuva how she had come home and cried for days afterward. Faigy took to calling Ahuva every night and would talk to her in school as well. *I guess she doesn't mind being labeled "teacher's pet,"* Ahuva thought.

*   *   *

Shmuely Friedman listened to his voicemail, and was surprised to hear Avigail's voice. *Are these my messages? But this has to be the study line, Zalman Schwartz called on it.* He listened closely to the message, and was hit with a sense of foreboding. "Hi, Tatty. This is Avigail. I wanted to speak with you about something. I guess I'll call back."

Why was she calling on his private line? What could possibly be the matter? Shmuely dialed Avigail's house and when she answered, he asked in a voice full of concern, "What's the matter, Avigail?"

There was no immediate answer.

"Avigail? Is everything okay?"

"Yes. We're okay. I wanted to tell you about a decision Baruch and I have come to, and I wanted to hear what you have to say." Avigail took a deep breath. "We spoke to R' Shua about this, Tatty. Baruch is looking for a job."

"Looking for a job?" Avigail's statement caught Shmuely off guard. Baruch, the dedicated *masmid*, looking for a *job*?

"I wish him much *hatzlachah*. The search should go well, and he should find something good." What else could he say? Avigail was not calling for his advice; she had already explained that this was a decision they had both come to after speaking with Baruch's Rosh Yeshiva. But what did she mean by job? They usually called it a *shteller*. "What kind of job, Avigail?"

"We're not really sure yet. That's part of the problem. He has no training and no special skills. He is going to sit down with someone who knows about these things and discuss what kind of options there are."

"Can I ask what prompted this decision, Avigail? It's a pretty drastic one, and we haven't heard anything about it until now."

On the other end of the line Shmuely heard his daughter take a deep breath. Then it all came out in a rush. He heard about their tight finances. "I'm not asking for money, Tatty. I'm just explaining." He heard about her weariness and how she would find a way to manage but… there was also Malka.

Sifting through his daughter's words, Shmuely understood that Malka was a helpful girl who did not complain, but Avigail felt bad for her. On top of that there was Avigail's own exhaustion, and money problems. They had spoken to Baruch's *rebbe* and received direction.

Somehow Shmuely realized that Avigail had expressed her worry about Malka to Baruch, and that it was Malka about whom Baruch was concerned. He also understood that Avigail wanted it to stay that way. Well, Shmuely was nothing if not discreet.

"How does he feel?" Shmuely immediately regretted his question as it brought forth a flood of tears.

"Bad, Tatty. Of course he feels bad. I feel awful about it. He is so sheltered; I don't really want him in the workforce either. But it's just that… I don't know," she wailed.

"I understand, Avigail. Don't worry. It needed to be done. Look, most people are not able to stay in *kollel* as long as you managed to. The years aren't wasted because Baruch is leaving the *beis midrash*. He'll take the past fifteen years with him to wherever he goes and he'll use it as a springboard for growth. I understand how you feel, but if you believe this is the right decision for the good of your family then you have to be happy with it. If you aren't happy, and want to ask R' Shua again based on how you feel now, that's one thing, but if you don't…"

"I don't," she whispered quickly. She said it as one who saw freedom within reach and wanted to grab it before it was snatched away.

"That's fine. But you have to be happy, Avigail. Deal? We'll let people know about Baruch's search, and it will be good. Don't worry."

"Thank you, Tatty. And Tatty? You'll tell Mommy?"

"Yes, don't worry." It was obvious to Shmuely that she was scared to tell Miri, and he understood. He was a bit apprehensive himself.

Well, Moshe had a date the next night, and they were meeting the girl with him. Shmuely would inform his wife of Avigail's news after the date. Nothing like a little procrastination.

*   *   *

The Friedman/Hirsch *shidduch* was a fiasco. Miri Friedman did meet with Dina Hirsch, but not until the night Moshe and Dina went out. The Hirschs were not as accommodating as the Steinhardts had been.

"Mommy, that's normal," Miri's oldest daughter, Esther, told her. "I mean, none of us met our in-laws before we went out. Certainly not alone! And to tell the truth, Mommy," Esther mused, "I don't know if I would have married Aryeh if his mother had done that to me."

"What do you mean?"

"I mean, I love my mother-in-law, but only because I love her son. Nothing bad, you know that, Ma, but *stam,* we are not the same type at all. But I married Aryeh, not his mother, and so I met Aryeh and *then* his mother. If I would have met my mother-in-law first, I never would have met my husband! The only reason I was able to handle it was because I was warned by Aryeh about what to expect. And we love each other now, and we respect each other, and I have a great relationship with her, Mommy. But it is only because I worked on myself, and I did it because she is my husband's mother and the grandmother of my children and I owe her for that."

Miri saw the wisdom of her daughter's words, but was

unprepared to give in. "Well, I am happy I met the first girl he went out with. Imagine where we would be if I had only met her on the night of the *vort*!" She shuddered.

"Why, Mommy? What happened?"

"I'm telling you, Esther, you don't want to know. It turns my stomach each time I think about it."

"But I do want to know, Mommy. What was so terrible that she was dropped cold turkey like that? If it's something you don't want to tell *me*, I understand. It's probably not my business, even if I am curious. But to do what you did and not even tell Moshe why? I never spoke about this to you, Mommy, but he was really hurt. I think he feels that you don't trust him enough to decide for himself. He feels that if he is old enough to marry, he is old enough to choose his life's partner and to determine for himself if whatever it was that bothered you would also bother him.

"And Mommy," she said, cutting off her mother's interjection, "Let me just say this. I think that the way it was done allows for no closure on his end, if you know what I mean. He did not say no to her; he liked her. But the way you ended things — cutting it off like that — he will compare every girl he goes out with to Steinhardt, wondering what *she* would have said and how *she* would have reacted."

"Sounds like your social work is rubbing off on your personal life," Miri said wryly. "I hear you. Okay, I'll tell you what made us drop it, and then you'll tell me what *you* think."

Miri paused. Then, "Their date was right before Journeys, remember? And Tatty spoke that week at Journeys, and… we saw her. Esther, I can't tell you what she looked like and who she was with, but it was *not* Bais Yaakov. Remember, she's going for her degree."

"Oh." Esther was stunned.

"Exactly. And don't try to make excuses for her. I don't know how it could be, and I agree that it doesn't make sense. Why would she go to a Journey's Seminar of all places? But she was there. Tatty saw her also and confirmed that I hadn't mistaken the girl."

"Oh." Esther tried to come to grips with her mother's revelation. "There's really nothing to say, just as you knew there wouldn't be. But is there no way to tell Moshe? So that he can put it all behind him?"

"Tatty and I discussed it, Esther. So just trust us that we know what's best for our own child."

Chapter 10

 MOSHE CAME HOME FROM his date about an hour after Miri's conversation with Esther.

"No, Mommy. Not for me," were his first words as he walked in the door.

"What did you talk about?"

"Whatever you are supposed to discuss on the first date. JIFS: Job, Israel, Family, School. But I am not going out with her again."

"That bad?" Shmuely asked, coming into the kitchen where the conversation was taking place. Miri was cleaning cabinets; Pesach was coming soon.

"Worse."

"Take the other girl out of your mind, Moshe," was Shmuely's advice to his son. "I thought we discussed that before you went out."

"We did, and I did. Even though I still have no idea why. But this girl was still a disaster. Sorry Ma," Moshe smiled. "Your job is still not over."

"Forget about my job, and hand me those plates to put back in the cabinet, please. I wonder if we should hear from the other side first before we make a decision," Miri mused aloud. "Could be she also doesn't want to go out, and then we'll have nothing to talk about, but first dates should not necessarily be conclusive. It's a bit awkward at first and you can't always get a feel in three hours. Sometimes if you go out again, and you have a little background, it helps things flow and you can get a better idea of who she is…" Miri trailed off at the look on her son's face. "What?"

"Nothing, Mommy. But I am not going out with her again. Even if she is ready to marry me tomorrow." He turned to his father and added, "You won't tell me the issue, but you also won't let me continue with Steinhardt. I put her out of my mind and gave this girl a fair chance… I understand that you only want what is best for me and I'm telling you that a second date is not best." There was more on his mind, but Moshe stopped there and handed his mother the stack of plates on the counter.

*   *   *

Shmuely was too quiet at supper, and something about his silence bothered Miri. "What are you thinking about?" she asked her husband.

"I have some news to share with you. Avigail called a couple of days ago."

"And?" Miri prodded.

"Well, it seems that their Malka is a very hard worker who has no time to be a kid. They've discussed it and they've reached the conclusion that it's because Avigail is never home. Malka takes care of all the children until she gets home, and then she is a big help to Avigail with supper and things."

"Okay." Miri thought that Shmuely seemed to be picking his words too carefully. What was wrong with Malka's helping out at home? Of course Avigail worked hard. Her husband wouldn't be able to learn if she didn't. "So why did she call?"

"Well, it seemed to be getting out of hand, with Malka neglecting homework and things. They spoke with Baruch's Rosh Yeshiva, R' Shua, and Baruch is looking for work."

"What? Leaving *kollel*?"

"Yes."

"Now? Now they've decided that they're overworking the kids and Baruch needs to work?"

"Now? What does that mean?"

"You know very well what that means. We have two kids in *shidduchim*, Shmuely. One actively, and one who will be on the market in less than a year! Couldn't they wait?" Miri's voice was shrill. Shmuely would no doubt tell her she was overreacting, but honestly, she wasn't. Shmuely was a smart man but he could be really thickheaded sometimes. Didn't he understand what this meant for their family?

Shmuely was looking at her, waiting for her to explain herself. "Seriously, Shmuely. We've always been known as a family wholly committed to learning. How will it look if our children are not solid in their commitment? Especially now, when Moshe is actively dating?"

"Are you serious, Miri?"

"Do I sound like I'm joking?"

"I hope you are. That is completely ridiculous. Not solid in their commitment? Avigail has been supporting her family in *kollel* for fifteen years! Fifteen years! And this is now the best thing for her family. Isn't family a commitment? Shouldn't her family be foremost on her mind? Don't you want her to continue to raise happy, successful children?"

The question was rhetorical, but Miri answered anyway. "Still, must it be now, when we are trying to marry off Moshe and then Chani?"

"Miri, I hope you aren't planning to say anything like that to Avigail. That's the last thing she needs to hear."

"Shmuely! What do you take me for? I may not like what they are doing, but you know I'd never deliberately make my children feel bad!"

Shmuely nodded and the conversation, apparently, was over. But it was all Miri could think about. *How could Avigail do that to her? Working? Baruch? Now?*

Avigail called the next day, just to schmooze, and Miri forced herself to be cheerful, acting as if nothing had happened, but inwardly she was seething. *It will be* your *fault if Moshe and Chani have a hard time with shidduchim.* She wondered if the only family who would be willing to take them now would be the Steinhardts. And Miri would never agree to *that*!

*   *   *

"Rachel, I think we are doing the *seder* this year and I need your help," Linda Bergmann said to her daughter. "The *seder* is on Wednesday night, but I want you home on Tuesday so we can get everything ready. I don't want to be rushed and I want everything done before everyone comes." Rachel was lying on the bed in her dorm room twirling a piece of her hair through her fingers.

"Why, where are Aunt Karen and Uncle Eric?"

"Eric's dad is not doing well and they are busy with him. She doesn't have time to organize the *seder*. I offered to do it for her. There will be about twenty people here. Hannah is coming with her new baby and they will be sleeping over." Linda said, referring to Aunt Karen's oldest child, the cousin Rachel had idolized as a youngster. "And Sammy will come, and I think he may be bringing his friend, Jenny. She doesn't live so far from here, so he is going to take her home afterward. You know, I think it is her first *seder*."

"Cute."

"What about Ian? Do you want to invite him?"

"Yeah, that would be nice. But I am sure he has his own *seder*. The way he talks about his mom, she would never let him opt out of any family gathering that had to do with Jewish tradition. They sound very observant. I think she even lights candles."

"Invite him and we'll see what happens. I like the fact that his is a very close-knit family, but you will be coming to *our seders,* and I hope you realize that!"

"Mom, chill. We'll work it out when it comes to that. Maybe we can get really observant and do both *seders.* Then we can go to one and one. Or maybe I'll make the *seder* and I'll have both of our families."

"Then you'd better get home quickly and help me prepare. You need practice."

*   *   *

In time, the school found out about the divorce and as Ahuva predicted, there was a memo sent to the teachers to inform them and to request some leeway for Faigy. Ahuva felt herself becoming a crutch to Faigy Baum; it made her impatient with her. She found herself becoming short with her during their nightly conversations and soon took to ignoring Faigy's calls whenever she could do so without feeling completely callous.

"I don't know what's wrong with me," she told Michal. "I don't want to be mean, and I do want to help her. She feels that there's no one else who cares about her. I don't want to harm her self-esteem, but this is a bit ridiculous. I'm on the phone with her every single night, and she writes me notes in school and stuff. I can't handle it!"

"Sounds like she's stifling you. You should set boundaries. Let her know you're available for her at specific times."

"But what if she's going through a really hard time but I'm not available because it's not between 8:30 to 9:00 PM?"

"You're smarter than that, Ahuva. Of course she can call you in an emergency! But at this point it sounds like she's using you and that is not healthy for either of you."

"Michal, how do you know everything?"

"Come on, Huv. My mother counsels all these people... you pick up a thing or two from living at my house," Michal laughed.

"Yeah, I guess. So what do I do?"

"You'll have to take it slowly. But you're her teacher, so it should be easier to do than if you were trying to limit a regular friendship. Why don't you speak to my mother and ask her?"

Ahuva spoke to her aunt and learned some valuable tips. But there was one which gave her a hard time. "Why don't you put her in touch with someone who has been in her situation or has dealt with divorce before?" Tante Devorah asked. "It's very nice of you to help her and to be there for her, but in this kind of situation it's important to have the support of others who can really empathize. I'm sure you do wonderful things for her, but *Baruch Hashem* you have no experience in these matters."

Ahuva had given her aunt a noncommittal "hmm" as a response to this, and told her she'd think about it. She did think, and she knew it was probably the right thing to do. In fact, that had been her immediate reaction when she first found out about Faigy's home life. But now — *I can't just hand Faigy over like that! I'm finally getting through to her and making some progress. Now I should "put her in contact with others who have been in similar situations"!? It's true, sometimes she grates on my nerves, and she calls me at the most inconvenient times, but I worked hard bringing her to where she is now, helping her to handle her situation, to get involved again in school, to hang around with friends… I don't want to hand all that work away on a silver platter. I'll have to learn how to deal with her neediness so that it doesn't overwhelm me. It's all part of being a good teacher and showing your students you care. She needs to learn how to recognize boundaries? I'll teach her how; that's an important lesson to learn!*

Chapter 11

THE HARDEST PART WAS telling his *chavrusa*. "Mendel, I have some bad news," Baruch began. He told his *chavrusa* of five years about the latest development and added that if he knew of any open positions he should let Baruch know. "I'd like us to remain *chavrusas* until something comes through, but it's up to you. I may not be so steady; I'll have to go to interviews."

"What kind of job are you looking for?" Mendel Gross wanted to know.

"Anything, I guess." Baruch spread out his hands. "What do I know about business and fields and kinds of jobs? A job is a job, and anyone who is willing to hire me has got me."

"Have you thought about *hashgachah*?"

"*Hashgachah*? No."

"Well, think about it. My brother-in-law works in *hashgachah* and it sounds to me like they are always looking for competent *mashgichim*. You'll have to take a *bechinah* before being hired, so if you want, we can crack open *Yoreh Deah* and start studying."

"Let me talk to my wife and I'll get back to you. She's the boss, you know." Baruch's grin was partly rueful and he hoped Mendel understood that it wasn't he who wanted to give up learning. "And

give me your *shvugger's* number so I can speak to him and find out
the *matzav.*

Business taken care of, the pair sat down to learn.

*   *   *

It was about two weeks before Pesach and Ahuva was preparing a Pesach worksheet for her students. She decided she needed a
break; she'd been working on this project for hours, and since she
was already on the computer she thought she might as well check
her email. It wasn't something she did often — she hardly used her
account — and now there were over a hundred messages to sift
through. It was time-consuming, and Ahuva had almost given up
wading through them when one jumped out at her. It was from her
friend Penina Kestenbaum and the subject line was, "Guess Who?"

Intrigued, she opened it.

Ahuva opened the attachment and was horrified. It was a picture of herself, sitting on a piano bench in the center of a room.
She was dressed in decidedly non-*tzniyusdik* clothes, and the girls
surrounding her looked even worse. There was another picture of
her, this time sitting at a lecture — and dressed even worse. Ahuva
grabbed the phone on the desk and dialed her friend's number.

Penina was all ready to catch up on the latest news. "I'm sorry,
Penina, I can't schmooze now, I have no head for small talk. What
is the meaning of that email you sent me from Journeys?"

"What email? Oh, that? I don't know. I do Pathway Partners so
they send all the promotional things to me, and I was bored one
day so I went through the newsletter. What are you doing at the
seminar dressed like that?"

"It's not me, Penina! You know that. Who else saw those pictures?"

"I don't know, whoever gets the newsletter I guess."

"Who makes them up? This is crazy! Why would they do that?"

"Do what?"

"Photoshop me like that!"

"You mean you went to the seminar?"

"Penina! Do you really think that is me?"

"Of course not! It has to be photoshopped, but how would they have a picture of you if you didn't go to the seminar?"

"I have no idea," Ahuva exclaimed. "Who do I know in Journeys that has a picture of me so they could do that? And why *would* they do that?" Ahuva wailed.

She ended the conversation quickly and called her parents into the study. They were furious. The next day, Dovid called Journeys from his office, and asked to speak with Rabbi Lazarus. He was told Rabbi Lazarus was not available; he was out of the country and would not be returning for another week. Dovid could not wait a week. He asked for Rabbi Lazarus' email address and promptly fired off a letter, attaching the picture of his daughter at the seminar, taken from the Journeys website.

*   *   *

"What are you doing for Passover, Sarah?" Susan Lankry asked.

"I'm not sure. I have a term paper due right after the holiday, so I haven't decided whether or not to go home," Sarah responded. *As if you made your decision because of the term paper! You're not interested in going home and seeing how happy everyone else is to be together, knowing you could have been just as happy if you hadn't been determined to cut off your nose to spite your face.* Holiday time was always hard for Sarah. As much as everyone tried to include her in the banter, she was not privy to the inside jokes that flew back and forth at the table, and she knew she had no one to blame but herself.

"I'm going home for the *seder*, and I don't live far from here. You're welcome to come to my *seder* if you want."

"Thanks," Sarah replied. "I wouldn't want to intrude on your family's *seder*."

"Oh, please, Sarah," Susan replied. "My mom and dad love having new people at the *seder*. It's a tradition my older sister started. She brought home an exchange student one year, and ever since then, we have not had a *seder* without a new face. Actually, the girl married my brother! My mom loves when we bring home *seder* guests. She tries to match them up. And you know," she continued thoughtfully, "she's pretty good at it. My cousin is dating the guy my brother brought home two years ago." Susan laughed and Sarah joined her.

"Actually, the Hoffmans invited me to their *seder*," Sarah responded. "If I don't go to my aunt and uncle, I'm going to stay on campus and go to them."

"Oh. Yeah, you go there like every other week."

"For Shabbat."

"Shabbat? Like at the seminar we went to with Rachel and Beth?" Susan wrinkled her nose. "Is that when you started going to the Hoffman's and doing Shabbat?"

"Yeah." Sarah did not say anything else and silently berated herself for having said even that much. *Oh, who cares? So, she'll think you're weird. Your whole life people thought you were weird. And now that you're finally becoming happy, you still care what people are saying?*

No, Sarah answered herself. *But I also don't see a reason to assist them in finding me weird. It'll be bad enough informing Grandma and everyone that I am not going to her seder. I don't have to explain myself to anyone else.*

She called her grandmother that night. *May as well get it over with.* As predicted, Grandma was upset. "Who are the Hoffmans? A *seder* is family time. Why would you spend it with someone else's family?" Sarah explained her term paper, and she came to a truce with her grandmother. Schoolwork was something her grandmother could understand, and Sarah found it an easy and convenient excuse. *I just better do really well!*

*   *   *

In Israel for the wedding of a nephew, Rabbi Menachem Lazarus checked his email, just in case there was something he needed to know about and deal with. "I run a business for people, and I need to be there for the people" was his refrain.

There were the standard emails: inspiring messages about the approaching holiday, announcements and letters promoting up-coming speeches and speakers, some questions from his secretary and other Journeys representatives — and an email from someone named Dovid Steinhardt.

> Rabbi Lazarus,
>
>   I want to start out by thanking you for the work you do for Klal Yisrael. While the rest of us sit here and tell ourselves, "some-one else will take care of it," you are that person.

Oh no, thought Menachem. *What happened now? What did Journeys do wrong?* He continued reading.

> I have only good to say about your work, but I am disturbed by the following: Recently, I saw a picture of my daughter in at-tendance at one of your seminars. The issue is that she never attended any of your seminars. Further, the picture (attached) borders on slander. My daughter is a Bais Yaakov graduate, and the girl in the picture is obviously not. I am not sure how this

happened but was told by my daughter that it was "photo-shopped." (My daughter is the girl on the piano bench.)

I am sure you will take the necessary action immediately. I trust this will include finding those responsible for this picture and dealing with them appropriately, as well as apologizing to my daughter for the *agmas nefesh* caused to her.

Thank you, Dovid Steinhardt

Menachem opened the attachment and immediately understood the harsh tone of Steinhardt's letter. This was why he opened his email while away from the office. It wasn't right for this girl to have to wait until he was back in the office for him to deal with this problem.

First things first, though. Menachem emailed Mr. Steinhardt and asked for a picture of his daughter, the girl in question. It wasn't that he didn't believe Mr. Steinhardt; on the contrary, why would anyone make up a story like that? But it was strange and unlike any previous complaints. He wanted to get to the bottom of this and a picture would help.

"I also want you to know that I am out of the country and will be back next week. I will do what I can from abroad, but if I do not respond right away, please do not think I am not taking this seriously. I hope to have this resolved by Pesach. And I will call your daughter to apologize as soon as I get back. As a matter of fact, it will be the *first* thing I will do on my return," read his email.

Menachem sent the picture to his secretary and told her to forward it to the Journeys employees, asking if anyone knew who she was. When no one in the office responded, the secretary forwarded it to some Journeys college campus employees, and received the answer just as she was turning off her computer for the ten-day Pesach break. She quickly forwarded the email to Rabbi Lazarus, who, although had put this on the top of his list as promised, was busy coordinating the Pesach Retreat and didn't see it until *chol hamoed*.

Menachem was tempted to put the email aside and deal with it after Yom Tov, but he thought of Dovid Steinhardt, sitting at home not knowing what was happening, and he called Yudi Hoffman, Brown University's Journeys representative.

"Hi, this is Menachem Lazarus. I got an email from Toby Jakubowicz saying that you know the girl in the picture from the Presidents' Day Seminar."

"Yes, Rachel Bergmann. What do you need to know about her?"

"Who is she?"

"Nice girl," Yudi answered. "Comes to my classes every once in a while. She went to the seminar with a couple of friends, but there's not too much potential; her father is the president of their Reform Temple. I think she is a waste of time. There was another girl in the picture, Sarah Kessler. I am having some *hatzlachah* with her."

"No one is a waste of time, Yudi, and all *neshamos* have potential." Menachem's voice suddenly got cold.

"You're right, I am sorry. I should not have said that. And I will try harder with her in the future."

"Good, but that is not why I am calling," Menachem said, his tone reverting to its previous warmth. He proceeded to explain the situation. "I have a picture of Miss Steinhardt, and there's no mistaking it, they do look alike. I wanted to make sure someone really did know the girl in the photo and can vouch for her."

"Strange. Send me the other picture and I'll get to the bottom of this after Pesach."

Chapter 12

"HOW ARE YOU DOING, Faigy?" her aunt Miriam asked.

"Fine."

"Really?"

"Yes, really." Miriam was her favorite aunt, and Faigy loved talking to her. Miriam was her father's sister, and she had come with her family to spend the second days of Yom Tov with her parents, Faigy's grandparents, along with Faigy, her siblings — and Faigy's father. They were alone in the kitchen, peeling potatoes, again. The ambience invited confidences, and Faigy blossomed under her adored aunt's attention.

"It was very hard in the beginning. It still is hard, having no father in the house. But we're getting used to it. In a way... in a way it's easier." Faigy was horrified; she could not believe she had actually said that to her father's sister. But Miriam must have known about the tension that was always right below the surface. Miriam was her father's youngest sister and Faigy remembered how often she used to come to their house for Shabbos before she was married.

"I can understand that, Faigs. It's hard when everyone is always on edge. It's okay, you don't have to be embarrassed to talk about it. I'm sure things must have hit you the hardest because you're the oldest, and sharing it will help."

Faigy nodded.

"Do you have anyone to talk to?" Miriam asked.

"Yes!" Faigy's eyes sparkled, and she told her aunt about the teacher she adored. "She really knows how to put everything in perspective," Faigy gushed.

"You're not speaking to her too often though, are you?" Miriam asked warily. She had been in high school recently enough to recognize the hero-worship in her niece's eyes when she spoke about Miss Steinhardt and was afraid of it.

"Oh, no! She's not married, so I don't have to worry about bothering her when she's home with her kids. She's really great. I'm so lucky to have her." Faigy sighed contentedly.

"What do the girls in your class say?"

"Well, some of them are jealous of me, of course! Everyone likes Miss Steinhardt." Faigy glowed with the knowledge that others were envious of her. "But I don't really mind being called a teacher's pet. She's really helping me in my time of need, and if others don't like it, that's their problem."

"That's a good attitude in general, Faigy, but make sure you are still left with friends. What about your friend Mindy?"

"She's great, Miriam. She encouraged me to talk to Miss Steinhardt and helped me go over to her and break the ice. She's happy for me that I have someone like her."

"Great, Faigy. I'm also happy for you. I just want to warn you — don't get too close to her."

"What do you mean?" Faigy demanded.

"Just that you make sure to keep a bit of a distance. It's not healthy to rely on someone so much. Get used to talking to other people, making other friends. Not only teachers. Not that you should broadcast your problems to the world," Miriam hastened to dispel the notion before Faigy thought it a good idea, "But don't get too familiar with one person. It's not healthy." Miriam said no more. "You're a smart girl, Faigy. Think about it and you'll understand."

Faigy reflected on what Miriam said as she ground the potatoes in the food processer. *Nah, Miss Steinhardt isn't like that.* She'd never betray Faigy's confidence if that's what her aunt meant.

*   *   *

Rabbi Lazarus called Dovid Steinhardt and gave him the good news. The girl in the picture was real, and she was not Ahuva. Dovid hung up the phone and joined his wife and daughter in the den. Ahuva was at the piano and Rivky was reading a magazine.

"Mommy? Do you think the Friedmans saw that picture?"

"Ahuva, I thought we were past that," Dovid answered for his wife.

"We are. But there is a picture of someone who looks like me floating around and anyone might have access to it. Maybe they saw it and got nervous."

"Unlikely. They canceled before the second date. There is no way the picture circulated that fast."

"Oh." Ahuva was silent. Suddenly, she flew upstairs to her room and leafed through her calendar. Yes! the dates worked. Running back down to her parents, she cried, "But, Abba, I just *chapped.* Rabbi Friedman speaks at Journeys! He probably saw this girl in real life!"

"You think he spoke on Presidents' Day?" Rivky asked doubtfully.

"Well, our date was the week of Presidents' Day. I just checked. And they canceled on *Motza'ei Shabbos,* so it makes sense."

"Do you think so? I guess it makes sense." Rivky was uncertain.

"Abba, can you find out?"

"Ahuva, do you really want to go ahead with this? They dropped you cold turkey." Rivky winced at her choice of words, but there was really no other way to describe it. "And without an explanation. What if this was not the reason? Do you want to find that out?"

Ahuva looked at her father, pleading. "I think I do. Abba, what do you think?"

"I guess we can try to find out. But Ahuva, if the answer is no, I want you to forget they exist. I don't want to hear another word about it. I don't think they are worth any tears if this is the way they do business. We are expecting an answer from Cohen after Pesach, and I…"

"But Abba, whatever it is, and whether or not this picture has anything to do with it, I know he had a good time. And so did I. I'd like to try again."

Dovid turned to Rivky, a question in his eyes. "I think so, Dovid," she said slowly. "It's worth a try. If not, then not, but at least we'll know."

Chapter 13

"WHAT DOES YOUR FATHER do?" Marc Bergmann asked. As predicted, Ian had spent the *seder* at home but came to East Hanover from Long Island to meet Rachel's parents before returning to college. Ian smiled. *So, Rachel had been correct about the cross examination,* he mused. But his dad would do the same to anyone who so much glanced at his sisters, and he was prepared.

"He's a pediatrician." Before Marc had a chance to grill, Ian preempted the query and explained that he was following in his father's footsteps but was considering specializing in pediatric cardiology.

"What's taking you so long to decide? Aren't you starting your residency next year?"

"Two years actually. And it isn't taking me so long to decide; I have focused all my electives on pediatric cardiology. I haven't decided yet if I want to continue and specialize, or if I'll join my father's practice. But I have time to decide, and I will continue to do research so that if I decide to go with that specialty, I'll already be halfway there."

The interview continued and when Marc was finally through with the interrogation (it could be called nothing else), Ian grinned again. "Can I take your daughter out now?"

"Nice guy, your friend Ian," Marc Bergmann teased his daughter, as the men turned the conversation to include Linda and Rachel.

"Thanks, Dad. You approve?" Rachel grinned back.

Ian offered to drive Rachel back to school, but there was the problem of getting her car there. "Have Beth drive it," Linda suggested. "Didn't you come with her?" Rachel decided she'd rather not do that and, after going out for a coffee with Ian, parted ways and went back to school with Beth.

*   *   *

In the car on the way up to Rhode Island, Rachel informed her friend that Ian had her parents' approval. "Really? When did they meet him? Didn't he spend the holiday at home?"

"He came down today to meet my parents and they really like him." Rachel sighed contentedly.

"You're so funny, Rachel. I mean, here you are, twenty-one years old, and you still need your parents' approval of your boyfriend."

"Yes and no. I mean, I knew they would like him, but even if they didn't, I would probably still see him. It's just that they do so much for me, and I want to be able to give back to them. I want them to approve of what I do." There was so much hidden meaning behind this statement, and Rachel wondered if Beth understood.

Judging by her reply, Rachel concluded that she didn't. "Parents do that for their children, Rach. They want them to be happy in life, and they want to give to them."

"It's different for me, Beth. I am an only child. As much as they want what I want, my parents also want me to, I don't know, continue their legacy." Rachel sounded very uncertain, and it was not in character. "I mean, who will take over Bergmann Holdings?"

she tried to lighten her tone with a joke.

"Ian will," Beth said promptly. "Yeah, I see why you need your parents to like him. Lighten up, Rachel. You know they would do anything for you. If anyone has parents who love her, it's you."

Rachel kept quiet, her eyes on the road. There was so much she had not said. It was somehow too frightening to talk about, as if speaking about her feelings would make them real. Rachel wanted her parents' approval as a proof of their love. They had raised her with everything and more that a child could ask for. They had anticipated all her needs and her wants and supported her through life. She had never tested their love; she had never felt the need to do so. But now, after the fiasco with Brad, she was frightened. If he, who had professed to care about her, had dropped her, perhaps Marc and Linda could drop her too. After all, they were not her *real* parents.

She wanted to know who she *really* was. And, if what Beth had said was true — that parents loved their children unconditionally — how could her real mother have given her away? She *had* to find out. She had to find *her*.

But she felt it would be like stabbing Marc and Linda in the back after all they had done for her and all the love they had shown her. And truth be told, she wasn't sure if she had the courage to put their love on trial.

As she drove up I-95 toward New England, she felt as if her mind were a battleground.

They love you. So just quit it. If you really wanted to find your birth mother you know they would help you. What's this bit about testing them?

They would help, but it would hurt them. They don't deserve to be hurt. They've given me so much. And do I want to hurt them? Isn't that what I'm afraid of? Or am I really afraid that they'll find someone else to love, like Brad did.

Don't be ridiculous! They're your parents. Why do you want to find your birth mother anyway? She's the one who abandoned you. She didn't want you. Why would you want her?

I don't want her to be my mother, Rachel answered herself. *I have a mother.* At the back of her mind she understood she was contradicting herself. *I want to know why she abandoned me. It doesn't make sense. Mothers don't do that. And my mother is the greatest proof.* In Rachel's mind there was *mother* and *woman who abandoned me* and she wanted it to stay that way.

Exactly. Your mother loves you, always and forever, the first voice declared. *They'll love you no matter what. So just do it if it means that much to you. And don't tell them if you are so scared.*

That is much worse, Rachel found herself answering back. *I can't do something like this behind their backs!*

So don't do it behind their backs the voice of reason interposed. *Send a petition to the state, and if anything comes of it, you'll discuss it with Mom and Dad.* Rachel had reviewed the process for reunion already, and she knew what steps to take.

I'll talk to Ian. Rachel decided. *He'll know what to do.* Somehow, it seemed the natural course of action. Despite the fact she had known him only three months, Rachel felt he would react differently than Brad had and would stand behind her. She calmed down after reaching her decision.

Beth had noticed neither the war that had just taken place nor the peace treaty Rachel was on the verge of signing. Turning suddenly to her friend, Beth exclaimed, "We are totally stopping at the outlets in Westbrook. I need a new bag, and I want to look in Off Fifth. Allison came by yesterday to say hi," she said, referring to a mutual friend, "and she had a really gorgeous yellow one from there."

"No, I want to get back." Rachel vetoed the shopping expedition.

Life was on hold until she spoke to Ian, and she wanted things to get back to normal as soon as possible.

*   *   *

Sometime over Yom Tov, the idea popped into Faigy's head. Her aunt's words were on her mind constantly, and she wondered, *Did Miriam mean it's not healthy for me?* She thought back to the week before Pesach when Miss Steinhardt had not returned her call at all one night and had told her the next night that she couldn't talk. *Is Miss Steinhardt getting tired of me? Is that what Miriam means?* She decided it wasn't. *After all, I spoke to her on bedikas chametz night for two hours!*

*   *   *

"Ian," Rachel called him as soon as she got back to her apartment. "What's your schedule?"

Ian heard the urgency in her tone and was concerned. His voice came clear and calm through the line, "What's the matter, honey?"

"I don't want to talk now, but do you have time tomorrow? I know you have lots of catching up to do from the past week…"

"Your wish is my command, Rachel. Now that we know your dad approves, I am at your beck and call," said Ian, attempting to alleviate her obvious stress.

Rachel found herself close to tears on the other side of the line. "Thank you," she whispered. And to herself, she added, *I'm cracking.*

Chapter 14

"HELLO, IS RABBI FRIEDMAN available?"

Shmuely picked up the phone in his study. "Hello."

"Hi, my name is Yossi Steinhardt. I am a brother of Dovid Steinhardt." Yossi was met with silence and so he continued talking. "I know my niece, Ahuva, was *redt* to your son a couple of months ago…"

"They went out, actually, as I am sure you know. It didn't work out." Shmuely cut him off.

"Right, I do know that. I was wondering if I could bring up the *shidduch* again."

"I'm afraid not. Thank you for thinking of us."

"Can I ask you why it was dropped? The way I hear it from my brother, there wasn't any reason given as to why you said no, and it sounds like your son had a nice time on the date."

"I'd rather not get into it."

"I had a feeling you would say that," Yossi smiled through the wires. "The story I have is that it was a great first date and both parties were looking forward to a second one. And then you called back and said no, without warning and without explanation. My brother and sister-in-law understand that you have the right to say no, but based on the way the events unfolded, it seems as though you must have heard something that made you change your minds. If you did, they'd like to know what it was, to be able to rectify it for the future." Yossi picked his words carefully. He was on a mission and wanted to do it right. He did not want to supply Friedman with any excuse, but he did want an answer, and so he needed to lead him. As a *menahel* in *Mesivta*, Yossi was a pro, but Shmuely Friedman wasn't a recalcitrant sixteen-year-old and needed to be handled with kid gloves if he was to become Dovid's only *mechutan*.

"I guess you could say that," was Rabbi Friedman's equally careful answer.

"Care to elaborate?"

"My wife and I made a decision not to talk about it. We did not even tell the *shadchan,* as we did not want to ruin your niece's chances. I am not sure if our decision was proper, but that is the way things stand right now."

"I guess I am with you on one thing here. I also wonder if it is the right decision." Yossi paused to allow Friedman a chuckle, and when none came, he continued, "If there is someone spreading *lashon ha'ra* about her, I hope you would give her the chance to defend herself. *B'emes,* there is nothing bad you can say about Ahuva."

"Listen, I understand your feelings about your niece, and she did impress us when we met her. It wasn't something we heard about her, it was something we saw." Shmuely instantly regretted his words. He had not meant to say that; he had not wanted to say anything.

"I can't think of anything that would paint Ahuva in a bad light."

"If I told you, you would understand. And it's hard for me to imagine that Miss Steinhardt herself doesn't understand. But really, I don't want to talk about it."

"Rabbi Friedman, you said this much. So tell me one more thing: Does it have anything to do with your son not thinking that my niece is a *shidduch*? Only your son."

"I..."

"Good. And once we have gone this far, just give me a hint."

"I am not sure why I am doing this, but you can tell your brother that I spoke at the Journeys seminar the Shabbos after their first date."

"And you saw my niece, and she wasn't *frum*."

"I told you she'd know." Shmuely was triumphant.

"I can explain."

"I don't need an explanation; my wife and I saw her. There is no excuse for how she looked. I am on the rabbinical board of Journeys, and our policy on *kiruv rechokim* is that there is no compromise in your own *frumkeit*, even if it will bring someone else closer."

"I am with you all the way. And so is my niece."

Shmuely did not hear Yossi's interruption and continued. "That is not the type of girl we want for our son. And what I said earlier about not being sure we made the right decision, it's because I think this *is* something others should know about when they are looking into her. Listen, I am sure she had the best of intentions, but it is not for us."

"Rabbi Friedman." Yossi stopped him.

"Yes?"

"Would you believe me if I told you that the girl you saw was not my niece?"

"What?" Shmuely was nonplussed. "We saw her."

"I know you did, and I am having trouble understanding it

myself. But it's the truth. Did you wonder why they never brought this up until now? I mean it's been two months and they never said anything."

Shmuely was silent in the face of that logic, and Yossi continued with the story. He explained how Ahuva had come across the picture two weeks ago, right before Yom Tov, and had been horrified at the thought that someone would want to portray her in so bad a light, until they found out that the girl in the picture was really someone else. They certainly understood that others might make the same mistake that they had, and, if that was the reason the Friedmans broke off the *shidduch*, there was a reasonable possibility it could be resumed. Ahuva was interested and she seemed fairly confident that if this was the reason, Moshe Friedman would also be interested in a second meeting. Dovid had asked his brother Yossi to find out.

Shmuely understood immediately. He had always felt the situation hadn't made any sense and he told this to Yossi. "I mean, the girl waved to my wife. The whole thing was strange." He promised to speak to his wife and bring things back on track. "Can you call me tomorrow?"

"Sure, and thank you."

Chapter 15

SHMUELY CALLED MIRI INTO the room to speak privately with her. This was no easy feat as it was *chol hamoed,* and the house was teeming with children and grandchildren. A quick synopsis of the phone call was all that was needed to restart the *shidduch.*

"Oh, I am so much happier now. I always liked the Steinhardt *shidduch* the best. They were the first ones we said yes to, you know. And it makes me feel so much better; I couldn't believe Rivky Miller had raised her daughter like that. Of course, it will be up to Moshe."

"And of course he will say yes."

"Of course. But we have to prepare ourselves for the fact that he may have deemed it a lost cause by now, and for good reason. Maybe he wants to move on to bigger and better things."

"Bigger and better? Than a *shidduch* with Steinhardt?"

"Well," Miri said reflectively, missing the teasing note in his voice, " He may have tried to convince himself it wasn't worth it and by now he could have gotten over it…" She trailed off, noticing her husband's grin. "Shmuely Friedman, you are the most impossible person I have ever met!"

*　　　*　　　*

Moshe jumped at the opportunity. "But what happened?" he asked his parents. "I thought it was written in stone."

"We found something out."

"*Nu?*"

"Nothing," Miri answered shortly. "We didn't want to tell you what it was that was negative, and now that we are back on, what would be the *to'eles* in saying anything at all? You just take her out on a second date as though nothing happened."

Miri turned to her husband as Moshe walked out of the room. There was a broad smile on her son's face, and his evident happiness contributed an edge to Miri's voice. "We'll have to tell them about Baruch."

"Baruch?" Shmuely was confused. "Baruch who?"

"Baruch Greenberg. Your son-in-law who is looking for a *job!*"

"Huh? Why should they care about Baruch? Didn't we go through this once, Miri? There is no reason in the world that we need to tell people that Baruch is looking for a job unless it will help him in his search. We certainly don't have to tell potential *shidduchim* as though it were a disease!"

"We must tell them." Miri was adamant. "They are going into this *shidduch* thinking one thing, and I don't want it to come back to haunt us later. I won't be happy until I know they know."

"Whatever you want, Miri."

*   *   *

The second date was scheduled for the Sunday night after Pesach. Ahuva walked into her closet and pulled out a black wrap jumper she had gotten for Yom Tov. Nice and conservative. She wore it with a white gold and diamond spiral pendant on a thin chain. Her manicured nails were pale pink, glowing subtly, but the color not discernable unless one looked really closely.

Dovid answered the door for Moshe and invited him in. "Have a seat, my daughter will be down in a minute," he said. "We already went through the whole *farher* thing, so just sit down and relax. Maybe a drink while you're waiting?" Moshe declined. He didn't need to soothe his nerves by playing around with a drink. He wasn't nervous — at least not *very* nervous.

Ahuva came down the back stairs into the kitchen where her mother was waiting and they walked into the living room together.

Introductions were unnecessary, and the young couple went outside into the crisp April twilight. Moshe opened the car door for his date, and they were off.

After the preliminaries were over ("Let me know if you are cold or hot so I can adjust the temperature..."), they were both silent. As they turned the corner, Moshe grinned in the darkness. "This is awkward," he said. "How about starting from the beginning, and pretending we never did this before?"

Ahuva laughed, the sweet sound of her voice filling up the car. "That's a good idea. So, how many siblings do you have?"

"Well, before we get to that, I do want to apologize for the past couple of months."

Score one for the boy, Ahuva thought, elated. She had discussed it with her mother before the date, and they had concluded that an apology was not required, but if he did apologize it would prove he is a *mentsch.* "Oh, it's fine. Very understandable."

"It is?" Moshe blurted before he had a chance to think.

"Well, yes. I mean, I would probably have done the same if the situation were reversed."

"Well, I must confess my ignorance, but I do not even know the reason it was called off. My parents sort of told me that it was not *noge'a,* and there was no *to'eles* in my knowing."

"Oh!" Ahuva was thrown off balance. "That was nice, I guess. I mean, it wasn't *noge'a* before, and now, you don't know the issue, so..." She stumbled while trying to express her thoughts. What she meant was that if he had not known the reason it was called off, then he had never thought anything bad of her. She found that thoughtful of his parents.

"I'll take your word for it," Moshe tried to put her at ease.

"It's not really such a big deal, truthfully," she said. "Now that it's over," she amended and she told him what had happened.

Moshe was silent. And then, "I guess it's a lesson in trusting your parents then. Mine kept telling me to believe they knew what they were doing and they only wanted the best for me..." he trailed off, and Ahuva picked up the thread and brought it to *tachlis*.

"I hope I would know what is best for my children. What do you think you would have done in this case if you were your father?"

"I don't know... I sort of hope I would never be in this situation... and I also hope I would learn from mistakes, and do some research before just stopping the whole thing. I mean, there had to be some plausible explanation... you know, you have to give me a little time to digest the situation. I can't be expected to come up with an answer in thirty seconds."

Ahuva conceded and there was silence in the car until Moshe resumed talking. "It's really a tough one. I mean if that girl really looks like you? So that the whole Shabbos they were convinced it *was* you? Then I don't know. But," he continued reflectively, "how did that happen? That she should look exactly like you? Maybe she's your long-lost sister," he said. He had meant it as a joke, but then, remembering who he was talking to and what the implications were, Moshe instantly regretted his words.

"I... I'm sorry... I... that was completely uncalled for... I..." It was Moshe's turn to stammer.

"It's okay," Ahuva said quietly. "My adoption is no secret. And I wondered the same thing myself." She was disinclined to continue the conversation, though, and was happy for the diversion Moshe created by asking her if she would rather the Hilton or the Sheraton.

The rest of the drive was uneventful. The young couple covered topics from things to do in Israel to funny dating stories. Moshe had no stories of his own, as this was only the third date of his career, but he did have six sisters, five of whom were married, so he was able to contribute some of their best.

They found seats in an inconspicuous corner of the hotel lobby, and the conversation turned back to *tachlis*. "What was one of your most memorable teaching experiences?" Moshe asked. *Someone has a list of topics in his pocket,* Ahuva thought with a grin. But it was a good start for a "greener," she acknowledged. Besides, she liked him and wanted to share with him. "It wasn't an actual teaching experience," she began, "but when I was a counselor in a camp in the Ukraine, I had a girl who was mean. Plain, outright cruel. She knocked a bunkmate onto the floor once and refused to apologize. So I made her sit out the rest of the day until she did.

"You have no idea what kind of day that was. First of all, it was a *ta'anis*. And here I was, with an eleven-year-old girl with whom I could not really communicate, and I had to punish her. And she wouldn't stay in the chair; I had to practically hold her down. It was crazy. We were in the dining room, with people going in and out, and she bad-mouthed me to each one of them so they all thought I was this crazy American who was holding Anya — that was her name — hostage. And I couldn't even say anything in my defense, because I don't speak their language. Not that I would have, because I think that is bad *chinuch,* but…" she paused, reflectively.

"And I felt helpless, like I *was* a monster, but I knew she needed it. She was never taught right from wrong, and enough was enough. But," she ended thoughtfully, "I'll never know if I did the right thing."

"What do you mean?" Moshe asked. "It sounds like she needed to be taught a lesson."

"She did. I am not telling you the whole story, so you might not understand…"

"Try me."

"What?"

"Tell me the whole story. We have time, and it sounds interesting. I didn't know you went to camp in the Ukraine."

Ahuva appreciated his sincerity and started from the beginning. She told him about going to camp and speaking the "language of the heart." "The point is to love the kids and show them what a *frum* Jew is like," she said. "Most of these girls did not come from loving families, and here was a chance for them to feel loved. It was our job to shower them with hugs and kisses and prizes and nosh, and to tell them that we love every one of them because we love every Jew. And that they are family with every other Jew, and that Hashem loves them. And we were told that even if we don't see that they changed in any way because we were there, our hope was that they will remember our time with them and how we related to them, and maybe that remembrance will stop them from marrying a *goy.*

"I personally think that love needs to be tempered with discipline, and I hated when on *Erev Shabbos* the campers would bang down the door, already asking for the Shabbos party. We gave it to them so they would associate Shabbos with good things and come to love it, but I found that it created an attitude of *"hakol magi'a li"* in the girls, and I hated that. Yet we were told to give, give, give. I thought it was the wrong kind of giving, but I was not the boss," she smiled, and Moshe nodded his head to show he was listening. "What happened with Anya, though?" he asked.

"Anya came from the dorm, which meant she didn't have a family. And she was so crazy mean. Well, sometimes she could be really cute and sweet, and other times… Whoa!"

"This was the other time, I guess."

"Right. And as I said, enough was enough. This was the straw that broke the camel's back, if you know what I mean." Moshe nodded again in understanding, and Ahuva continued. "So I sat her down and told her that she must apologize, and she refused. I sat with her for at least four hours, and I watched her like a hawk, because every time I turned my back she got up to leave. I had to forcibly bring her back, and I felt like a tyrant. And even the other girl, the one Anya kicked, told me she didn't care and Anya could come back to the bunk. But I still made her sit there."

"Why?"

"Because I told her she must sit until she apologizes, and she just refused to say she was sorry. And I was not going to back down, because if I did she'd think she won. She needed to be taught a lesson."

"So why aren't you sure you did the right thing?"

"Because," Ahuva explained, and it was obvious this still bothered her, "we were supposed to give them love. This wasn't love."

"Tough love. That's what my mother would call it."

"Right. But does tough love work if it's used only once? If this were to be the only time she'd be disciplined — *really* disciplined — then what was the point? She wouldn't get the feeling that I loved her, and who knows if I turned her away?" To her own ears she sounded overly distressed; she hoped it didn't sound that way to him. She wondered if it was a smart idea to have brought this up. It meant so much to her, but was it too early to get into such a discussion?

"This can't be the first time you are telling the story. What does everyone else think?"

"That I did the right thing. At least that's what they told me, but I just thought of that last part now. If this is the only time she was ever disciplined, who knows if it caused more harm than good?"

Ahuva took a mental step back and found herself feeling disembodied, as though she was floating above the two of them, sitting in the hotel lobby sipping their drinks. She wanted to view the scene from the perspective of an observer, to see how her date would respond to the situation. She could learn much from his reaction.

"But if you had to do it again, would you?"

"What do you mean?" Ahuva asked. The question threw her off balance.

"If you were back in the same situation, how would you react?"

"It would bother me so so much not to do anything to discipline Anya. I mean, she was crying for help. But, as you said before, I hope I would learn from the past, and I… I don't know…" she found herself answering candidly and mentally kicked herself. She had wanted the ball to be in *his* court!

"It sounds to me like you would do it again — because it had to be done. She needed the discipline, and you were the one on the scene to give it to her. And let's say that this *would* be the only time she ever got it. She would just think that you are a crazy American, not that all *frum* girls are monsters and that this is a reason to stay *frei*."

"I guess," Ahuva was comforted. She had never thought about it like that before. And he had taken it well; that comforted her, too. "But what would you have done?" she asked, turning the situation back to him.

"You're doing that to me again," Moshe said, wagging his finger in mock chastisement. "How do I know what I would have done over there with that girl? The way you presented it, I think you did the correct thing." Ahuva smiled and opened her mouth to say something, but Moshe cut her off. "What you really want to know is if I believe in discipline. And the answer is yes, as long as it is accompanied with love. And sometimes it has to be tough love. Of course, the key is to raise your children with discipline when they are young so they won't need the *potch* when they grow old."

"Do you believe in *potching*?" Ahuva asked. Things sure were getting heavy for a second date.

"Sure do. My parents *potched* us when we needed it and I think we all turned out okay. There needs to be a balance, as with everything in life. Too much *potching* is of course no good, but none at all is also bad. What about you?"

"You know about me, you saw it from my story. Of course I couldn't hit Anya, she isn't my daughter, but I think that a few good smacks would have set her straight. I think that is one of the problems of today's generation. People are so scared of turning their children off that they throw discipline out the window and then wonder why their kids are so *chutzpadik*.

"I mean, look at me. I am an only child, and I could have had anything I wanted... But my parents were smart, and they made me earn things so I would see the value of money. There was no such thing as an allowance when I grew up. If I wanted something that I didn't *need*, I babysat, or saved up birthday money or something."

"But that's not *potching*."

"No, but it goes under the heading of Discipline. Children need to be shown authority from when they are young so they can grow into it." She looked at Moshe pensively.

"*Maskim*. A hundred percent. My story would be a bit different than yours because I was not an only child, and my parents had no money, so we always knew the value of a dollar. But we were *potched* and put in the corner and taught to respect our elders."

The conversation continued and Ahuva and Moshe discovered that they had much in common and that they shared ideals. When Moshe got up to refill their drinks he glanced at the clock and noticed that almost five hours had passed since he had picked Ahuva up at her house. "I think we better head home," he said as he returned with Ahuva's water. "It's late."

The third date was scheduled for Wednesday night.

Chapter 16

"AVIGAIL, I GOT TWO offers today, *Baruch Hashem*!"

"Oh, really? I'm so excited! Which ones?"

"One is with Menorah. They need someone in the area but they also need someone to travel to their out-of-town places. Because I'd be the new guy, I'd have to travel. The guys who've been with them longer have first choice, so they get the local jobs. But after a while I might not have to travel so much."

"Travel?" Avigail sounded dismayed. "How long would you be away?"

"I would be home every Shabbos. And they will try not to schedule me to be away two weeks in a row."

"Oh."

"But the job seems pretty easy. You know, they give *hashgachah* on processed foods, so I'd be working in factories. I'll be able to learn while I'm there, so that's good. I must thank Mendel again for giving us the idea of *hashgachah*," Baruch added.

"What's the other offer?" Avigail asked.

"Lakewood Kosher. One of their *mashgichim* is retiring. He works in a restaurant — they won't tell me which one," Baruch answered.

"What does that entail?"

"It's only at night — from 5:00 to 11:00. So I could learn morning *seder*," Baruch smiled at the thought. "But the work is much harder. You need to be much more on top of things in terms of making sure the ingredients are okay, and I'll be responsible for checking every piece of lettuce and whatever else they use."

"Oh." Neither prospect sounded exciting. *Travel?* How would that make Avigail's life any easier? She wouldn't have a husband around to help if things got out of hand at home. But working at night, every night, from 5:00 to 11:00? That meant he wouldn't be home at suppertime. That was when they discussed all the events of the day. That hour was sacred.

Avigail despaired. She wished she had never made a fuss about Baruch going out to work. There wasn't going to be a 9-to-5 office job; with either of the available options, she was losing the little help her husband had been able to provide.

"What do you think, Avigail?" Baruch asked. "The pay is about the same in either case, and I don't know what I'd prefer. On the one hand, traveling sounds terrible, but I'll be able to learn — on the plane, in the hotel, at the plant. With the other job, I'll be learning in the morning, but my nights will be very difficult."

"I don't know," Avigail answered. "By when do you need to give an answer?"

"Three days."

"So we'll think about it."

*   *   *

And think about it she did. *Why, oh why, did I ask him to leave kollel?* Her father's voice rang in her ears. "*It might be k'dai to go back to the Rosh Yeshiva and ask him again, based on how you feel now.*" But she didn't *want* to. Somewhere, deep down, even now after these latest developments, she still felt pleasure in not having to be the family's chief breadwinner. She'd be able to cut her hours, be there for the kids. She'd wash breakfast dishes after *breakfast* instead of saving them, along with Baruch's lunch plate, until after supper. She remembered how she had felt when they were told that Baruch should look for work. A stone had been lifted off her shoulders, and she was able to breathe easier. For months now she had been waiting for an offer to come through that would enable her to lighten her load.

But — travel? I'll never see him. On the other hand, though, if I do cut my hours, and I am able to get things done around the house, maybe I'll be able to go to sleep early, at least one night. If he's out of town I won't have to wait for him to come home. If he worked locally until 11:00, I wouldn't be able to go to bed before he came home. How could I do that in good conscience when I'm the one who caused him to go to work in the first place? So maybe Menorah is a good idea.

Avigail, she scolded herself. *Don't always think of yourself. Think of Baruch! What does he want?*

I'm not only thinking of myself, Avigail answered herself angrily. *But I don't* know *what he wants. To learn in the morning and then to work really hard at night? And then he'll still need to daven Ma'ariv. And wake up early enough in the morning to get all the kids out in time. Or to have to travel — but the work is quiet and he can learn in peace. Besides, this whole thing is about me! The reason he's leaving kollel is to make my life easier! That's what the Rosh Yeshiva said.* She clung to this last line. She needed to remind herself that she had the Rosh Yeshiva's validation for her desire to make her life easier.

But... what *would* make her life easier?

"Baruch, I think you'd better ask R' Shua what you should do," Avigail told her husband the next night. *Let him make the decision.*

Then, whatever happens, it won't be on my head.

*   *   *

The fourth date took place the next Sunday. There was familiarity now in the way Moshe and Ahuva got into the car and eased right into conversation. There was comfort in the fact that they had a shared past, even if it was only three dates. "Remember my friend whom we saw last time?" Moshe asked, "He got engaged last night."

"Oh, *Mazal Tov!*" Ahuva responded. "That's so nice!" Conversation flowed and Ahuva pinched herself more than once to make sure this was real. And to think it almost didn't happen!

It was a beautiful afternoon, and they strolled through a park, enjoying the scent of spring in the air. Ahuva asked Moshe about his family.

"My brother-in-law starts his new job tomorrow. It's really very sad."

"Yeah, I heard about it."

"At least he found a job pretty quickly. But of all people to have to go out to work, he's the last one I would have chosen. A bigger *masmid* you won't find anywhere. I feel very bad for him."

"Mmm."

"It makes you think. My sister never thought she'd have a working husband, but life changes people, you know? And her job was taking a toll on the family."

"I hear you," Ahuva answered, and she was quick to reassure him. "That won't happen with me."

"How can you be so sure?" Moshe wanted to know.

"Well, for one thing, I work in a school setting. I have summer vacation, and Yamim Tovim, and vacations throughout the year. I'll be off whenever my kids are off. And I teach in high school, so I'm at work only a couple of periods a day. Besides, if I ever felt that it was too much for me and I needed a sabbatical or something," she laughed apologetically, "well, my father could support me for a year if I needed him to." No, Ahuva would *never* force her learning husband to go out to work, no matter what the circumstances.

Moshe was silent. Then he asked "What about his business?"

"What about it?" she asked, her guard up, as always, when anyone spoke about Steinhardt Design.

"Well," Moshe seemed embarrassed to say what was on his mind. "He does plan on, uh, retiring someday, no? What are his plans for the business? I, uh, I mean, he has no sons, and, uh, you're not involved at all, and…" he trailed off.

Ahuva felt suddenly deflated, as though someone had stuck a pin into her dreams. *Is that the kind of person you are?* She knew that some people married girls whose fathers were Roshei Yeshivos to ensure themselves of a *shteller*. And she so clearly remembered her one and only date with the Klein boy. He had had designs on her money and her father's business. *But I thought you were different! You're supposed to be the best guy out there. "They don't make them like him anymore," were the words of his Rosh Yeshiva to her parents when they had checked into him. Well, his Rosh Yeshiva was mistaken. Obviously what Moshe really cares about is wealth and status. Well, he won't get it through her!*

"Oh," Ahuva answered with forced gaiety, "I have a cousin in the business. He has no head for learning, but he is very smart. He started about seven years ago, and my father is making him go through every aspect of the business. When he started he was doing deliveries, then customer service, then outside sales." Ahuva tried her best to make it sound really challenging. "My father says you can't effectively run a business unless you know the ins and outs of each department. My cousin acted as a secretary, and I think now he's in the accounting department. My father is very hard on him and doesn't let him make *any* mistakes. And he's not even promising him the business when he's..." Ahuva stopped. *Yes, he is promising him the leadership reins. At least, it doesn't matter, but he's not giving them to my husband. Certainly not to a guy who doesn't have the decency not to show how hungry he is while he's still dating!*

The enjoyment of the day, of dating Moshe, was killed for Ahuva. She tried not to show him how upset she was, but she couldn't find any more to say. She was listless and answered his attempts at conversation in monosyllables.

Moshe got the message; how could he miss it? After an hour of trying to bring the date back on track, he turned to Ahuva and said, "I guess we should head back."

She left the car with a "thank you," leaving out the "I had a nice time." Actually, she had had an awful time.

*   *   *

Rivky was surprised. Ahuva's dates with Moshe had all lasted at least five hours, so when Ahuva returned home after barely two, she became concerned. "How was it?"

"Awful, awful, awful! And it's over. Over. Over."

"What happened, honey?"

"What didn't happen? He wanted to know whom Abba is planning on leaving the business to. Straight out! You thought the Klein boy was bad? Needed to learn the art of subtlety? Well, compared to Friedman he was a model of tact!"

"Oh." Not having been on the date, and hearing only Ahuva's perspective, Rivky could say nothing. But she saw how upset her daughter was, and it tore at her heart. Things had looked so promising! After the first fiasco with Friedman, now this? "What was that?" she asked Ahuva, who was muttering under her breath.

"Nothing. I'm going to change."

"I thought he was different!" Ahuva told herself. "And I've already had so much *agmas nefesh* because of him. Mommy," she called from the top of the banister, "Please call Uncle Yossi and tell him it's over. OVER!"

But she had liked him. She really had. Was there no one in this world to trust? She couldn't trust the boys she dated who wanted her only for her last name… "Who's your *shver*? Oh, Steinhardt," and the eyebrows disappear. And now she couldn't even trust her own instincts. She had liked Moshe Friedman, and she had thought he was different. Of course, if someone had accused his *mother* of being mercenary, well that she could have believed. But that wouldn't have mattered; after all she wasn't going to marry her. But *him*!

She flew to the piano, but her fingers played by rote, her mind elsewhere. She had had enough of Moshe Friedman. In fact, she had enough of all boys!

She was so *mad* at him.

And at herself.

Chapter 17

RACHEL AND IAN DID not meet the day after their return to school, nor the next day. Both were too busy catching up on schoolwork. Ian insisted he would drop everything and run to help her, and Rachel was touched but felt that if she had already waited this long, nothing terrible would happen if she waited a few extra days. It was not until Saturday night that they went out for dinner and Rachel explained what was bothering her.

"You know I am adopted," she said as she picked at the salad on her plate.

"You're what? No, I did not know that," Ian looked up from his soup bowl at her revelation.

"Oh, I thought you might know. It is not a secret..." Rachel was at a loss as to how to continue. She did not know how Ian would react and so much depended on his reaction.

"Well, that's neither here nor there. What's up?"

"It is quite relevant actually," she smiled. *Yay!* she thought. "It is the reason I'm so uptight. I want to find my birth mother." Ian didn't respond. "So, the thing is that I love my parents..."

"And they love you. No question about it. When I think how

your father grilled me on Sunday..." Ian grinned ruefully. "I know you warned me Rachel, but not enough!"

Rachel smiled, but the smile didn't reach her eyes. She put her hands in her lap and smoothed her skirt, hoping Ian couldn't see how nervous she was. "I know they love me, and I am afraid they will be hurt if I want to find my birth mother. I love them, and I don't want to hurt them." She did not say anything about the rejection she was afraid of; it sounded childish to her ears when she had so much proof her parents loved her.

"But isn't that a normal thing? Whenever you hear stories of adoption, people are always looking for their birth parents. Your parents don't strike me as the type to mind if you want to find your roots."

"But I am sure that deep down it would hurt them. They've given me so much. Why can't I be happy to just be Rachel Bergmann?"

"I got you. But from what I know, which admittedly is not much, it sounds like a pretty valid thing to want." He paused and absentmindedly thanked the waiter who brought them their next course. He appeared to be thinking, and said presently, "Can you talk about this openly with your parents?"

"What do you mean by openly? I grew up knowing I was adopted, and I can't tell you how many times I heard the story of how they wanted a baby, and then it turned out to be me, and how they are the luckiest people in the world to have gotten me." She gave an embarrassed grin. "They never really talked about how *she* was crazy to have given me up — not in so many words, but that was the idea. And they are so thankful to G-d for answering their prayers and giving them the best daughter a person could ask for.

"And now I should be like 'Thanks, Mom. Thanks, Dad. But now I want to find the woman who gave me up'?"

"Like I said, I understand your feelings, but let me ask you this: How does it work? It can't be that simple to find your birth mother, can it?"

"Well, there are websites where you register and tell your story and if the person you are looking for also posts you can find each other, but I don't think I want to do that. What I can do is send a petition to the court that finalized my adoption and ask them for my real birth certificate, which would have my birth mother's name. I am over eighteen, so they should give it to me. Or I could hire an intermediary to send in the petition and he would then find my birth mother and let her know that I would like to meet her."

"Hmm."

"I am not sure what I would like better. On the one hand, if it's done through an intermediary you are really out of the loop, but on the other hand, if you do it yourself you get so involved you become obsessed and start jumping on planes left, right and center to chase any dumb lead."

Ian smiled at the image she painted. "Why don't you send the petition and once you get the birth certificate we'll worry about the next step? Let's take one thing at a time."

We'll worry about the next step. The implications were not lost on Rachel and she felt a bubble of happiness rise within her. Rachel ran her fingers through her dark hair, not wanting Ian to see what his words had done to her. "That works, I suppose. I sort of came to that conclusion myself."

"Just needed my blessing, huh? Glad to be of service. And now I'll give you another good idea. Eat your food; it's delicious hot, but I can't vouch for it cold."

Rachel laughed and picked up her fork.

*   *   *

As he did after every date, Moshe drove down the Parkway back to Lakewood. He usually called his parents immediately after the first toll, but now he didn't want to. What had happened to get her so upset? Moshe drove a bit more and then bowed to the inevitable. There would be no use in pretending to his parents; the date had been awful and as puzzled as he was, he was glad to be on his way home. He made the phone call.

"Finished so soon?" Miri exclaimed. "What happened?"

"I'm not sure," Moshe answered truthfully. "Is Tatty home?"

Miri called her husband to pick up the phone. "Moshe, is that you? What happened?" Shmuely asked, echoing his wife.

"I'm not really sure" Moshe repeated. "We were talking and all of a sudden she just clammed up. Wouldn't say another word. It was really strange." He tried to sound nonchalant, but his attempt sounded flat to his own ears.

"Well, what were you talking about? Maybe you hit a raw nerve. Maybe it was something she doesn't like to discuss," Shmuely tried to look at the situation rationally.

"But even when I tried to change the subject it didn't go. It just didn't go. I had no choice but to take her home."

"What were you talking about?" Miri asked.

Moshe hesitated. He did not want to tell his mother about the conversation that had triggered Ahuva's mood. He knew how his mother felt about Baruch's going out to work, *now, when we're trying to marry Moshe off and then Chani.* He, like his father, felt that Miri was going a bit too far. How could it hurt his prospects if his brother-in-law, in *kollel* for fifteen years, was working? But that *had* been what they were talking about!

"What were you talking about?" Miri demanded again.

"Working," Moshe said miserably.

"Avigail and Baruch." It was not a question. His mother would have gone on, but Moshe heard a quiet, firm, "Miri!" from his father, and his mother was silent.

"That's it?" Shmuely asked.

"Yes."

"What did she say?" Shmuely wanted to know.

"I don't know." It was Moshe's turn to answer in monosyllables, and his tone reflected his mood.

Shmuely tried to question him further, but seeing that he was getting nowhere, ended the call. "Let me think about this. Call me back when you get to Lakewood."

Chapter 18

"I KNEW IT!" MIRI burst out as soon as Moshe hung up. "Oh, why did Avigail need to do this *now?*" she wailed. "Miri, enough!" Shmuely was uncharacteristically sharp. "We've discussed this a million times. Avigail is doing what is right for her family. It was a difficult decision to make, and she needs your support. What she does not need is for you to be worried about some faceless people who might or might not care about whether or not a sibling-in-law of a potential spouse is working. It's completely ridiculous! And it's beyond me why it matters so much to you. Anyone who turns down Moshe or Chani because Baruch is working — *Baruch*!" Shmuely shook his head, "We don't need them!"

"Ahuva Steinhardt is not faceless!" Miri shot back. "She is an excellent girl, comes from a wonderful family, and Moshe *likes* her! He liked her from the minute he saw her!"

"Her own father is working, Miri!" Shmuely exclaimed. "And doing very well, I might add. No, there is more to the story." *I'll call him later, alone,* Shmuely decided. *We'll have a man-to-man and get to the bottom of this. Women!* He shook his head. *There is no understanding them.*

*　　　*　　　*

126

Baruch would be starting his job the next night, and Avigail prepared his favorite supper for his last one at home. From now on, it would be restaurant meals for him. R' Shua had *paskened* that Baruch should take the job in the restaurant, and every time she thought of the look of delight on Baruch's face as he told her, she felt stabbed anew.

"R' Shua wants me to go with the restaurant," Baruch had said. *"This way I can still learn in the morning. I'll be home every day from two to five and I'll be able to help you out then, after lunch (and a nap, of course!). The nights will be harder, but R' Shua thinks this is the best for both of us."*

In hindsight, Avigail knew this *was* the best for them, and she wanted to kick herself for her utter selfishness in wanting Baruch to travel. Why make his life any more miserable than she had to? She was already taking him out of the *beis midrash*. Must he also travel, and sleep in hotels and eat tuna fish? Must he also be around *goyim* in factories all day? So, she'd have to wait up for him. Was that so terrible? *I won't even have to make supper. I'll eat with the kids and we'll clean up the kitchen only once a night. And, I start my new hours tomorrow. Home at 3:00. Yippee!* She felt like a ten-year-old. What would she do with all her free time? Somehow, though, Avigail didn't think she had to worry about that.

*   *   *

"Yossi, it's Dovid."

"Dovid! I was expecting your call. *Nu?*" Yossi sounded happy, excited.

"It's over." Dovid sighed.

"Over?" Yossi was puzzled. "But things were really going well. I had such high hopes for this one."

"Ahuva refuses to consider it, Yossi. They had a bit of a fallout today, and that's it. Have you heard from Friedman?"

"Not a word. Let me call and see what's going on. I always tell my *talmidim* that if things have been going well, not to let one bad date ruin it. What was the, er, fallout about?"

"Apparently he asked Ahuva about Steinhardt Design and where it's going when I retire," Dovid laughed. "Really, were we so immature when we were younger? If I had been after a father-in-law's business, I would have waited until after the knot was tied before trying to get my hands on it. He's not the first boy to ask her, you know."

Yossi laughed. "Strange. It really is, because remember I told you how important it was to Mrs. Friedman that you know upfront that one of her sons-in-law is going to work? She was so hysterical about it. You'd think growing up in such a family he'd be against working like the plague. Funny. Let me get to the bottom of this. I'll call you back."

Chapter 19

YOSSI WAS A *SHADCHAN* who earned his fee. He called the Friedman home and would speak to no one but Shmuely. He was laughing so hard when he hung up the phone that he had a hard time dialing the *bachur,* Moshe. He spoke briefly with Moshe and laughed even harder. It was good to hear the relief in Moshe's voice as they ended the conversation, and he promised the boy to get back to him. "I'll call you directly, Moshe, okay? You'll hear it from the source," he chuckled.

Yossi proceeded to call his brother. "Hi, Rivky," he said when she answered the phone. "Dovid there? And you know what? Get Ahuva on the line as well. She'll want to hear this."

"Good news?"

"The best."

"Ahuva," Yossi said as soon as everyone was assembled. "He wanted to confirm you *weren't* expecting him to join the family business. He has no interest in being the CEO of Steinhardt Design. But after his brother-in-law had to leave *kollel* he saw that things don't always work out as planned, and he just wanted to be sure that you are on the same page as he is and that you don't want *your* husband going into business."

Yossi was met with silence. "You there?"

"Yes," Ahuva answered. "And he did a really bad job if that was his point. Sounded to me like he wanted to take over!"

"I spoke to the *bachur* himself," Yossi responded. "He was bewildered. He had no idea what it was that he said wrong. He didn't think that you would get upset about his brother-in-law going to work, and it didn't even occur to him that you were upset about the business."

Silence.

"Listen, Ahuva. Listen, Dovid, Rivky. I'm on your side in this, you know that. You're my family, and you're the guys I'm going to protect. He's happy with Ahuva, and you with him. This is standard miscommunication. If you don't believe me, ask him yourself. You're smart enough to be able to tell if he's lying. And he is ready to pick up where you left off and get to the bottom of things.

"You'll be doing yourself a disservice if you don't listen to me. Don't throw away a good thing because of a bad choice of words. Hear him out and then make your decision. Give him a chance to explain. Call me back when you've decided what to do." Yossi hung up to give his brother and niece the courtesy of privacy.

Rivky and Dovid left Ahuva alone with her thoughts.

You know he's right, Ahuva. Listen to Uncle Yossi and talk it out. He's a smart boy and he knows how to defend himself.

You're a wimp, Ahuva, she answered herself. *You want Uncle Yossi to be right because you still like him. Even if he's money hungry.*

That's not fair.

But it's true.

Who cares?

You do. Because you don't want a status hungry fellow for a husband. You want someone who will make you proud because of his Torah. You want someone who understands, like your father does, that money is only money, but the important thing is Torah.

Ahuva's father was unique, and she recognized how special he was. He had gone into business only because he had had no other choice. He had become successful because he was smart and he worked hard, yet from her earliest years he had brought her up to know that the business was the *taffel* and Torah was the *ikkar.* This was the principle that guided his every action.

He hired as many *frum* employees as he could. He was closed all through Yom Tov — even *chol hamoed.* He had *shiurim* set up at the office and offered bonuses to those who attended. He organized and supported a *kollel* located in his building. If there was ever a business dispute, large or small, her father went to a *rav,* and accepted the *pesak* with a smile. He dreamed of finding someone competent enough to take over the business so he could devote more time to actual *limud haTorah,* and he instilled a love for Torah in his daughter as well.

Well, Ahuva's mental debate continued, *why can't I ask him outright and see what he says? I'm smart enough to figure out if he's being two-faced.*

You are smart enough in cases where it's not so personal. Do what you want, Ahuva. But don't say I didn't warn you. You'll interpret everything he says to his benefit. Of course you'll be dan l'kaf zechus! You like him and you want to continue liking him.

Not true! Yes, I like him, but I didn't take his words and interpret them to his benefit, did I? I took them at face value and look where it got me.

Do what you want, the voice sounded resigned, *and I'll refrain from saying I told you so.*

Ahuva wiped her tears. She hadn't even realized she was crying. She went to find her parents who were in the den speaking quietly. It wasn't hard to guess what they were talking about.

"What should I do?" Ahuva cried.

"It seems strange," Rivky answered. "I know it does. But Uncle Yossi would never try to hurt you, honey. And he is very good at reading people; you know that. That's why we asked for his help. We think you should go out with the boy again. Talk to him openly about it."

Ahuva turned to her father for confirmation. He nodded his agreement.

"Do something fun this time," Rivky suggested. "An afternoon date. And pay attention to how he acts," she told her daughter. "Does he thank the ticket man? Does he hold the door for people? Does he push to go first? You can learn a lot about people from the way they interact with others."

Chapter 20

"I'M SORRY, MRS. BROWN, there doesn't seem to be any more I can do for you." Dr. Williams said.

"Nothing at all?" Michelle pleaded.

"I'm afraid not. You've completed every treatment that I could give you. You've exhausted all I have to offer. I'm really sorry."

"Didn't you say there's an 87% success rate with the specialized treatments?" Michelle's husband, Steven, broke in.

The doctor nodded regretfully. "That means that 13% of the time they are unsuccessful."

"Are you sure?" Michelle asked. "Can't we try again? I don't care about the cost."

Michelle was frustrated; she was not used to being denied the things she wanted. She had brought herself to where she was through disciplined, determined hard work. She had set difficult goals for herself and achieved them. Now it seemed she was being deprived of something that was every woman's right.

"The only thing I can do at this point is to recommend that you try Dr. Lieberman. He has some specialized methods that even I do not know of. He practices in Boston, and it might be a year until you are able to see him. But he would be your last stop.

Very unconventional, Dr. Lieberman, but he might be able to help you."

"What's his number?" Steven asked. "We'll try him." Anything to keep Michelle happy. Steven would never tell this to his wife, but he had already given up.

Chapter 21

RIVKY STEINHARDT HELD HER breath and spent her time baking. She had fun with a new cookie recipe, and baked them in multiples. Some she decorated with the words *Mazel Tov*, and others with a miniature *chasan* and *kallah*.

She could always give them away to her friend's *gemach*, but Rivky prayed that they would be used at *her* daughter's *vort*.

* * *

There was an air of anticipation in the Friedman home. Miri called Chani in Israel and urged her to start dieting *right now* because it looked like there was going to be a *chasunah* pretty soon. She agonized over the bridal party's color scheme until her daughter Leah calmed her down and said, "This is their only child and they have money. So if I were you, Mommy, I'd wait to hear from them. I'm sure they'll want to marry her off in style. And didn't you say that the mother has taste?"

* * *

"When was the last time you spoke to Miss Steinhardt?" Faigy asked her friend Mindy one night as they studied for a test. Faigy was sprawled on Mindy's bed holding her notebook above her head, while Mindy, the more studious of the two, was sitting at her desk.

"*I* never speak to her," Mindy answered, her tone somewhat derisive. "You're the one who calls her every night."

Faigy rolled over on to her side. "Not anymore I don't. She told me I shouldn't call her at night unless it's an emergency, and she doesn't seem so interested in talking to me at school anymore. She always has papers with her and makes it seem like she's so busy." The truth was that she had spoken to Miss Steinhardt the night before, but Miriam's words were weighing on her mind, and she was curious about what Mindy thought.

"Good, because you were way too into her and the girls were getting nervous. You were being a total teacher's pet."

"I don't care!" Faigy retorted. "Let them think what they want. They're jealous because Miss Steinhardt paid attention to me." Faigy used the same line of defense she had used with Miriam. "Besides," she continued as the full impact of Mindy's words hit her, "what do they think? That I am happy my parents got divorced so I could talk to her?"

"Of course not!" Mindy quickly dispelled that notion. "But you are happier, right?"

"It certainly is a lot more peaceful at home now," Faigy said, and she sat up on the bed and sighed. "Now that my father is not there, my mother is much calmer, and things run more smoothly, but she's out of the house a lot more because she needs to work more hours. And I do miss my father, and Simi asks for him every night. Also, it's really awkward on Shabbos and stuff, because there is no one to make *Kiddush.* So it's good *and* bad, I guess. We went to my grandparents' house for Pesach, so that was good."

"Oh."

"But anyway, what do you think about Miss Steinhardt? She's never available anymore," Faigy steered the conversation back on track.

"I think that's good. My mother said it's not healthy the way you have a crush on her, and she thinks you talk to her way too much." Mindy colored as she realized that she had given herself away. *Well it's good for her to know,* Mindy thought, defending herself. But she knew her friend and was aware of her temper. Mindy cowered in her seat as she watched Faigy process what she had just told her.

"What does your mother have to do with this?" Faigy sat up, her eyes shooting sparks. The fact that Miriam had said essentially the same thing did not help matters. It only made Faigy more upset as she realized the truth of what Mindy was saying.

Mindy said nothing.

"How does she even *know* that I have anything to do with Miss Steinhardt? What else do you tell her when you talk about me? And who else have you discussed me with?" she cried.

Mindy felt bad for her friend who had gone through such hard times. "I'm sorry, Faigy. I don't discuss you with anyone, but my mother noticed you weren't around so often," Mindy improvised quickly, "and she wanted to know how you were doing."

"I'm doing very well, thank you," Faigy interrupted.

"I care about you, and I wasn't sure if I liked the way you were so into Miss Steinhardt. It didn't seem healthy to me."

"Jealous, that's what you are!" Faigy spat. "And talking about me behind my back to make yourself feel better! Don't you worry about my health. Worry about your own first. I want to know who else you spoke to!"

"No one, Faigy. Honestly. Calm down. You're blowing this way out of proportion."

"You're blowing this way *under* proportion!" Faigy retorted. "I thought we were friends, and I could share things with you that wouldn't go anywhere else. I *trusted* you, Mindy!"

"Faigy, please. Sit down, and let's talk about this rationally."

"Rationally, my foot." Faigy jammed her notebook and folders into her knapsack. "What sort of excuses are you going to come up with that you expect me to believe? You already told me that everyone thinks I am the teacher's pet and that they talk about me. You obviously talk with them. How else would you know what they talk about?" Faigy stuffed her feet into her shoes, and before Mindy could say another word, she had thrust open the door and flown down the steps.

As the front door slammed shut behind her, Mrs. Glassman came up the steps and gently knocked on the door to Mindy's room. "Mindy, honey?" she asked quietly. "What's the matter? Why was Faigy in such a rush to leave?"

"Nothing. It doesn't matter. She got mad at me."

"Would you like to talk about it?"

"No. I have to study," Mindy responded and she made a point of looking at her notes. *I certainly can't discuss this with Mommy. That would be like sticking my foot even deeper into my mouth.*

*   *   *

On Sunday Rachel sat down at her computer to write the petition and put it in her bag to mail on Monday. She felt lighter, as though by sharing her load with Ian she had lifted it off her chest — although, as she made sure to tell him, he had not advised her to do anything she hadn't previously decided. But it was with a spring in her step that she walked to Rabbi Hoffman's office on Monday afternoon.

Rachel had gotten a text message from Daren, Beth's boyfriend, that Rabbi Hoffman wanted to see her. "Huh?" she replied. "Idk," came the answer. "He askd me 2 find u. 1 pm wrk?"

Entering the office at his prompt, she sat down and waited for him to begin speaking.

"How are you? How was your Passover?"

"Very nice, thank you," Rachel said warily. She was not sure where this would go. She had no relationship with Rabbi Hoffman and had no real interest in creating one. If this was going to be the outcome of the few lectures she went to, she would tell Beth that she was done with Journeys, and Daren could find someone else to help make them look full.

"Where were you for the holiday?" Rabbi Hoffman asked conversationally. "I didn't see you around campus."

"I went home to have the *seder* with my parents." Rachel's answer was defensive. What did the guy want from her?

"Very nice! Where is home?"

Rachel made a point of looking at her watch. "Look, I am really sorry, but I have a class this afternoon…"

Yudi Hoffman smiled. He picked up a picture that was lying on his desk and handed it to Rachel. "Do you recognize this girl?" he asked.

Rachel took the picture from his hands and looked at it. It was a picture of herself, only it wasn't her. Just the head and shoulders were visible, but she would never wear a neckline that high. High necklines made her feel claustrophobic. Her gaze moved up to the face. Nice haircut, she noted, but not her style. It was layered, and fell around the girl's face like a halo. The makeup was light, only a hint of brown eye shadow around the clear blue eyes. *That might be a good idea*, Rachel thought, *instead of my purple*. The effect was soft, almost ethereal.

But all that was completely beside the point. Rachel looked

up at Rabbi Hoffman, anger flaring. "I do not find this humorous, thank you." She dangled the photo in her thumb and forefinger. "You have no right to use me as your poster child, turning an American Jewish girl into an Orthodox Jewish American. You have Sarah Kessler for that. Seems to me she's doing a fine job." Sarah had been a steady at the Pathway lectures since the seminar and had become very close with the Hoffmans in the ensuing months. She had most recently spent the *seder* with them.

Rachel stood up and thrust the picture into her bag. She was *not* going to give it back for these people to use against her. *I'm sure they have more where this came from anyway.* She turned and walked to the door in three angry strides.

"Rachel." Rabbi Hoffman's voice was soft and arresting. She turned around, hand on the doorknob. "What if I were to tell you that the girl in the photo had the same reaction as you did?"

"Excuse me?"

"She is a real person. And she saw a picture of you at the Journeys seminar back in February. She felt the same way you feel now — angry that someone would use her that way."

"Huh?" Rachel turned around, and walked back to sit in the chair she had just vacated.

Rabbi Hoffman explained as much as he knew of the situation and Rachel nodded slowly, unsure of whether or not to believe it.

"I am not sure who she is. I was given her name, Ahuva Stein-hardt, and I wondered if maybe you knew her. Could be she's a cousin of yours or something."

"Yeah, I'll ask my parents, I guess. Uh… thanks for bringing it to my attention, and… uh… I, I'm sorry for the way I acted." Rachel felt like she had been hit in the stomach. *Could be she's a cousin of yours.* The words echoed in her mind and suddenly

Rachel did believe. She felt a tingle of excitement. Could this be a lead?

"No problem. It is completely understandable. Let me know if I can help you in any way… with this, or anything."

"Yes, thank you." Rachel regained her composure and stood up. "I must get to class, but I will let you know if I need anything."

Chapter 22

BETWEEN PREPARING AND TEACHING, and school, homework and term papers, Ahuva didn't have much free time. Whatever time she did have was spent with Moshe Friedman; either in the flesh, going out with him, or virtually, reliving her dates with her parents. Her grandparents and her cousin Michal were also privy to the finer points of Moshe's personality and their experiences together. When she was not with him or discussing him, she was thinking about him and had come to the conclusion that Ahuva Friedman was a very nice name. She hoped to wear it soon.

There was a wedding dress to dream about, and an apartment in Lakewood. She found herself noticing china and linen patterns, and she leafed through catalogs of furniture from Steinhardt Design.

There was really no time to think about the picture that had made these dreams possible, nor the girl in the picture whose existence had almost toppled them. But at night, when she couldn't fall asleep, Ahuva found herself wondering about the story behind the story.

Who was this girl who looked so much like her that she

managed to fool Ahuva herself? *Maybe it's your long-lost sister,* Moshe had said. She wondered if Moshe realized the implications of that statement. *Maybe it is.* Ahuva wasn't sure if she wanted to find out. Sure, she had always been curious — and now even more so — about her birth mother, but she had made a conscious decision at age eighteen not to think about the woman who had given her up but to focus on becoming the best Ahuva Steinhardt she could be, so that in time she could become Ahuva… Friedman.

Now, just when her dreams were coming true, she felt herself torn. Moshe Friedman or Rachel Bergmann? Or Rachel Bergmann's mother?

Moshe Friedman won, certainly. But she wished there was a nonthreatening, noncommittal way to walk up to Mr. and Mrs. Bergmann and say, "Hi, I'm Ahuva Steinhardt, and I'm your daughter."

*   *   *

As she went about her day, the picture of Ahuva Steinhardt burned a hole in Rachel Bergmann's salmon colored bag. Suddenly, it became unimportant to find out who her birth mother was, or why she had abandoned her. *A long-lost cousin,* Rabbi Hoffman said. If only life would be that simple. She wanted to run into the arms of her mother and cry. Her real mother, the one who waited and prayed for her. The one who dropped everything and ran to her. Who raised her and praised her. Calmed her fears and soothed her cries. The mother who had given her everything a girl could ask for and more.

The picture was in and out of her bag many times a day. She studied it intently. It was a small comfort that she would not want to live the way *that girl* did; *she* was obviously Orthodox, like Rabbi Hoffman, and that was something Rachel would not want to be.

But I suppose if my parents were Orthodox, I'd be happy with it. Living with my real parents, I wouldn't even know any other way. She hated the girl in the photo who looked so happy, so comfortable, and so peaceful. This girl, who was raised by her *real* parents and had no notion of what it was like to grow up unsure of who you really were. Sometimes she just wanted to tear the picture apart. Ahuva Steinhardt. Such a soft face. Such soft eye shadow. No brown eye shadow for Rachel Bergmann.

The music coming from her dorm room keyboard these days was loud and angry.

"What's with you?" Beth wanted to know. "You look like you are ready to kill someone."

"I'm fine," she lied glibly. "*Get a grip, Rachel,*" she told herself fiercely. And she sent her mother a text. Luv u Mom. Thought u shd know.

*   *   *

Faigy Baum had been demoted to the bottom of Ahuva's priorities and she felt bad about it. She was sure Faigy still needed help and someone to talk to. But there really was no time. Maybe it was time to hand her over as Tante Devorah had suggested. Ahuva was sure she would be getting engaged any day and still she had to prepare for school and continue with her fieldwork in special-ed. There would be a *vort* and many things to take care of, and part of her wanted to tell Faigy she just didn't have time for her right now, but here was someone else who could help. But did she *really* want to do that? Wouldn't it be more praiseworthy if even as a *kallah* she still had her head on her shoulders — neglecting none of the responsibilities she had had before her engagement? It would really not be right to wrap herself up in her own excitement and leave everyone else out in the cold. Besides, Ahuva noticed vaguely that

Faigy and her best friend Mindy Glassman seemed not to be on speaking terms. She forced herself to focus on the issue.

"Faigy," she called out as the girls filed out of the room for lunch. Faigy looked at her and the smile that used to spread all over her face when she talked to her favorite teacher was noticeably absent.

"What do you want?"

"We haven't spoken in a while, and I wanted to find out how things were doing."

"Fine."

Ahuva looked at her. Things were obviously not fine, but she wasn't sure that she had the mental energy to pull the story out of her student. Handing her over was becoming more and more a welcome alternative.

"Come on, Faigy. What's the matter? Where's my loquacious teen?"

"I'm fine. I appreciate your concern." Faigy looked impatiently at the door. "I have a vocab test right after lunch," she said pointedly.

"All right," Ahuva laughed. "I know when I'm not wanted! Go have fun with your friends." *Well, at least she is not stifling me anymore. Michal would be proud. And I don't have to feel bad about not being there for her 24/7. That's a relief.* But Ahuva wondered what she had done to turn Faigy off. *Had someone told her off for being a teacher's pet? I'll have to talk to Mindy,* she decided. But it would have to wait. There were other things to take care of.

*   *   *

"Got anything back?" Ian asked conversationally. They were in the car on the way to a movie, stealing a few hours from studying for finals to spend some time together.

"Not yet. And I decided I don't really care," she told him about her meeting with Rabbi Hoffman. "I keep the picture in my bag," she said and she pulled it out to show him.

Ian whistled. "Nice. Yeah, I see what you mean. You'd rather stick to your nice, easy parents than go there and be forced to observe 500 crazy rules. But aren't you curious about why they gave you up?" he asked candidly, and watched out of the corner of his eye for her reaction.

"I guess so, but like you said last week, we'll take one thing at a time. And now that I know who she is, I guess I am satisfied and happy to be Rachel Bergmann again."

Chapter 23

 "SARAH, CAN I RECOMMEND Neve Yerushalayim?" Mrs. Hoffman asked one Shabbos afternoon.

"Sure, you can suggest it. What is it?" Sarah wanted to know.

"It's a school for beginners. It's located in Israel, and it's geared toward teaching girls and women everything there is to know about Judaism. It is much more extensive training than I am able to give you."

"What are the rules?" Sarah asked nervously. "I mean, I am still learning, and I try to keep kosher and to come here for Shabbat and stuff, but that's it."

Mrs. Hoffman laughed. "Most of the women who go there know less than you do. Don't worry. They'll teach you everything you need to know. Everyone is placed into a class where she'll fit comfortably, according to her level of knowledge. They really have an excellent program and the teachers are exceptional. It's open all year, and they have a special summer program. And a great dorm. I think it's something you should look into."

Sarah promised to do so. *Why not?* she thought. *It's not as though I have anything better to do in the summer, and I really do want to learn about life the way the Hoffmans live it. But Israel? Do I really want to go so far? On the other hand, it's a break. What's keeping me here in the US? What friends do I have that I don't want to give up for a summer?*

Sarah made up in her mind and called Mrs. Hoffman for the number of the office to register for the summer program.

*   *   *

"We are making a *vort* tomorrow night, *im yirtzeh Hashem,*" Miri was on the phone with Shira Becker, a neighbor. "It will be in the *kallah's* house, in Monsey, so I don't expect you to come early to help out like you did for all my other girls." Miri laughed. "The *kallah* is Ahuva Steinhardt. Her father is Dovid Steinhardt from Steinhardt Design." Miri paused to hear the gasp she knew would come; it had come from everyone she had spoken to. *Yes, I, Miri Weiss Friedman, am marrying my son off to Steinhardt.* "Actually, it's quite adorable; I know the *kallah's* mother from way back. We went to Bais Yaakov together!"

*   *   *

"*Mazal Tov.*"

Rivky smiled her thanks and murmured the good wishes back to her *machateniste.* Funny to think that the word applied to her now. She welcomed Miri and Rabbi Friedman into the lower level of her home. Even with a *mechitzah* the room was spacious and comfortable. It looked as though it had been designed to be used for *simchahs*, and probably was.

Miri took in her surroundings. As with everything Rivky Steinhardt touched, the space was classy and tastefully decorated. Nothing ostentatious, but Miri could feel money oozing from every corner of the room. She took careful note of everything she saw, though she knew she would never be able to duplicate any of it in her own home.

She was excited and could not wait for her family to come to see everything. And she certainly couldn't wait for the wedding. If this was the *vort*... Leah was right; she had no need to worry about color schemes. She would quietly accept all Rivky's instructions and would write everything down, so that when she married Chani off — well, she wouldn't want Ahuva to be embarrassed at her sister-in-law's wedding.

She glanced nervously at the table that stood next to the *mechitzah* and breathed a sigh of relief. The flowers made a nice showing. Miri had wanted to get an even more expensive bouquet, but Shmuely did not allow it. "It's one thing to break the bank over the jewelry we're going to have to give. I am not spending that kind of money on flowers that will be dead tomorrow," he had said, and all Miri's protests were for naught.

"Wow, these cookies are beautiful," she enthused, inspecting them. "You made them, right?" Rivky smiled demurely. "I love to bake, and there is no greater joy than baking for your daughter's *vort*."

Ahuva and Moshe entered the room to accept the hugs and kisses and *mazal tov* wishes from their parents. They looked cute together, she thought; Moshe especially, in his freshly pressed suit and hat. His shoes were polished till they shone, and his tie was brand new. Ahuva wore a navy taffeta dress with a diamond spiral necklace to add some sparkle. Her wrist was adorned with a brand-new diamond tennis bracelet, a gift from her *chasan*. (Miri was gratified; she had *known* the new *kallah* would prefer the tennis bracelet above the other two bracelets she had brought. As she had told her husband and daughters, "The Steinhardts have *class*.") "We are so excited to welcome you into our family!" Miri gushed.

"I'm happy to become part of it," Ahuva responded courteously.

"The photographer should be here any minute," Ahuva said to her. "Oh?" Miri's eyebrows went up. "I didn't realize. I would have told my children to make sure to come on time."

"It's only my sister," Rivky explained, and she looked somewhat reproachfully at her daughter. "She takes great pictures and promised to come early."

*   *   *

The *vort* was beautiful; Rivky was a gracious hostess, and the guests came from all over. Ahuva was beautiful and unpretentious, doing her best to make all those who came feel welcome and wanted.

Her students came in groups; they were excited, as all students are, to have a teacher who was engaged. They planned the *shtick* they would pull on her and discussed whether or not she was "the type to have her head in the clouds and totally forget how to teach."

A few of the bolder students went over to Miri to wish her *mazal tov*. Miri beamed with pride and she listened eagerly as the girls told her what a great catch she had gotten as a daughter-in-law.

*   *   *

Mindy Glassman came over to her teacher and wished her a shy *mazal tov*. "Thank you, Mindy," Ahuva smiled. "And don't think I have forgotten about you. I actually want to talk to you, okay? Next lunch break?"

Mindy nodded in response. She quickly ran over to a group of her friends and informed them with shining eyes that Miss Steinhardt was *not* in the clouds. "Trust me, I know," was all she would say.

But Faigy was not there. *She ruined my friendship with Mindy,* she told her herself over and over again. She was trying hard to convince herself not to go to Miss Steinhardt's *vort,* sure that everyone would make fun of her for attending. *They think you're a teacher's pet.* Mindy's words reverberated in her brain. In the end they weren't convincing enough to keep her home, and she dressed hurriedly and ran out of the house just in time to catch a ride with another girl on her block.

*   *   *

As they drove home after the *vort,* Shmuely commented to his wife, "Well, it seems you got what you wanted in a girl for Moshe." Miri was too tired to take the bait and merely sighed contentedly.

*   *   *

The day after her *vort,* both of her classes made a party for Ahuva, and the whole school danced for her during lunch break. So there was no time for her to speak with Mindy. But true to her word, Ahuva sought her out at the next opportunity.

"What's going on?" Ahuva asked her student. "How are things with you and with Faigy?"

"Fine," Mindy responded uneasily.

"Fine?" Ahuva asked. "I've noticed you don't sit near each other anymore. Class has certainly gotten much quieter. Was that Mrs. Feldman or Mrs. Kessin's doing?"

Mindy smiled sheepishly. "We're fine, really. But Faigy's a bit mad at me. It's happened before, and it'll happen again."

"You're sure?"

Mindy nodded again, and cocked her head to the side, thinking. *Oh whatever. Maybe she can help. She helped Faigy before.* Throwing all caution to the wind, Mindy burst out, "I told her that my mother was worried that she talked to you too much and that it was not healthy, and she got really mad at me for talking to my mother about her, and wants to know who else I talk to behind her back."

Ahuva smiled encouragingly.

"I don't talk about her to people! But my mother is my mother, and of course I talk to her if I am nervous about something! You're supposed to talk to your mother."

"Of course you should talk to your mother if something is bothering you. Your mother should be your first address. I understand, Mindy. Let me think about what we can do, but somehow we'll have the two of you back together. I want to dance together with both of you at my wedding, you hear? Go tell that to Faigy. I want just you two, and I want it to be a happy, smiling dance. Got it?"

Mindy glowed. "Thank you," she whispered, too excited to talk. She floated out of the room, and Ahuva smiled to herself. *Flattery always works.*

Chapter 24

"MOMMY, WHAT DO YOU think I should bring to my mother-in-law for Shabbos? I have an album of pictures of the *vort*, but it's such a *nebby* gift. Everyone does it!"

"Well, everyone gives a bracelet, Ahuva. Is that *nebby*?" Rivky answered.

Ahuva's eyes flew to her wrist and her *kallah* bracelet. Certainly *hers* wasn't *nebby*. How many *kallahs* are given a tennis bracelet? Briefly she wondered how they had afforded it. Moshe always said they had no money. Well, what was she to do about it? She couldn't refuse it once it was given! That would be the height of bad manners. Besides, what would she say? "Moshe told me you don't have money. I can't imagine how you were able to pay for this beautiful bracelet. Take it back, I'll ask my father for one instead."

"How about a salad bowl? That's a nice gift, and useful," Rivky suggested.

"Mommy! That's what you give people when you stay in their house for Shabbos!"

"Well, what are you doing if not visiting them for Shabbos?"

"Yes, but it's my *mother-in-law!* You don't give your mother-in-law a salad bowl!"

"Why ever not?" Rivky wanted to know. "With a nice set of

tongs? I think it's a wonderful gift. It can be pretty, it's useful, and it's quite generic."

"Exactly, Ma. It's generic. I want to give something *different*."

"How different? You can give her a framed *Birkas HaBayis* if you want. I saw a really beautiful one, but it was a bit expensive. And I don't necessarily think it's a smart thing to give to someone before you really know what she'd want. Maybe she doesn't hang things on her wall, and now you'll have put her in an awkward position because of course she'll have to hang it up before you come back. Or maybe she has no wall space, and she'll need to take down her favorite picture to put this up, and she really hates it."

"Okay, so not a picture."

"You don't really know her yet. Did Moshe tell you anything about what she'd like?"

"No."

"So if I were you, I'd go with a dish. You'll have plenty other opportunities to buy her different gifts, Ahuva."

"But…"

"And," Rivky became serious. "It's not such a good idea to set yourself up as *different* from your in-laws. For many reasons." She stopped for a moment before ending: "They are not used to what you have. So get used to what they have."

Ahuva looked at her mother with an expression of curiosity. She opened her mouth to say something and then shut it. There was a moment of silence and then Ahuva asked, "Will you help me pick out a nice bowl?"

*   *   *

The answer to her petition finally came, and Rachel opened it with a detached curiosity. She already knew who her mother was. She was the mother of Ahuva Steinhardt. Rachel had googled the name Steinhardt, and had found that the exclusive Steinhardt Design living room furniture that her own mother loved was Ahuva's father's business. Well, she couldn't be entirely sure, but the blurb about the founder said he had a wife and one daughter. And from his picture it was clear that he was obviously Orthodox. Rachel thought about the coffee table in the living room that she had chosen to complement the couches and felt used. *They gave me up and I gave back to them.* She pulled out the picture of Ahuva Steinhardt from her bag. *Why did they keep* her, *though? And why did they have to choose between me and her?*

Her birth certificate named her mother Michelle Stern. Her birth date, which she knew, was July 10.

It was Ian who suggested she do a separate search on Michelle Stern. "Why are you so sure your mother kept one daughter and gave another away? That seems weird to me. I would think that if she was excited to keep one child, she'd want both."

"Maybe she felt bad she gave me up, so when she had another baby she kept her."

"But you look identical! You've got to be twins," Ian said.

They sat together in one of the student lounges and googled Michelle Stern.

There were three websites whose owners shared the name Michelle Stern. The first, michellestern.com, depicted a young party planner in New York City. From the client testimonies it seemed that she was successful, and Ian joked, "What would happen if you used her for your next party and said, 'By the way, I'm your daughter'?"

Rachel laughed dutifully, but answered, "She's too young. Look at her. How can she possibly have a twenty-one-year-old child?"

The second Michelle Stern was a life coach in Chicago. "That's got to be her!" Rachel said. "I was born in Chicago." They examined the website closely, but there were no further clues. There was no blurb about Michelle; the website seemed to be only half completed. "Write down the number, and we'll figure something out," Ian suggested. "Let's take a look at the last one."

"Why? We found her already."

"Why not? It's not hard to look up, and we may as well follow all clues."

Michelle Stern Brown was the senior partner in Michelle Stern Law. She lived on the West Coast and was involved in many high profile cases. Ian clicked on the "About" tab, and they read:

Michelle Stern Brown, originally from Chicago, Illinois, and educated at UCLA, opened her law firm in Los Angeles in 2003. Michelle had been practicing in Northern California with Patner, Patner & Morris and had quickly risen as one of their most sought-after attorneys.

There was more about Michelle's education and the awards she had received throughout her career. Rachel skipped to the last paragraph of the blurb and read:

When she is not studying law, Michelle plays piano. Her favorite vacation spot is Venice, Italy, where she and her husband Steven honeymooned in 2004.

There was a picture of Michelle. She was a tall, thin woman with dark hair. "*This* is your mother!" Ian cried. "Not the other one. She looks exactly like you, except for your eyes."

Rachel nodded, stunned. "And she's from Chicago," her voice was barely audible. "And she plays piano. This has to be her."

They sat in silence, and Rachel felt tears coming to her eyes. *This is the woman who abandoned me. To become a successful attorney in LA.*

"Don't worry," Ian said. "We'll figure out what to do with this woman, but don't get too hung up on her. She doesn't deserve it."

Rachel smiled through her tears. "You're right, of course. But putting a name and face to her makes it much harder."

She had started down the path to finding her birth mother because Brad had left her and her old feelings of rejection were fed by this new hurt. But somehow, as she told Ian, putting a name and a face to the woman who abandoned her, not to mention that she had lost a sister as well (for what else could Ahuva be?) made it much harder. *You have parents, and you have Ian. Give it up.* She repeated Ian's words to herself over and over again: *She doesn't deserve you.* The idea, and the fact that it was Ian who said it, comforted her.

Chapter 25

RACHEL DECIDED TO DO nothing for now, and life returned to normal. Summer came, and with it the end of school. She went back to New Jersey and interned in a psychiatrist's office in Long Branch three times a week. The doctor was a friend of the family, known from a lifetime of summers spent on the Jersey Shore, and Rachel was happy.

Ian spent the summer in his dad's office and came down to meet Rachel in the Bergmann's summer home on most weekends.

Beth had stayed in Rhode Island. Having graduated from dorm life she was now looking for an apartment, and she would have Rachel in mind. Her summer job was in Rhode Island, and she was thinking of taking permanent residence there.

Sarah had surprised them all by going to Israel for the summer. "Why is it a surprise?" Susan wanted to know. "Sarah always did her own thing. And she was so into the Judaism bit."

"Yeah, more than Daren," Beth concurred. "He's giving up the Hillel next year. Said it was too hard to arrange those events and then have to beg people to attend. He said he did it for the resume, and now that it's in there he's done with it."

"Good for him," Rachel said. "And good for the rest of us who won't have to attend those events."

"C'mon, Rach, you make it sound as though you'd never have had anything to do with Hillel if I hadn't dragged you to Daren's events. Your own dad's the president of the Temple at home! Your family is one of the most consciously Jewish ones I know."

"I would have been involved in the Temple things, maybe. Certainly not in Hillel things and the Orthodox things we went to," Rachel shot back.

"But then we would never have gone to that seminar," Susan pointed out. "That was fun."

"We didn't even go swimming!" Rachel said in mock dismay. *And if we hadn't gone to that seminar I'd still be blissfully unaware of anyone called Ahuva Steinhardt.*

Would that be blissful? Rachel asked herself. Somehow, knowing that her lawyer-mother had given them both up made her feel better. *It wasn't about me; it was about her.*

*   *   *

"The *kallah* is coming for Shabbos," Miri said to her husband conversationally one night during supper.

"Right," Shmuely answered. "Anyone else? Leah will walk over, I imagine, but are any of the other girls coming?"

"Well, I thought I'd tell them not to. And to tell Leah to just come for *shalosh seudos*. I was thinking, I mean, Ahuva's an only child, and she must be used to quiet. Our house can get pretty rambunctious when everyone comes over. I thought maybe for her first Shabbos we'll keep things more, I don't know, under control?"

Shmuely nodded. "I hear you. I think you're right. There will be plenty of opportunities for her to get to know the rest of the family, *im yirtzeh Hashem*. Did you speak to the girls? What do they say?"

"Oh, I'm sure you could guess what they said. Avigail agreed with me, Esther thought I'm being overly cautious and that 'this is our family, take it or leave it.' Leah's fine, she's coming anyway. Blimi was like 'whatever you want, Mommy.' You know it's hard for her to pack up her kids and come here. They don't sleep well away from home, she hates going away anyway. And Yocheved didn't really care either way; she's still googly-eyed over Yankel and she's happy to spend a quiet Shabbos at home."

Shmuely nodded again, "Can I have some more soup?" he asked. "It's really delicious."

As Miri got up to refill his bowl, she resumed talking. "Anyway, I was thinking that maybe I should update the Shabbos china."

"Update the china? What does that mean?" Shmuely asked. "What are you going to tell them? That Ahuva's coming?"

Miri ignored Shmuely's comment. She placed the bowl of hot soup before her husband and absentmindedly accepted his thanks. "You know we don't really have a complete set," she continued. "I mean, we have I think four whole place settings of china. Everything else is chipped and mismatched. I thought maybe I would just, you know, buy more place settings. Our design is pretty classic and I think I will be able to find matching pieces. That won't be as expensive as getting a new set."

"Why do we need new china? We never use it anyway when the kids come home, and when it's just us, we have enough."

"I know," Miri seemed reluctant to continue. "But, I'm sure Rivky Steinhardt has never used disposables at her Shabbos table, and I want Ahuva to be comfortable here." *There, that sounded altruistic.*

Shmuely wasn't convinced. "But we have four settings, you said.

And you told the girls not to come this week, so it's perfect."

"Yeah, but she'll come again, and we will invite the kids."

"But we won't be using china then anyway."

"Well, I thought maybe we should use china. Just for the adults."

"Why, so you should have to work harder when you have company? After the *seudah* the girls are putting their kids to bed and you're cleaning up with one or two helpers. Who is volunteering to wash dishes?"

"I don't know, we'll work it out. I thought it would be nice, and I think Ahuva will appreciate it…" Miri trailed off at the look of skepticism on her husband's face. He wasn't buying any of it. He knew she wanted the china because she was embarrassed to use throwaways with Ahuva there.

"We can't afford new china now, Miri. Especially not if you want nice jewelry for Ahuva. As it is, we'll need to borrow something for the ring you want. I'm sorry. There is a limit to how much money I will spend on this wedding, and new china is not on the list."

"Just like the flowers I wanted for the *vort* didn't make your list, and new candlesticks. I'm going to be so embarrassed as I *bentch licht*," Miri moved on to another point of contention. They had had this discussion before, and there was no use pretending she wanted new *leichter* for anyone other than herself. *"As it is, my leichter aren't silver — can't I at least have crystal that matches?" she had said.*

"The flowers we had looked nice. You told me so yourself after the *vort*. All this makes me wonder if marrying into a family that has money is such a good idea," Shmuely mused. "Seems to me you want us to spend more on this wedding than on all the others combined. Sorry, Miri, I do feel bad, but we can't afford it. We may as well initiate her into the family right away," he echoed his daughter Esther's words.

Miri didn't answer. She stood up to clear the soup bowls, a mutinous expression on her face. Her husband was right, of course, but that didn't make it any better. What was the use of marrying into money if you didn't get any of it for yourself? Miri was not even going to bring up the new *shaitel* she wanted for the wedding, because she knew it would make Shmuely upset. And catering the *aufruf*? Forget it. *Baruch Hashem*, there would only be their side of the family at the *aufruf*, except for Ahuva's father. Ahuva was an only child. There wouldn't be any brothers.

Miri loved her family and was proud of the way she had brought them up. She was proud of her husband's commitment to Torah. Her children had their priorities straight (except, recently, Avigail). She had taught them to recognize what was truly important in life, and they were prepared to live a *kollel* lifestyle, having grown up with one. There were many things Miri would never change. She was proud of the family's *yeshivish* car, proud that she never spent money on brand name clothing for her children.

She had never dreamed of going away for Pesach. When Shmuely was offered a nice compensation from Journeys to be their main lecturer one Pesach, they had turned it down, and he had gone to speak only one night of *chol hamoed*. Pesach is always a strain on a family's finances, and staying at a hotel for eight days — free — plus the compensation, would have helped the family's perpetual financial crunch. But they had turned it down; Miri would not compromise on her Yom Tov for all the money in the world. (Of course, she had dropped a hint here and there to friends. Part of the enjoyment in making the sacrifice was in knowing that others were impressed by her convictions.)

And she was proud of her jewelry — all of it "faux." "You can't tell the difference," she'd tell her friends, "and this way I can wear things I like without breaking the bank." She was acquainted with more than one woman who insisted on new jewelry for every Yom Tov, and who wouldn't dream of wearing costume pieces. She would never become one of *those*.

But what did all this matter now, when she was welcoming a girl to her home who was born with a silver spoon? Well, not quite born with it, Miri conceded. She was adopted, and more than likely born into poverty. But she had grown up in the lap of luxury. Miri was sure Ahuva had never been to a home like the Friedmans' and she wanted to make a good impression on her future daughter-in-law.

She served the rest of supper in silence. Shmuely knew his wife well and didn't make any attempt at conversation.

Chapter 26

"SO, HOW DID IT go?" Rivky asked as soon as Ahuva came home from the Shabbos spent at her future in-laws.

There was a pause before Ahuva answered. "Nice. I don't know. Weird."

"Weird?" Rivky sounded puzzled. "What does that mean?"

"It was so different."

"Okay…"

"I don't know. First Moshe warned me that all his siblings would be coming and I was nervous. I thought I would be on show in front of all his sisters, and also I'm not used to so many little kids around, I guess. But in the end they didn't come, except for one sister for *shalosh seudos*, and it would probably have been much less awkward if there were people there the whole time."

Ahuva laughed suddenly. "It was a good thing I brought that salad bowl. You were right, Mommy. A picture would have been a disaster in that house. Actually, nothing decorative would have been right. It is the most *yeshivish* house I have ever been to. Seriously. A lot worse than Malky Miller's," she said, referring to a cousin of Rivky's. "But I'll get used to it, I guess. Anyhow, I probably won't really be staying there so often. That's sort of what my mother-in-law said. They don't have room for everyone to come at the same time, so if his sisters come for a Shabbos and there will be lots of kids, we'll stay at the neighbor's. That's good, I guess. She put me up at a neighbor's house this Shabbos, and it was much more my speed."

Ahuva paused, reflecting, and Rivky said nothing. "They didn't really have any dining room chairs. Just two that were left from their original set. They used folding chairs that were hiding behind the breakfront and they weren't hidden so well, if you know what I mean. That doesn't really bother me, I think. Not everyone can afford Steinhardt furniture, and I'm really fine with that. It will be a little awkward though, when my in-laws come to me. I mean, our standard of living is so different."

"Okay," Rivky said again. "But what was *funny* about it?"

"It wasn't funny, I guess, just really awkward. It was just the two of us, my mother-in-law and me, Friday night before the *seudah*. And there really isn't that much to prepare for four people, so there wasn't that much to schmooze about. She's supposed to be a good schmoozer, but she didn't schmooze; she just apologized. That was what was so bad about it. She just kept apologizing to me about everything. First, because her *leichter* don't match. Big deal! I hadn't even noticed. Then I offered to set the table, and it turns out she thought she had four place settings left of her china and she only had three, so she apologized for that. Then she made a salad, but she hadn't had time to *toivel* the "beautiful bowl" I got her, so that was another apology. The couch in the living room was almost brand new, and the grandchildren are not allowed on it, so at least I had someplace to sit. That's how she put it. They have a piano. My mother-in-law can't wait for me to play, but it hasn't been tuned in years, she's so sorry. They'll have to remember to do that before the next time I come. I said I don't play on Shabbos anyway so there's no need to worry." Ahuva chuckled at her own joke.

"Finally the men came home and things got more relaxed. The *seudah* was fine. I really like my father-in-law. He's so unpretentious. He was just so *normal*. He didn't care if the items in his house matched or were worn-out. Things really *were* quite worn-out, I'll admit. But my mother-in-law was bringing unneeded attention to everything!"

She changed the subject at the look on her mother's face. "Would you like some water, Mommy?" As she brought the tray with pitcher and glasses to the table, Rivky looked at her daughter and tried to assess the effect her words would have on her.

"You have to look at things from her perspective, Ahuva. Here she is, living on whatever little income they have from Rabbi Friedman's lectures and the small salary that comes with being a *rav*. She knows you're used to having much more, and she's apologetic. It's not usually the best course of action because, as you mentioned, it brings attention to things the other person may not have noticed, but people are always defensive that way. This can't be the first time you've encountered something like that."

"But, Mommy, the point is why should she be uncomfortable with me? I know they don't have money, and I knew their house wouldn't look like ours. You didn't let me grow up spoiled! Moshe once told me that his sisters used to want to do all these fun things during midwinter break that they couldn't afford, and I had to laugh because you wouldn't let me do half of them even though we could afford it. Come on, Mommy, I was practically the only one in my class who babysat when I was young! I never even went to Florida, where a lot of the girls went during break, until Shevy got engaged and I went with her and Michal. I've never been to Europe, except to the Ukraine for the summer, and that was camp, but it was *work*! You know I'm not spoiled, Mommy, you raised me!"

"True, and I hope I did a good job. I'll never know until you're married and I'll hear it from Moshe. I did all I could to teach you how to value money, and how to recognize that it's really not the most important thing. But with all that guidance, you still never knew what it was not to be able to have everything you need, let alone want. You didn't grow up the way I did, Ahuva. I was one of seven, and of course, it's no one's fault that you have no siblings, but you don't. My father was a Rosh Yeshiva, not the owner of an upscale furniture company. When you think of my parents' home, the picture in your mind is how it looks *today*. Of course it's in perfect condition. There aren't any little children jumping all over the elegant furniture from Steinhardt Design! That's not the way it looked when I was growing up. Did you ever take a good look at Bubby's old pictures? Or Bubby Steinhardt's? Abba and I grew up much the way Moshe did. We were forced into decisions that ultimately brought us to where we are today, but telling me you never went to Florida doesn't mean a thing in this context. You *could* have gone to Florida; you had the wherewithal. You simply are the product of a different kind of lifestyle."

Rivky paused. It was important that Ahuva understand the consequences of a meager income on one's outlook on life. "Florida? That wasn't even on the radar when I was young. There was no money for any extras. On my fifteenth birthday, I became responsible for my own wardrobe! My parents bought me the basics, which consisted of one Shabbos outfit and three or four weekday outfits. There was no such thing as a uniform back then, or believe me, my wardrobe would have been just one Sunday outfit."

"Okay, but Mommy, times were different back then. All Moshe's sisters went to Florida in their senior year."

"Look at it from their point of view. Today's world is very

different, just as you said. And they had no money for other things they wanted to do. Your in-laws didn't want them to feel deprived. They didn't want their daughters to grow up thinking that a life of Torah meant you couldn't have what your friends have. So they managed to give their kids a couple of extras. I'm sure it wasn't easy. You didn't have that *nisayon*, Ahuva. You had access to so much more than they did! That's why we were able to set stricter guidelines."

"If you ask me, they went because my mother-in-law wanted to keep up with the Joneses," Ahuva muttered.

"What was that?"

"Nothing," Ahuva had the grace to blush.

"Good, because it seems to me that maybe I didn't do as good a job as I thought in raising you to be unspoiled. I think becoming a Friedman will be good for you, Ahuva. You'll see what life is really like."

The phone rang, and Ahuva was grateful for the diversion.

Shabbos was unnecessarily awkward, she thought as she swished the ice left in her glass, *but if I'm going to be honest, I guess there is truth to what Mommy is saying. Not that my mother-in-law did anything for anyone but herself — to keep up with the Joneses — but maybe I am not as untouched by my wealth as I like to think I am.* She stood up and her bracelet caught the light. *How on earth were they able to pay for this?* Ahuva wondered for the umpteenth time. *I'd rather not know,* she decided.

Chapter 27

 IT WAS ALMOST A month after the *vort* when Ahuva approached her parents during dinner one night. "I was thinking," she began, "about the girl in that picture. Rachel Bergmann."

"Yes?" Dovid prompted after a long silence.

"Well, I'd like to meet her."

"Oh?" Rivky tensed.

"It's quite obvious that we're sisters. What else could we be? We look exactly alike. I wonder how old she is. Do you think the Bergmanns are my birth parents?" she asked, and exhaled. She hadn't realized she was holding her breath and wondered absently if she had been holding it since that night on Pesach when Rabbi Lazarus had told them about the girl in the picture.

"Why don't you focus on getting married now, Ahuva, and wait to find your birth parents afterward?" Rivky suggested.

"Mommy, I'm not getting married for another two months and it doesn't take long to buy pots and pans. I can take an afternoon off to meet them."

"It may not take time, but there is the emotional aspect as well."

"But after I get married I will need to focus on being a good wife and a good daughter-in-law. It will be *shanah rishonah* which does not seem to be the right time to go looking for your birth parents…"

"But while you're engaged it is?" Dovid wanted to know.

Ahuva smiled at the contradiction. "No, I guess not. But somehow I think it makes more sense." And she wanted both of them at her wedding. For some inexplicable reason, she wanted them to be there, to show them how beautiful a Jewish wedding is. *And to show them that although they had given me up, I thrived as a Steinhardt.*

Ahuva was determined, and her parents finally understood that the emotional energy expended in dreaming about them might be more draining than actually meeting them.

Dovid contacted Rabbi Lazarus, who in turn contacted Yudi Hoffman and asked him to arrange a meeting between the two young women, Ahuva Steinhardt and Rachel Bergmann.

*   *   *

Rachel looked up from the paperwork she was busy with and glanced at her ringing phone. The area code was 401, so it was obviously someone from Brown, but she did not recognize the number. Curious, she answered the phone and was taken aback by the voice on the other line. It was Rabbi Hoffman from Journeys/ Pathways. He had gotten her number from Daren Gelman and hoped he was not catching Rachel at a bad time. Apparently, Ahuva Steinhardt wanted to meet her. Does he have her permission to forward her cell phone number?

"I'd rather you give me hers, if that's okay." It was fine, and Rachel hung up the phone with the number in her hand.

She wasn't sure if she wanted this meeting and clarified her feelings while on the phone with Ian.

"I decided not to do anything," she said, lying on the beach. "I haven't even told my parents about her. I… I sort of wanted my life to get back to normal. And I managed to curb my obsession a bit. Is this going to bring all those feelings back?" *Why am I telling this to Ian?* Rachel asked herself incredulously. *He's not my therapist, he's my boyfriend!* But she knew the answer to the question. For one thing, there was no one else to talk to; as she had told Ian, Rachel's parents knew nothing. Second, and even more important, she wanted to assure herself that Ian would stay with her through every circumstance — even one as difficult as this.

"I think you should call her," Ian said. "She's in the same boat as you, you know. Somehow or other the two of you were given up by the same woman. Meet her and see what she's like. Meeting her doesn't mean you must meet your mother."

"But that's the obvious next step, isn't it?"

"So just don't take the next step," Ian retorted. "See what this girl wants. Maybe she's already met her mother. Maybe, just like you, she doesn't want to meet her. Maybe she doesn't know she's adopted and is curious about how you look so much like her. Maybe she *isn't* adopted and this whole thing is one big coincidence."

"Maybe." Rachel ran her fingers through the sand. "I've got to break the news to my parents somehow. I am a bit scared to do that, you know."

"I'll bet. I wish I could help you, Rach, you know that. But you know I'm behind you whatever you do, right?"

"Thank you, Ian." Rachel felt a wave of happiness spread through her. "I know, and I appreciate it."

*   *   *

"So how is the *kallah*?"

"*Baruch Hashem*, great, Bubby. How are you doing?" It was *Erev*

Shabbos and Ahuva was lounging in the hammock in the Stein-hardt backyard while on the phone with her grandmother.

"Good. So, what are you up to these days? We haven't spoken in a while. It's not your fault, you call me faithfully, but your life has become so busy that even though we talk every week we're not really *talking*. Last week, it was because you went to Flatbush for Shabbos and were rushed, and the week before was Shavuos, and before that, the *chasan* came. Of course, that was a treat, and I spoke to him... Really nice boy... But you, Ahuva. What are you thinking about?"

"I don't know, Bubby. My gown, my apartment, a job. Really, I could keep my job here, but I don't think I want to travel an hour and a half every day from Lakewood, and I have to find out if any of the high schools in Lakewood are looking for teachers. I really can't see myself teaching elementary school, even though I am doing my fieldwork in a third grade classroom now and I love it. You know what I mean."

"I sure do. You stick to what you are good at, Ahuva. Stay in high school. I am sure there is an opening for you. There are so many schools in Lakewood; you can't tell me none of them need teachers. Bais Yaakov will put in a good word for you, won't they?"

"Of course they will. I am planning to look at a few apartments next Wednesday, and I hope to talk to a few principals then."

"Anything else?"

"Nothing really. Did I tell you that we finally went shopping last week? I got most of my kitchen things and chose my linen."

"You told me that last week, Ahuva, and your mother told me when you came home from the store. What else is on your mind? Finals are coming up. Have you made a killer test for your students?"

"Bubby, I don't make 'killer tests.' I am too fresh out of high school to believe in failing my students with a test on things they didn't learn. I had enough of that myself."

"Then what?"

"Did my mother talk to you?" There was a pit in Ahuva's stomach and she got off the hammock and sat down in the freshly mowed grass. She ran her fingers through the blades of grass and scattered those that were cut.

"Talk to me about what? Your mother hasn't told me anything, but I should hope I know my granddaughter well enough by now to hear in her voice when she is preoccupied. And I don't want to hear 'it's because I'm *flechting challah* now.' Tell me the truth, sweetheart. What is going on?"

There was no getting around it, and Ahuva bowed to the inevitable. The truth was that Ahuva would be happy to talk and get this particular load off her chest, but her grandmother was very strong-minded, and Ahuva wasn't sure she was ready to hear what Bubby had to say. Had she already spoken with Rachel Bergmann, it would be easier; it would be a fait accompli. But right now, she was not sure she wanted Bubby's opinion.

"I've been thinking about the girl in the picture. You know, the one who is probably my sister." Ahuva stopped and waited for Bubby to say something. Apparently, Bubby was waiting for Ahuva to finish.

"I want to meet her, and her parents." Ahuva spoke in rush, the words tumbling one after the other as though she wished they would go so fast they would get lost somewhere in the phone line. "I contacted the Journeys rabbi who knows her, and he gave her my number to contact me. I think it is important to do this before I get married," she defended herself. "I want to meet them and find out the story of my birth before I walk down to the *chuppah*. And

I want them to see who I am, and that I've thrived in my parents' care." Her voice was high, as though she needed to convince herself as well as her grandmother.

"Okay," Bubby responded. Her tone did not register protest, and she did not seem to mind as much as Dovid and Rivky had; it was a relief to Ahuva. "That makes sense to me. I guess Mommy and Abba aren't so happy?"

"They think I should focus on preparing myself to get married, but I think that now that this has come up, it needs to be one of my preparations. I know they had given me the choice three years ago, and I turned it down. I still would turn it down. I love them, and I don't need to be the daughter of anyone else..."

"Except the Friedmans, of course."

Ahuva smiled. "But really, I only feel like this because of the way things happened. I mean, it was because of her that I almost didn't get engaged to Moshe, and it sort of brought the whole business of being adopted to a head now, if you know what I mean."

"I do, and I think you are correct. I'll talk to your mother if you want me to."

"You don't have to. They already told me I could call her. I want to meet her first, and then her parents. I think it will be less... I don't know... intimidating..."

"So what's the problem? It seems like a good idea to me, and it sounds like you have it all worked out."

Ahuva took a deep breath and dropped the bombshell. "I don't know if I should talk to Moshe about it."

"What do you mean?"

"If I should tell him before or after I meet her."

"What are the pros and cons?" Bubby asked.

"I don't know..." Ahuva began.

"Does he know you are adopted?" Bubby interrupted.

"Of course. It's not a secret. Everyone knows."

"You know he knows because everyone knows, or because you discussed it with him?" Bubby demanded.

"We discussed it. But he knew beforehand." Ahuva remembered the conversation clearly. It was their fifth date and they were in the Liberty Science Center. Passing the 'Computer' exhibits on their way to a lightning show, Moshe had turned to Ahuva.

"Can I ask you a personal question?"

"You can ask," Ahuva answered with a smile.

"What is the story of your adoption?" Moshe wanted to know.

"Story?" Ahuva repeated. "There's no story. My parents couldn't have kids and so they adopted. It's why my father went to work. You know he is the only one on both sides of my family not in chinuch. He needed the funds to go ahead with the adoption." Ahuva had heard the story countless times but had never told it to anyone before. "The call came in that I was born and they went to get me. That's it. Nothing major."

"You knew?"

"Knew what? I was a baby, three days old, when my parents brought me home."

"So when did you find out you were adopted?" Moshe asked.

Ahuva told him about wanting and praying and waiting to become a big sister. "Even after my parents told me, I still davened. I didn't really understand the implications, and I wanted to become a big sister so badly. I was the only kid in my class who was an only child, you know."

"But I mean, how did you react? Was it a shock? Not when you were seven, but when you were old enough to care."

"Well, seven is old enough to care, and it bothered me that I

was an unwanted baby, but I got over it. My parents wanted me very badly, you see." Ahuva paused and, preempting his next question, said, *"I never tried to find my birth mother. I have parents who love me, and that's what matters."*

Ahuva turned back to the present and the grass running through her fingers. Her parents' love was no longer all that mattered now that the woman who had given birth to her was so close, now that it was likely she had a sister. *Maybe even a little sister,* Ahuva thought self-mockingly.

"So if you tell him before you meet her, then what?" Bubby was asking, and Ahuva turned her focus back to the conversation at hand.

"Then nothing, I guess, but I don't know if I want to consult him about this now. So then I would tell him after, and it would be a conversation, not a consultation. On the other hand, this is a pretty big part of my life, and he will be sharing it, so…" Ahuva stopped, trying to gather her thoughts.

"It doesn't sound to me like a consultation, sweetheart. You're not asking for his advice. Unless you are and are prepared to take it. Which I'm not saying you should do, but I also don't know that it would be a bad idea.

"But the way you presented it to me, you'd be telling him that she has your number and you're waiting for the phone call. I think you should tell him. Get it off your chest, and be open with him, because you're right. You will be marrying him and this is pretty major in your life."

"I guess."

"Ahuva, sweetheart, are you comfortable with your *chasan*?" Bubby asked suddenly, concerned.

"Of course, what do you mean?"

"So why wouldn't you want to tell him? What are you afraid of?"

"I'm not afraid, but I am not married, yet. I don't want to scare him off…"

"What does that mean?"

"I don't know… but most girls don't have to deal with this sort of issue…" Ahuva got up to sit back on the hammock. Swaying gently back and forth, she struggled to put her feelings into words. "We… well, we're engaged, but he doesn't *really* know me yet, and… I don't know… I guess I'm afraid he won't think it is a good idea, and where will that leave me? Because I don't think I am prepared to listen to that…"

"You're scared he'll say no and you'll do it anyway? Is that it? You don't want to scare him by causing him to think that you won't listen to what he says? I'm a little confused."

"I guess you could put it that way. I guess I'm nervous because it is possible that he might say that, and also that he might think I should be focusing on my marriage — to him — and worry about this later. But as much as he knows me, he doesn't *really* know me; I mean we got engaged after, what, fifty hours together? So who knows if his advice would really be correct, even if it sounds nice?" Ahuva got off the hammock and started pacing the backyard. "I don't know what do, Bubby. I'm so nervous!" Ahuva burst out, and she could not stop the tears that had been threatening at the corners of her eyes from flowing.

"Well, the nervous part I got," Bubby said dryly, and Ahuva sniffled in response to the humor. "And it's okay to be nervous. But I have to wonder if you are making an issue where there is none. You got engaged after fifty hours because you felt he would make a good husband, and part of marriage is discussing your issues and feelings and working them out. Here is a perfect opportunity.

"But if you're nervous because you're determined to meet this girl no matter what, then that's okay, too. You're a smart girl, and if this is bothering you now, then I do agree it is better to take care of it now, rather than later. But still you should inform him. No, you don't need to go to him to review your *Chumash* final — save that for marriage. But this is big, and in some way involves him, and he should be a part of it. It will be a good experience for both of you."

Ahuva wiped her tears. "Th-thank you."

"Will you listen?"

"I th-think so."

"Let me know how it goes, okay, sweetheart?"

"Okay, Bubby. Thanks. Good Shabbos."

Chapter 28

"MISS STEINHARDT, UH, I just wanted to, um… thank you, uh, for, umm…" Mindy broke off with a blush that crept up her cheeks.

"You're welcome, Mindy," Ahuva saved her the embarrassment of continuing. "I'm happy to see that everything worked out. I was scared there for a while."

She had been. She had begun the journey with Faigy because her heart had gone out to her, and she wanted to ease her pain and help her navigate the frightening waters that she was plunged into with her parents' divorce. But truthfully, she also liked the picture she saw of herself as the kind of teacher who really made a difference in her students' lives, as being caring, and capable — and yes, as being indispensable to her student's happiness. But Faigy's neediness quickly began to stifle her, and it was no longer so much fun to feel so all-powerful. And then, after her talk with Mindy, when she realized that, due to her intervention, the girls' friendship was on the brink, she had taken stock of the situation and finally listened to what Tante Devorah and her better self had been trying to tell her all along. She gently pulled back from Faigy and put her in touch with an organization devoted to helping children and adolescents whose parents are divorcing. She had focused her attention on getting the classmates to speak to each other again, and had felt a *real* satisfaction when she had succeeded. There was no ego involved, and Ahuva knew she had finally done the right thing.

Faigy had been really angry at what she considered to be disloyalty from her best friend, and although Ahuva didn't blame her, she also understood why Mindy had voiced her concerns to her mother. Faigy's relationship towards Ahuva had been bordering on the unhealthy, and it had taken maturity and insight on Mindy's part to recognize that. There were other students in the class who were jealous that Faigy enjoyed such a close relationship with their adored teacher, but Mindy had not acted out of jealousy.

"Continue speaking to your mother, Mindy, only don't tell Faigy, okay?" Ahuva said, a smile in her eyes.

"Thank you, Miss Steinhardt. I, uh, really appreciate everything." Mindy turned and left the room quickly. She had only approached Miss Steinhardt because her mother told her it was the proper thing to do, but boy was that embarrassing! *Pretty soon they'll be calling me teacher's pet if I continue speaking to Miss Steinhardt during lunch. And then we'll dance together at her wedding, and I'll be doomed for life!*

*   *   *

"So, how's it going, Baruch?" Shmuely asked his son-in-law.

"Not bad, not bad. The work is hard, and the hours are long, but it could be worse. Listen, this way I am able to learn first *seder.*"

"Yes, that's a big thing."

"I've learned a lot from this, Tatty," Baruch told his father-in-law seriously. "I never fully appreciated how hard Avigail worked to keep me in *kollel*. You know her, she's a perfectionist. The house was always spic-and-span and things were always under control. I took it for granted and I went off to learn.

"Now that she works part time, she's so relaxed, it's mind-boggling! The house had always been under control, but now her smile is real. The kids are thrilled to come home to a mother; Malka is happy to study with friends. Do you know that she is able to find the time to read a book every once in a while!" Baruch shook his head with wonder and Shmuely smiled appreciatively.

"The years I had in *yeshiva* were great, they really were," Baruch continued, "But I am so happy to be able to give back to Avigail some of what she gave me all those years. The work is hard, that's true. But it's worth it."

*   *   *

"Rachel, you'll never believe the apartment I found for us!" Beth was ecstatic.

"Hmmm."

"It's on the East Side, so it's a bit more expensive than I had planned, but it's stunning. And there are three bedrooms so we can invite another girl in, and make it cheaper for us all. Do you want to hear about it? You'll love it! It's a ground floor..."

"Hmmm" was the only response Beth got for her efforts.

"Rachel, you there?"

"Yeah... Um, yeah, so the apartment, what about it?" Rachel was clearly distracted.

"What are you doing, Rach?" Beth demanded.

"I'm going through my closet. I can't decide what to wear."

"For what? Where are you going?"

"I'm meeting that girl, Ahuva Steinhardt, tomorrow, and I need something to wear. I may just have to go to Nordstrom tomorrow.

Too bad you're not with me, Beth. I could use some help."

"Who're you meeting?"

"I told you about her, remember?" Rachel answered, although she had not told Beth about her. She had not told anyone besides Ian and her parents about Ahuva, and she only told her parents last week. Marc and Linda had been supportive of her search, as Ian had predicted they would be. Still, she didn't want to go into the whole discussion again. She still felt a pit in her stomach when she thought of it. "She's the girl from the picture that Rabbi Hoffman gave me. I don't think jeans will do, but I am really not sure what to wear."

"Rachel, *what* are you talking about? I didn't know you were so close with Rabbi Hoffman that he gives you pictures."

"You do know," Rachel lied, sighing. Sometimes the best way to go about this sort of thing was to pretend innocence. "Don't you remember when Daren told me Rabbi Hoffman wanted to see me and he gave me the picture?"

"Rachel, *what* are you talking about?"

Rachel sighed and told her. "*Don't* scream," she implored when she finished. "Don't shriek. Don't do *anything*, Beth, please. I am really sorry that you didn't know… But just don't make this any harder for me than deciding what to wear tomorrow. I know I have my parents' encouragement, and Ian's, but I am so nervous. I don't have any clue in the world about what to say to this girl."

"Where are you going?"

"There is a kosher coffee shop in Teaneck."

"Why so far? Where is she?"

"She's somewhere in New York. Monsey. I've never heard of it. Anyway, she is Orthodox, so she needs kosher. And this is sort of halfway for both of us. Do you think I can do those khaki capris from Abercrombie with a T-shirt?"

"A T-shirt? I don't know... How about that zip-up from Hollister? You got the white one, didn't you? But tell me more. I did not even know you were looking for your birth mother. And you told Ian?"

"I am not wearing a zip-up, Beth. I don't want to look like I am sixteen years old! She's Orthodox, for goodness sake!"

"What about a zip-up makes you look more sixteen than a T-shirt? And what does her being Orthodox have to do with it?"

"Come on, Beth! Have you ever seen an Orthodox girl in a zip-up? They are always dressed — like at that seminar we went to, or like Mrs. Hoffman when we went to her house for that party she made which you dragged me to."

"Truthfully, I don't really know any Orthodox girls to know what they wear. And I would so not want to look like Mrs. Hoffman — always in black, bundled up in long sleeves and stockings in the summer. Who really cares what they wear anyway? Wear what you always wear. Be yourself."

"Whatever," Rachel responded. Beth's reaction convinced her that she had been justified in never having spoken to her about her longing to find her mother — or about the picture of Ahuva she had kept in her bag for months.

Rachel cared. She cared about what she would wear and the first impression she would make on Ahuva Steinhardt. This was her sister and the only link she had to the woman who had abandoned her. Her birth mother — the woman she had dreamed about for months.

"You know my ruffled tee from Banana? The grey sleeveless one?" Rachel tried to steer the conversation back to neutral ground. And it would stay there, or she would hang up. She was too tired and too emotionally charged to get into any sort of conversation now with Beth. Just telling her about the background to this had been draining. Rachel was itching to get to the piano. She wanted to get lost in her music, to unwind, to concentrate on a piece by Vivaldi. She knew from experience that it would help her. Music always helped; it was one of the reasons she believed in the therapy.

"Remind me."

"It's nothing major. Only a V-necked T-shirt."

"Oh, with the shirring? Sounds nice. I don't really see what the big deal is. Wear whatever you want."

"Beth, do me a favor. Don't go there."

"Gee, I'm sorry, Rach. Good luck then," Beth had been friends with Rachel long enough to know when it was time to hang up the phone. "Let me know how it goes. I'll keep my fingers crossed." She hung up and left Rachel sitting on the bed in her room in the Bergmann summer home, a pile of clothes surrounding her. One by one Rachel picked them up and brought them back to her closet. She'd hit Nordstrom on the way to Teaneck. Unless… there was a short-sleeved white cardigan peeking out from under a mountain of clothing. She had worn it with jeans, which was a no-no for tomorrow, but it would look good with khaki.

Decision made, Rachel breathed a sigh of relief and went down to the piano.

*　　　*　　　*

Ahuva's cell phone rang and she smiled as she looked at the caller ID. "One minute, Mommy, okay?" she asked as she excused herself from stuffing wedding invitations.

Try an hour, Rivky smiled to herself. Even if she hadn't heard his distinct ringtone, Rivky would have known who it was. Only Moshe got that wide smile from Ahuva, somewhat shy, definitely eager. And it was only when she was talking to Moshe that Ahuva's conversations suddenly became private.

Rivky laughed to herself as she thought of her own engagement. She too had kept every conversation with Dovid to herself. But phone conversations were scarce back then, and so precious. They had written letters, and Rivky loved rereading them. Nothing consequential, but written with such seriousness! They really thought they were solving the world's problems. *That must be what they do on the phone now,* Rivky thought. She felt sad for her daughter who would have almost no tangible mementos of her engagement — there were very few notes, let alone letters, that had been exchanged.

Ahuva went outside to the backyard to her favorite perch on the hammock. "I know I'm really not supposed to call tonight," Moshe was saying. "I'm breaking the rules… but I wanted to wish you *hatzlachah* for tomorrow. I'm *davening* for you, you know that."

"Thank you," Ahuva said. "That is so thoughtful of you." She was glad she had listened to Bubby's advice and had told Moshe about her upcoming meeting. She chuckled at the memory of her conversation with him. It had taken place in this exact spot on the hammock, and Rachel Bergmann had clicked in while they were talking.

"You keep getting cut off," Moshe had said. "Should I call you on another number?"

"I'm sorry. I have a click. For some reason it takes really long on cell phones."

"Do you need to take it?"

"Now, that would be rude. To hang up on my chasan and take another call!" Ahuva laughed.

"Oh, I'm used to it from my mother and sisters. I'll get used to it from my wife."

Ahuva laughed again and then said, "No. I don't recognize the number anyway."

"You think it's...?" Moshe had asked.

"Possibly. Probably. It's a 973 area code, so it makes sense."

"Do you want to take it? I can call back."

"Thanks, I appreciate it. But I am not ready to talk to her just yet," Ahuva had answered.

"Are you ready to meet her?" Moshe asked, bringing Ahuva back to the present.

"I've got my clothes laid out on the bed, if that's what you're asking," Ahuva said lightly. Then her tone changed and she answered the question seriously, "I really don't know. I am excited, but very nervous..." *Sort of like before a date.* "Every once in a while a swarm of butterflies enters my stomach to say hi, and I wonder if I should have listened to my mother and waited until after we're married."

"You don't really want that, do you? I thought you want her at our wedding."

"I do. This is something I need to do, but I'm nervous."

"Well, that's to be expected I suppose. But I'm sure everything will be fine. I know you, Ahuva. You'll be great. You'll enjoy it and you'll be happy you did it."

"Thank you. I appreciate it." There was nothing else to say.

"I'm counting on you, Ahuva. And I'll be calling you tomorrow night to find out how it went."

"It's against the rules, you know. You're coming for Shabbos. You're not supposed to call this week."

"I know. How does eight o'clock sound? I'll call you then."

"Thank you." Ahuva lingered on the hammock, enjoying the fresh June air, before going back to the dining room to complete the mundane task of stuffing envelopes. She rocked gently back and forth and lifted her eyes in prayer. *Thank you, Hashem, for Moshe. And please, please let tomorrow be good. Let me not need to stay too long for the final, and let the meeting go well... Please, Hashem.*

Chapter 29

MICHELLE STERN BROWN STOOD up from her desk in frustration. Coffee was not helping, the air conditioner was not helping, and music was not helping. Nothing helped these days. Michelle felt like throwing something, but was sure that if she did so someone would set up an appointment with a psychologist. *I should probably see one anyway,* she thought as she reached into the bottom of her purse for a cigarette. *And I don't mean Steven.* She didn't care who saw her smoking, though it was no secret that her husband had made her give it up when they married. *If anyone asks, I'll blame the Lewis case,* she thought grimly. It was only in extreme circumstances that she actually lit up.

Her tension had nothing to do with the Lewis case. She just couldn't concentrate on anything anymore. Except her babies. Or her lack of them.

Steven wanted to adopt. They had reached a dead-end; the doctors told her there was nothing further they could do, and she must accept the fact that she would never be able to bear children. *But I can,* she screamed silently, blowing out smoke rings. *I did!* Two little girls. She remembered the day she gave birth; it was almost twenty-two years ago. *I gave birth, and I gave them up.* She took a long puff and watched as the rings rose to the ceiling. *I had to! My life then* — she shuddered. She never wanted to remember how her life had been then. *I couldn't have taken care of them then. But now I can!*

Michelle tried to imagine what her life would have been like had she kept her babies. But it was unimaginable. She had been so young, so needy, with no one to help her. She had done everything — contacted the adoption agency, driven herself to the hospital, given birth — all alone. Had she kept her babies she would probably be on welfare now; certainly there would have been no law school, no internship at a prestigious law firm, no possibility of making partner, or of opening her own law firm. Michelle Stern, Attorney at Law. She loved how it sounded. She loved calling the office and hearing the receptionist answer, "Stern Law, can I help you?"

Michelle threw down her cigarette and crushed it into the fashionable carpet with the spiked heel of her shoe. She was not satisfied until it was thoroughly ground into the Berber weave. The cleaning crew would vacuum later. The satisfaction this provided her lasted only a minute, and she felt like a caged lion as she resumed her pacing. *What good does all this* — the corner office, the name recognition, the expensive, trendy home — *do me?* she wondered. She was doing work that she loved. She had all the wealth that came with being one of the top criminal lawyers on the West Coast. She had a wonderful marriage. *But no one to pass these gifts to.*

Michelle refused to look for her daughters. Steven thought that should be the next step. He thought it would afford her closure, help her move on with her life, allow her to think about adopting. But she refused. "No. I gave them up and I have to live with that. I don't want to mess up their lives. If we do end up adopting, I would *never* allow the birth mother to contact my children. She gave them up, and they will belong to me. Period."

She thought back over the years. *If I had known then what I do now — that I would never be able to give birth again — would I have given them up?* But then her whole life would be different — *she* would be different — someone else entirely.

Michelle was startled out of her reverie by the ringing of her phone and then her secretary's voice. "Michelle, there is a call on line 1."

"I am not available," she snapped, and was upset at herself for being annoyed at the interruption. She was here to work, wasn't she? She had come to work to distract herself, hadn't she?

"But it's Anthony Lewis?" there was a question in the secretary's voice.

"I am not available now. For anyone. In fact," she said, as inspiration struck, "I am leaving the office now, and I am not sure when I'll be back. Let Lewis know I'll call him at my first opportunity." There was such sweet pleasure in being the boss of a sought-after firm. *I call the shots.*

Michelle gathered her files into her Prada leather tote and marched purposefully out of her office. She smiled to her secretary in an effort to soften her previous tone and strode towards the building elevators.

She called Steven from her car and asked him to meet her at the steakhouse in Beverly Hills for dinner. "I need a pick-me-up," she explained. "I'm going crazy. And no, it is not the Lewis case."

*   *   *

Ahuva sat in the corner of David's Café in Teaneck. It was 2:15 PM, and she had come straight from proctoring her *Chumash* final. She had been in the café for an hour, grading papers, and contemplated getting a second cup of coffee while she waited. She decided against it; her meeting with Rachel Bergmann was scheduled for 2:30, and she would need another coffee during the meeting to soothe her nerves; three coffees within a couple of hours… Not a good idea.

The butterflies in her stomach got excited every time the door opened, and they seemed to come out in droves to say hello to whoever entered the café. Ahuva found that she was unable to concentrate on the tests in front of her; her mind was occupied with containing the enthusiasm of the winged creatures inside her abdomen. She put the tests in her bag with a sigh, and as she cleared the table of her things, the door to the café opened once more. Giving in to the butterflies and allowing them to take the lead, she lifted her head and saw her.

Rachel Bergmann. In the flesh. By now, her stomach was dancing, and nothing she did could contain the excitement of those butterflies. *Much worse than a date,* the thought came to Ahuva unbidden. The thought made her grin; her nervousness abated, and she lifted her hand in a wave.

Rachel saw the gesture, and was relieved to find Ahuva already in the coffee shop. The hour-long trip from Long Branch had made her antsy; what if Ahuva wouldn't show up?

Because she had been so concerned about what to wear, Ahuva's outfit was the first thing Rachel noticed. She was wearing a knee-length black skirt and an open cardigan in a smoky mauve color with a thin black belt and silver Tory Burch flats completing the look. As Ahuva stood up to greet her, Rachel noted that the skirt was below-the-knee, and the blouse Ahuva wore under the cardigan buttoned to her neck. Rachel congratulated herself for having chosen her most conservative cardigan, and capris instead of jeans, but still she wondered why Ahuva found it necessary to be so covered up. She remembered Beth's comment — *all bundled up in the summer.* She smiled in response to Ahuva's greeting, and put out her hand: "I'm Rachel Bergmann."

"Oh," Ahuva wrinkled her nose as she put her hand in Rachel's, "that makes it sound so official," she said, laughter in her voice. Rachel looked at Ahuva and cocked her head, unsure of what Ahuva meant. She didn't respond, and Ahuva, realizing her joke fell flat, let it go and continued, "Let's sit down. I've been here a while, doing paperwork. Grading tests and whatever… There is a menu here, and when you want to order, you go up to the counter, but they'll bring the order to you if you ask them…" Ahuva stopped suddenly as she realized she was babbling. She never babbled, which showed how nervous she really was. She sat down in her seat, and waited.

"What's good?" Rachel asked. "Oh, anything," was the answer. "Let me know what you want, and I'll order."

"That's okay, I don't mind going up. Let me know what you want."

Ahuva ordered a hot cappuccino, no sugar, and a cheese danish. "You also don't like sugar in your coffee?" Rachel asked. "I can't stand it. I think it ruins the taste. But most people don't agree with me."

"I don't think it has anything to do with our being related," Ahuva finally felt herself again, and was able to think coherently. "We just both have good taste."

Rachel laughed and went to order. She came back with their choices and as Ahuva took her coffee off the tray, Rachel noticed a solitaire diamond in the classic Tiffany setting adorning the ring finger of Ahuva's left hand. "You're engaged to be married?" she asked, as she daintily pulled apart the pastry she ordered and wiped her fingers on a napkin. "May I see?"

Ahuva extended her hand for inspection. "Beautiful," Rachel said. "Who's the lucky guy?"

"How do you know he's lucky?" Ahuva asked with a grin.

"Oh, anyone who marries the girl who is my carbon copy has to be lucky. It's almost like marrying me."

They laughed and then were silent as they sipped their coffees. Rachel broke the silence and said, "Can I ask you a question?" Without waiting for a reply, she continued, "When did you find out about me?"

"Oh, on Pesach. That is, uh, Passover."

"I know what Pesach is," Rachel said, and she wasn't sure if she should be amused or annoyed that Ahuva perceived her to be so Jewishly ignorant. "But that was in April. Now it's June. Why did you wait so long?"

"I was dating, and then I got engaged and the school year was ending so I had to finish up teaching. I don't know; I was busy."

"Oh. So now you aren't busy," Rachel's voice sounded deflated to her own ears, and she wasn't entirely sure why. Was it because she wanted Ahuva to still be busy — *very* busy — too busy to continue searching into their common past? *She* didn't want to continue.

"Of course I'm busy. I'm getting married in about eight weeks. I have to put my trousseau together, not to mention finding an apartment in a new city. I'm still busy grading finals, and the school where I intern for special-ed still has another month to go before they break for the summer. But I suddenly decided I couldn't get married without meeting my biological mother. Or at least you."

There was a ton of information to digest in what Ahuva had just told her. Getting married in eight weeks? Was that a rush job? Plus, finding an apartment in another city meant that Ahuva and her fiancé had dated long-distance. And finishing teaching? She was a teacher already? How in the world could she have gotten her degree so fast? As far as Rachel knew you needed a Master's to become a teacher. And what was the special-ed thing she mentioned?

All that would have to wait, though. Rachel did not want this girl to pull her into a search for her roots, and she wanted to make that clear. *I've lived on edge the past year. Every spare thought was devoted to that woman who just — abandoned me, and now I've had enough. I've already hurt my parents because I did not tell them anything about the petition and my search, halfhearted though it's been up till now; but even so, I know that they are there for me and will always be there. And I have Ian who has been my champion through all this. My life is finally falling back into place. I won't do it.*

When Rachel said nothing, Ahuva continued, "I never really cared about her. I have my parents. *They* are my family. And when I first learned about you, I didn't have any interest in finding out any more about you. I was just happy that now I could continue seeing the only boy I was ever interested in." She knew she must be thoroughly confusing Rachel who had no idea what she had done, inadvertently, to sabotage Ahuva's happiness. Ahuva wondered if Rachel even knew that her parents had given Ahuva up for adoption. She tried to keep things as simple as possible. "Now that things have fallen into place for me, I couldn't get you and your parents out of my head. I have this urge, childish really, to introduce myself to them and show them who I have become despite everything." *Whoa, that was tactless!* Ahuva bit her lip and waited for Rachel's reaction. *I did not mean to say that. If she storms out of here in a huff, I can't say I'd blame her.*

But Rachel only looked confused. "My parents? What do they have to do with anything?"

Ahuva stared, "Your parents? Your mother is my mother, isn't she?"

"But I'm also adopted," Rachel responded, and there was a wistful note in her voice.

"Oh." Ahuva was silent. *What did I need this for, then?* Ahuva thought to herself. *I still can't invite my birth mother to my wedding, because I still don't know who she is. Why did I make myself crazy?*

Rachel suddenly shook her head, as though to clear it. She took a long sip of coffee. "I don't want to meet her. I know who she is, and she doesn't deserve me, or you either, I would say." She sounded petulant, like a defensive child, and as Ahuva raised her eyebrows Rachel explained to her what the past year had been like. "Wow. I didn't realize. I'm sorry." Ahuva's voice was soft.

"It's pretty simple to find out who your mother is, if you're interested," Rachel said. "Just send a petition to the court where your adoption was finalized. Do you know where that is?"

"I was born in Chicago. I guess everything happened there."

"Well I would assume we have the same mother anyway. We're pretty identical. When's your birthday?" Rachel asked.

"July 10. I'll be twenty-two."

"So we're twins, then. And I've always wanted a sister." Once she understood that Ahuva wasn't on a mission to unite her with their mother, Rachel was content to put her newfound sister at ease.

For Ahuva, her initial disappointment was wearing off, and now she was excited to meet a sister, a *twin* sister. *I never really cared about my mother,* she rationalized over her cheese danish. *So why should I care now? But I have a sister. A real live sister. Let's be friends.*

Chapter 30

RACHEL'S GAZE RETURNED TO Ahuva's ring and she said, "Tell me about him. Do you have any pictures?"

The conversation flowed from there as the new-found sisters discussed Ahuva's engagement to Moshe Friedman, and then each girl related a condensed version of her life story. They studiously avoided the topic of their adoption as they got acquainted with each other. *As though we are on a date. Which we are, sort of,* Ahuva thought. Rachel was amazed that Ahuva was a teacher; a girl her own age, without a degree, teaching teenagers? But what she was most interested in was the fact that Ahuva was engaged. She took out her cell phone and found pictures of Ian to show Ahuva. "I can't believe you are engaged to be married!" she exclaimed. "And you knew your fiancé only five weeks before you got engaged?"

"Well, I actually met him three months before that. But I saw him only once and then the whole mess with you happened!" Ahuva answered with a laugh. At the look of obvious confusion on Rachel's face, Ahuva explained what had transpired behind the scenes as a result of the Journeys seminar.

"Oh my, I remember that lady!" Rachel exclaimed. "She kept

staring at us like she was furious at something we did! We had no idea what her problem was. This is too funny; I can't wait to tell my friend Beth."

"But listen, all's well that ends well," Ahuva philosophized. "Imagine if you hadn't gone there — we wouldn't be sitting here today."

Rachel was impatient with the tone of the conversation. She didn't want to talk about adoption and birth mothers — or even birth sisters. "Tell me how it works," she said, steering the conversation back to Ahuva's engagement. "What makes you think you are ready to spend your life with a guy you only knew for a month? I mean, I've known Ian about seven months now, and he hasn't dreamed of proposing!" *Although if he would propose, I would say yes.* But even as the thought popped into her head, it made her nervous. How could she know it would be the right thing? Would she have accepted Brad after five weeks? Or even seven months? Look where he left her after knowing each other for three years! *In a better place,* she decided. *Ian is different. And my relationship with him is different.* She turned her attention to Ahuva who was explaining the *shidduch* process.

"First you check out who the guy is and what kind of value system he has. Before you even agree to meet him." She did not mention that it was her parents who did the checking. "And once you are sure that you are on the same wavelength in terms of what you want in life, you meet. And if you like each other, and you know you agree on the important things in life — well, marriage is work. And you work together." She saw Rachel's skepticism, and said, "It sounds crazy, I know, but it works."

They continued talking, enjoying their conversation, until Ahuva glanced at her watch and saw that it was 5:00. "Oh my, it's so late! I have a *kallah* class at 6:00! I better run!"

Rachel did not ask what a *kallah* class was, and Ahuva did not explain. The young women wrapped up their discussion, and Ahuva seemed hesitant to ask, "I know you don't want to go any further with this, but do you mind if I ask you for the address and stuff to send a petition to the court? I just want to confirm everything we know already…."

"No problem. What's your email address? I'll send you the info," Rachel promised and the sisters exchanged information.

"When will we see each other next?" Ahuva wanted to know.

"I don't know," Rachel answered. "You're getting married pretty soon, plus you've got all those other activities you told me about, teaching and final grades and stuff. I'm just interning in the office on alternate days and swimming on the beach on others. When you have a free minute why don't you come down to our summer home and we'll spend a day together? You can meet my mom and dad, as you've always wanted to," she grinned.

"Thank you. I'll have to see what fits into my schedule," Ahuva replied. She was not ready for an invitation from Rachel to visit the Bergmanns. She would have to explain that she didn't swim on public beaches, that even drinking a glass of water at their home could be problematic, and that she certainly would not shake hands with Rachel's father.

"Great. We'll be in touch then. And you'll see those couches my mom just bought. Did I tell you that every piece of furniture in our house comes from your dad's place?"

"Really?" Ahuva asked smiling. "That's so neat. I'll tell my father. He'll be happy to hear it."

"Yup. My mom's obsessed. Tell him she's waiting for new patio furniture. She hasn't seen anything she likes yet."

Ahuva nodded, "Will do."

They gathered their things and went to the counter. A small

argument ensued over who was to pay, and Ahuva won when she said, "Don't be silly. I invited you here and got you nervous. It's my treat." She turned around to say goodbye to Rachel, and the latter stretched out her arms and enveloped Ahuva in a loose embrace. "I'm really happy we met. We'll be in touch."

The lady behind the counter looked confused. *Happy they met?* she thought. *They are carbon copies of each other.*

*   *   *

Rachel got into her car and slowly reversed out of her parking spot. She turned the radio on low and drove, unthinking. It was only when she reached the open space of the Garden State Parkway, and the speedometer read 75 mph that she gave into her thoughts.

She was startled when she heard her mother's telltale ringtone and, ignoring the law against using a handheld, Rachel took the call. "Rachel, where are you? How was it?"

"I'm on the way home, I just left. It was nice, I suppose, though that feels like the wrong word to use."

"Tell me about it. I was so nervous."

"Well, Ahuva was… well, she was nice, and down-to-earth, and seemed normal."

"Well, as normal as you can be if you're Orthodox," Linda Bergmann interjected.

Rachel found herself unaccountably annoyed. "What does that mean? Why can't she be Orthodox and normal?" Ahuva *was* normal… she was. *She was.*

She thought back to Ahuva's outfit. It was cool, and trendy; Rachel had the same pair of shoes at home, and a similar cardigan. *But why was she so bundled up?* Rachel thought. *With her neck covered and long sleeves,* and Rachel could have sworn she saw stockings; but who in her right mind would wear stockings on a day like today? The temperature, as it had been the past week, was close to one hundred degrees. *There must be a reason. And there must be a reason for the black skirt, too. All the Orthodox wear black.*

"She's engaged to be married, Mom. Did you know that?"

"How could I have known?" Linda shot back.

"Can you believe it? She is twenty-one years old and engaged to be married. And her wedding date is set for August, Mom. It's so… so…" she struggled for the right word. "She met her fiancé for the first time in January!" she burst out.

"Wow. I hope she knows what she is doing. Even in my days, we didn't do it quite that fast."

"Well, she's quite mature and besides, this is the way they do it in her circles." Rachel did not understand the sudden desire to defend Ahuva, but she felt like a mother bear protecting her cubs. "The divorce rate is much lower among the Orthodox than anywhere else, you know."

"They probably feel trapped into marriages their parents arrange for them and see no way out," was Linda's tart rejoinder.

"That is not true, Mom! I asked Ahuva about that, and she said that before any girl would even meet with a guy he is investigated thoroughly to make sure he's a good, upstanding citizen, but then when they finally do date it's totally up to the girl or guy if they get married. She said she dated many other guys before she met her fiancé. It doesn't sound much different than what you and Dad do by having me bring my dates home. It sounds quite sensible, actually. Then something like Ben and Mary wouldn't have happened!" Rachel was referring to a family sore spot. By the time her cousin Ben's parents had met Mary, there was nothing they could do to prevent their son's intermarriage.

"Would you like us to go about it that way, honey?" Linda's voice was sweet.

"Mom!" Rachel had to laugh. "All I am saying is that you can't deny there's some merit in their way of doing things. I think I'll do it that way for my kids."

"Oh, are you thinking of going Orthodox on us, Rachel?" Linda asked. "Because you can't pick and choose, you know. It's all or nothing. If you want to do things their way, you have to do the whole shmear."

"Maybe I am."

Chapter 31

 *KALLAH* CLASS LASTED UNTIL 8:00 and afterward, as Ahuva crossed the street to where her car was parked, Baila Cohen, another *kallah* in the class, asked for a ride home. As soon as she got into the passenger seat, Baila burst into tears.

"What's the matter?" asked a horrified Ahuva. She and Baila did not have much to do with each other. In fact, they had only met through *kallah* class and, because they did not travel in the same circles, Ahuva would not have thought they would have any connection outside of lessons.

"I'm really sorry," Baila sputtered, embarrassed at her outburst. "This was not supposed to happen. But my life is so crazy right now, and I am completely overwhelmed. I thought you might be able to help me."

"Oh. I am flattered that you think so!" Ahuva was a bit taken aback and was not sure what the proper response should be. Baila must be desperate. Ahuva could not imagine breaking down like that in front of a virtual stranger. "What's the matter? How can I help?"

"Well, my sister's friend from camp is in your high school class, and she thinks you are the best. She swears by you."

"Well I really am flattered, I guess." Ahuva answered, amused. "But hers are tenth-grade problems."

"Well, I figured maybe you could have some suggestions for me. She said you're really understanding. Worst case scenario, I'll have gotten things off my chest."

Ahuva raised her eyebrows. They were nearing Baila's block, and Ahuva was anxious to get home, to talk to her parents about her meeting with Rachel, to speak with Moshe who was supposed to have called at 8:00 — *I must have missed the call because my phone is on vibrate,* she thought suddenly. There was really no nice way to brush Baila off and tell her that now was not a good time to talk. Ahuva realized that at this moment Baila came first; she would have to put her own issues on hold for a little while. *It's going to be a long night,* she thought as she turned down a side street and drove aimlessly. "What's going on?" Her tone was warm and inviting, giving no hint that she would rather be a million miles away. Baila took a deep breath and began.

"I don't know if you know, but my brother is sick. My parents are busy with him all day, and since I am the oldest, everything falls on me. It's true that most nights we get supper sent from the Bikur Cholim, or sometimes by a neighbor, but I'm the one in charge of serving it, and then I have to clean up and give baths and put the kids to bed, and sign homework. Well now it's summer, but you know what I mean. I try to get my siblings to help me, and sometimes they do, especially Nechama whose friend Mindy Glassman told me about you. But they are not really interested in helping, and I can't really make them help me because I am not their mother, only an annoying big sister. My mother is always in the hospital, and when she does come home she is so tired and needs to rest. I am in charge of the kids and making sure they don't bother my mother when they finally catch a glimpse of her.

And my father is at work during the day, and researching doctors and things at night. So basically I am taking care of everything on my own."

The words came out in a jumble, but their meaning was clear. Baila, the *kallah*, was thrust into the demanding role of being the mother of a large and needy household.

"Meanwhile," Baila continued, "I'm engaged, and this is supposed to be a very exciting time in my life. I am supposed to be bonding with my *chasan;* I should be excited to get married. I'm supposed to drop everything and run when he calls, but I can't because there are too many things to do and I am too tired. Even if we make up a time beforehand, there is always something that comes up. Maybe it's laundry, maybe one of the kids had a tantrum. Last night whoever was supposed to have sent us supper never did, so the whole house went into chaos, and one of my siblings, who needs things to happen on time or else he goes crazy — well guess what, he went crazy. So I can't really be so excited about getting married — well, it's not that I'm not, there's just too much going on. And my *chasan* sometimes hears it in my voice. And then he asks me what the matter is, and I don't want to tell him, so now he thinks we are a dysfunctional family…" Baila stopped suddenly, and said, forcefully, "We are *not* dysfunctional." She sighed, "At least we weren't before Chaim Meir was diagnosed. His name was Meir, but they added Chaim.

"And that's another thing. I'm ashamed to say this," Baila turned her face away and spoke quietly. "I know this is terrible, but I can't help feeling upset at Chaim Meir for ruining everything for me and for taking my mother away just when I need her most. He got sick right after I got engaged," she explained, her voice sounding normal again, "so things were on hold for a couple of weeks.

"At first my in-laws were very understanding about the

situation, and my *chasan* was wonderful, and I was so grateful, but finally it got to the point where I guess their understanding ran out and they just were like 'pick a date, this is ridiculous already,' because it *was* getting ridiculous. I mean we were engaged for two months and we hadn't picked a date. So now I am getting married in six weeks... When we finally picked a date my mother wanted to give herself lots of time to prepare so she could give me 'the attention I deserve' — which was how she put it — but I am not getting any attention at all. She told me to take care of the invitations myself, and I hope they come tomorrow so we can get them out. I am supposed to get the guest list from my aunt and go over it with my mother in the hospital. As if she'll have the head for it sitting in the hospital next to my sick brother and all those beeping machines! I found Mrs. Goldberg for *kallah* classes on my own, and my mother told me to go to the caterer to pick out a menu with my father, and I went to get a gown with a friend of mine, and I have absolutely nothing else. No pots or pans or linen or towels. I'll be living in Monsey so I worked on getting an apartment myself, and *Baruch Hashem* that went easy..." Baila finally ran out of steam, and she burst into tears again.

Ahuva stopped the car on the side of the road and sat in silence while she waited for Baila to calm down. She was itching to change the CD in her car to something more appropriate, something like Project Relax, but she didn't want Baila to think she did not have Ahuva's full attention.

Should she get some of the *tzedakah* organizations involved? But she didn't know Baila's family's financial situation. That might be the *worst* thing to do. "I'm sorry, I'm not really sure..." she began and stopped as she was struck with a flash of inspiration. She turned to face Baila enthusiastically. "You know, I still have shopping to do. How about we go shopping together tomorrow?"

Ahuva mentally marked off her day. Was there anything crucial she was supposed to get done tomorrow? Anything that couldn't be pushed off? "The whole school is involved in finals now, so I have the day off tomorrow. Do you work? Do you want to go during the day or at night? I have coupons for Macy's and I know they have good kitchen things."

"*Could* we go together? I think that would be fun. I could take off. My boss keeps telling me to take off a day to prepare for my wedding. Day would be easier because at night I am busy with the house."

Ahuva thought quickly. Giving Baila a break from the night chores — even if only for one night — would go far towards helping her feel like a *kallah*. "I think the night might work better for me actually, so how about I send Mindy Glassman to your house tomorrow night and she and your sister Nechama can be in charge together? This way you'll have a night off. It *will* be fun. And if the girls are there you won't be pressed for time to get back to the house to take care of things."

"She doesn't need to study for finals?" The question ended with a sniffle as Baila saw the world light up and go dark again in a matter of seconds.

"I'll take care of her studying. Don't you worry. How about I pick you up at 5:30 and we'll grab a bite to eat before we go. This way we'll be home fairly early and give Mindy a chance to study. Give me your phone number and we'll be in touch tomorrow."

The girls exchanged cell phone numbers. Ahuva drove around the block and stopped in front of Baila's house. "Wait," she called before Baila got out of the car, "how many kids are in your family?"

"There are six at home now," Baila answered, "and I have a brother in *yeshiva* and Chaim Meir." Ahuva had timed the question so that Baila would not have a chance to wonder why Ahuva cared about the number of children in her family. But the kids would be thrilled to get an anonymous package in the mail with enough treats and prizes for all of them. Judging from Baila's story, the children — including Nechama, Mindy's friend — could also use a little extra attention. (She'd figure out something really special for Nechama.) And she also wanted to prepare some meals for Baila's family, something to pull out of the freezer when the expected meal from Bikur Cholim or whomever did not materialize.

Ahuva pulled into her driveway at 9:00. As she picked up her purse from under the passenger seat she felt it vibrating. Uh-oh. How many calls had she missed? Her caller ID identified this call as HOME, and she was glad to be able to tell her mother she was in the driveway. "I'll be right in."

She checked her messages and saw a voicemail and text from Moshe. "Hope everything is okay. I tried to reach you a couple of times. I am going into night *seder* now, so I guess we'll talk tomorrow."

Moshe was going to be with them for Shabbos, and Ahuva wondered if their talk would be pushed off until then. So many things had happened today, and she needed time to process it all and to put everything into perspective. Baila's problem was the most urgent right now, but it was Rachel she wanted to think about. It was hard to believe that she'd only met her a few hours ago; by now it seemed like days. She wanted to talk it over with her mother, and then they would discuss Baila. She thought of what Baila had said, that her *chasan* got pushed to the side, and she was determined not to do that to Moshe regardless of any issues she would have to deal with. *But our engagement is not at all like that,* she thought. *Moshe really wants to be involved in my concerns. And my problems — if you could call them that — are so different from what Baila has on her plate.* Ahuva silently blessed Bubby for her advice to be open with Moshe about Rachel. *It has brought us closer and made me appreciate him more.* She thanked Hashem for the life He gave her, *with* its issues, and she thanked Him for giving her the ability to deal with them. And then she went inside to conquer her challenges.

*   *   *

After the Friday night *seudah*, the *chasan* and *kallah* took the requisite walk. "So, what's been happening?" Moshe asked. "We haven't spoken in a while."

"I know. I've been crazy busy this week. But at least we've been following the rules. You weren't allowed to call, you know."

Moshe grinned in the dark. "Well, I think there were extenuating circumstances this week. How was your meeting?"

"Very nice." Ahuva spoke with a conviction that surprised her. She had not really had time to process the whole Rachel thing between grading finals, cooking for and going out with Baila, and gown fittings for both her mother and herself. "I'm very happy I met her. She seems like a really nice girl."

"Does she really look like you?" Moshe wanted to know.

"I guess so. Next to each other, I don't know. I wouldn't wear her kind of clothes, so I didn't feel I was looking in a mirror, but we definitely do look alike.

"I hear. I was only wondering, because my parents were so horrified when they saw her."

"I hope they like me now."

"Oh, don't worry. You can do no wrong in my mother's eyes. But tell me. What happened?"

"Nothing. Mostly we talked about me getting married. She was so shocked. She couldn't believe that at my age I would know what I want out of life and whom I want to marry. She thought it must have been an arranged match, and when I told her it wasn't really, and then I told her how the whole thing almost fell apart when your mother saw her and thought she was me, she was a little confused."

"Well, from her point of view it doesn't make sense. Why should my mother have been upset at seeing her? *She* doesn't see anything wrong with the way she dresses and talks and walks."

"True," Ahuva agreed. She had not thought of that. "She told me about herself. Her father is the president of their synagogue or temple or whatever they call it. She grew up in East Hanover, which is right here. Maybe an hour away. And her family goes to Long Branch, which of course is Deal, in the summer. Yet it took us this long to find each other!"

"But you don't travel in the same circles at all. You wouldn't have found her in Camp B'nos. So how should you have found her?"

"Yeah, but she could have come from California or something, or stayed in Chicago. But living right next door! I mean, come on. She even plays piano, and is taking music therapy in school."

"So I guess you have something else in common," Moshe interrupted. "Does she play as well as you do?"

"Well, she is continuing her music education, so I would imagine she's probably better."

"Unlikely," was Moshe's retort and Ahuva snorted, but was pleased.

"What else?" Moshe asked.

"Nothing, I think. She sent a petition to the courts to get her real birth certificate and find out who her mother is. Actually she was supposed to email me the information. I wonder if she did; I haven't checked my email in ages. She said our — well, *her* mother is someone named Michelle Stern, and that she was born in Chicago. I know about being born in Chicago; my parents had told me that. I'm sure I won't forget, but remind me when we talk next week about sending the petition. I am going to be really busy; I have to finish grading papers, and I am starting to do summer tutoring next month, for college. Plus, I still have Keren Orah — they are not done with school until the end of July. At least I'm done teaching and dealing with tenth grade politics," she said.

"Why do you need the birth certificate? You know you look alike, and you know where you both were born, and I assume you have the same birthday?"

"True, but I want to confirm it, and really, what's the big deal? All it means is that I'll have to type a letter."

"I hear. What about that other girl you met? The night you met Rachel?"

"Baila Cohen. Nothing much. My mother and I made some suppers for them. You should have seen her face when I knocked at her door with the pans in my hand. It was classic!" Ahuva chuckled at the memory. "I took her out to eat before we went shopping, and she was so happy. I was worried about how she would pay for the stuff we bought, because what if they have no money? I paid for supper, I told her it was my treat, but I couldn't offer to pay for her kitchen things. That would have been so awkward."

"So what did you do?"

"Well, I decided that I would observe the way she shops. If she's more concerned with price than with quality then I would have to do something about it. I mean, I don't believe in spending money unnecessarily, and I do look for sales, but my mother always says that sometimes spending money on a quality item is cheaper in the long run, because you don't need to replace it."

"Don't let Chani or Yocheved know that you look for sales.

They always badgered my mother to buy brand name stuff, like Tommy Polo."

Ahuva stifled a laugh, "No. They didn't. It's Tommy Hilfiger, or Polo."

"Whatever. What happened with Baila?"

"Nothing really. She looked at prices, but she didn't actually buy anything. I told her if she did buy anything not to open the packaging because she might get gifts and would need to return stuff, and I helped her make a registry."

"What's that?" Moshe asked.

"The store keeps a file of all the things you want, and then if someone wants to buy a wedding gift they ask the store for your registry and buy things they know you want, or need."

"Oh."

"My mother thought we should plan a grab bag shower for her, but I can't because I don't know who her friends are. I am *so* not asking her for a list of friends; that is worse than awkward. We thought we would just buy stuff anonymously, but I still don't know. If we take care of a lot of things on the registry, I'm sure it'll come out somehow."

"I hear, but it seems to me that with a sick child in the family, they could probably use the gifts."

"Right, I guess. I'm going to buy her something; I told her to put stuff she doesn't really need but would want on the list, and she wants a special set of goblets. There's someone in town who sells them so I can get them easily and give them to her as a surprise. The rest I'm going to leave to my parents. My father knows what to do in these kinds of situations."

They were back in front of Ahuva's house, and she invited him for a cold drink before they went their separate ways for the night.

Chapter 32

MICHELLE COULDN'T SLEEP. SHE got out of bed and went outside onto her bedroom balcony. She gazed at the starry sky and at the Pacific Ocean looming before her. It was July 9, and her thoughts, as they constantly seemed to do lately, turned to her daughters. *My own flesh and blood.* She looked at her watch. It was their birthday, wherever they were, although, in her time zone, they would not actually turn twenty-two for another hour.

Had so much time really passed? What were they up to? Michelle shook her head in disgust. *Enough philosophizing. It gets you nowhere — just makes you more depressed.* Well, tonight she *wanted* to be depressed. Michelle felt like a masochist as she sat down on a lounge chair and hugged her knees.

Had they stayed together? Were they adopted by nice families? Were they given the love and comfort that she now wished she could have given them? Were they aware of her? Were they aware of each other? What did they look like? Where did they live? What schools did they go to? Did they have friends? Are they happy?

Stop it. Stop it, she commanded herself. Steven would just glance at her face and know what she had been thinking, out there alone on the balcony. She lifted her hand and wiped her eyes with the sleeve of her robe. They had discussed it today, she and her husband. Steven had almost succeeded in convincing her to seek out her daughters, but at the last minute she had found the strength to refuse.

"I don't like to see you torturing yourself like this, Shelly," he had said. "Why not meet them and get it over with? It will give you closure. You'll be able to move on."

"I am not your patient, Steven," Michelle had answered her psychiatrist husband. "Don't talk to me about closure. You don't understand, I can't do that to them. I can't give them away and then surface twenty years later to claim my place as their mother. I don't deserve it, and it isn't fair to them, or to their adoptive parents. Let's just go down to Boston to this Dr. Lieberman. Let's see if he can help us."

"We can do that if you want. But I still think you should try to contact them. Look, they are adults now; they can make a rational decision about whether or not they want you in their lives."

"They might not even know they're adopted! And here I come upsetting them. I won't do it, Steven. You hear me? I won't. Case closed."

"If that's the way you feel…"

"It is. I am going to make an appointment with Dr. Lieberman tomorrow, okay?"

"I thought you wanted to wait until after the Lewis case?"

"Dr. Williams said it would be a year till we get in. Let's make the appointment, we'll go for an initial consultation and then we'll come back and wrap up the Lewis case. I assume we'll need to rent a place in Boston for a considerable

amount of time if he does accept us for treatment."
"Fair enough," Steven had answered.

Michelle was startled out of her reverie by the sound of the sliding door opening. "Come, Shelly," Steven said. "Dwelling on it anymore won't help. You'll call Dr. Lieberman in the morning, and we'll take it from there."

"Okay, Steven, but do you think I should try to push for an appointment sooner?"

"Sooner than what?"

"Sooner than a year. I don't think I can handle waiting so long."

"What about your practice? The Lewis case?" Steven asked.

"I don't know. Maybe I'll ask Anthony to take it over. He's very good in court, and he's been sitting in on all the sessions and working with me."

"I guess if you trust him enough, Shelly. Are you willing to bear the consequences if he loses?

Michelle understood why Steven said that. More than once Steven had suggested she tone things down, take a small break, and she always answered, "If we lose a case when I am in court, it's okay; people believe the guy is really guilty, and that's why I lost, so it doesn't hurt the business. If we lose and it was another attorney from the firm that worked on the case, potential clients will say that I must be losing my touch, that's why I let someone else work on the case. They'll say that I don't care about the firm anymore." Steven would have thought it was the other way around, but he couldn't deny that his wife was successful.

"I think so," she answered slowly. "When I thought children would come easily I had planned on keeping the same working schedule I have now and employing a nanny. Now that I see how hard it is… well, I'm not going to become a stay-at-home mom, and I'll still need the nanny, but I do think I'll finally cut back. Children have become too precious." She thought again of the ones she lost — no, gave away — and stifled a sob.

"You're growing up, Shelly," Steven told his wife. "Call Dr. Lieberman tomorrow and offer top dollar. We'll take the earliest appointment. And, get back to bed, it's late and you have a busy day tomorrow.

Michelle stood up and walked back inside.

*   *   *

Ahuva's phone beeped with a text message and she flipped it open. "Happy Birthday." It was from Rachel Bergmann, her new-found sister, and she responded with a birthday wish of her own.

How long does petition process take? Ahuva asked.

6-8 wks, was Rachel's reply.

Gr8. Will confirm we r sis's. Hopefully b4 my weding. Did u gt invite? Ru coming?

Ye so excited

Gr8. Me 2.

Gtg ttyl

*   *   *

Miri ran her hands under the sink before she answered the phone. *I hate talking on the phone while cleaning chicken,* she thought for the umpteenth time. Aside from getting a crick in her neck from holding the phone with her shoulder, she hated hanging up with hands full of chicken fat. And if she tried to be creative and hang up with her chin, the phone inevitably landed in the chicken. Leah told her to use gloves. She had gotten the idea from her mother-in-law and now used them for everything. While Miri did see the virtue of using gloves to protect her hands from getting dirty, she did not really see how it helped with chicken and answering the phone.

"Hello?" she answered with a question. That was something her Chani hated.

"Hi, Miri? It's Fraidy Goldman. How are you?"

"Fraidy, how are you? Thanks so much for calling me back. I know I'm early, but I want to make sure I have all the houses set for the *aufruf*. The wedding's in the summer and most people will be in the mountains, so I figure it's not too early to start lining them up. Also, I need to get nice places for the Steinhardts. You know, I can't have them sleep in musty basements. I think I want to place the *kallah's* father with you. Would that be okay?"

"Sure, no problem. Listen, I can't talk now Miri, but can I stop by tomorrow for coffee?"

"Of course! I have a dentist appointment at ten, so drop in after you get your kids off to day camp..." she cut herself off in midsentence as she processed what Fraidy had asked. "For coffee?" They never did that. Coffee was for characters out of Libby Lazewnik. "Is everything okay?"

"Not really. There is something I need to talk to you about." Miri heard the nervousness in Fraidy's voice for the first time.

"What's the matter? Is it one of your children?" Fraidy had asked her for advice before; it was how she had come to know the younger woman. But they usually spoke on the phone.

"No, it's... well, I'd rather talk in person."

"Is it something I did? Do you not want to give me your guestroom?" Miri had a one track mind; she mentally kicked herself as she said that. The guestroom certainly did not warrant such an official tête-à-tête.

"Well, it's... no, nothing about the guestroom... not really, anyway… it's… I don't know, I'm really not comfortable telling you over the phone." Fraidy was clearly uneasy.

"Of course not. Come on over tomorrow after my appointment. I should be home by 11. But what did I do? You have to give me a hint! I won't be able to sleep tonight. Is it me? My husband? Did he say something in *shul*?" Miri tried to remember what Shmuely had spoken about on Shabbos, and came up blank. "Is it one of my kids? Grandchildren?"

"Well," Fraidy took a deep breath, "It's about the *kallah.*"

Chapter 33

"THE *KALLAH?*" MIRI WAS taken aback. What could be with the *kallah*? "Is everything okay with her?"

"She's... yes, it's okay... I... I don't know. Look, I really don't want to talk about this over the phone. I am sorry I said anything, but I'll come over tomorrow." Fraidy seemed to have gotten her tongue back.

Miri hung up the phone with hands full of chicken fat. At the moment she did not care that the phone was slimy and made no effort to wash off the grease. *Something was wrong with Ahuva!* Could it be that she was hurt? But wouldn't the Steinhardts tell her directly? Could she want to break the *shidduch*? But how would Fraidy know that? Fraidy had nothing to do with the Steinhardts. What could Fraidy know that the Friedmans didn't? *Anyway, you are not allowed to give information once a shidduch has gone through!* Unless... unless it was really derogatory, and it was something that needed to be conveyed. Could Ahuva be... sick? But still, how would Fraidy be privy to such information? Well, she had stayed in Fraidy's house. Maybe Fraidy saw something then?

Miri shook her head to clear it and went back to the chickens.

She laid them neatly in a pan and dressed them. She looked at the pile in the sink and despaired. Thirty pieces left, at least. Was it even worth it to continue? Would there even be an *aufruf* after her conversation with Fraidy tomorrow? Miri sighed as she put the pan of dressed chickens in the freezer and attacked the fowl in the sink with a vengeance. Nothing like doing mundane tasks to allow your mind to wander.

Miri could not decide whether or not to bring Shmuely into her confidence. She could hear him admonishing her, telling her that this is what happens when you are so keen on procuring a classy *shidduch* that you miss all the red flags. *But it's not true!* Miri silently defended herself. *It's true that I wanted a classy shidduch, but I stopped it in its tracks when I thought Ahuva wasn't frum enough. At that seminar. Of course I love the fact that she is a Steinhardt and that she is Rivky Miller's daughter. I was always impressed by Rivky in school, she had real class — even then... I* was *relieved when I learned we could start over, but that was for Moshe's sake, too. He obviously wanted it.* Miri shook her head again. *No. If we're being honest, let's be honest. You were happy that your son was happy, but you thought he was taking things a bit too far. To be so captivated after one date?*

Miri was too honest to argue with herself. She laid another chicken in the pan. *But I, and Shmuely too, have since come to love Ahuva for who she is as a person. I love her kindness, the way she helps in the kitchen when she comes for Shabbos; and her thoughtfulness, the way she helped that kallah that Moshe told us about; her practicality in making sure to bring a gift she knows I want. She's great with kids even though she's an only child. She talks to people about the things they want to talk about and never dominates a conversation. She is poised and confident.* Miri remembered her very first meeting with Ahuva and her first impressions. *She's obviously geshikt, and she has a head on her shoulders. She's sweet and warm, and Moshe is enamored.*

No, Miri concluded, *Shmuely has no right to say anything.*

As if on cue, Shmuely opened the front door. "I'm back from *Ma'ariv,*" he called. "Is Chani home yet?"

"No, she's staying at Leah's tonight," Miri called back. "Chaim's grandfather is doing better, but it doesn't look like they'll be home till really late, so she decided to sleep over." Chani, just back from seminary, was babysitting so that her sister and brother-in-law could visit his grandfather in the hospital.

Miri stood by the sink in pensive silence. *If Shmuely asks,* she decided, *I'll say something. If not, I won't.*

"Any treats?" Shmuely asked. "I saw you and Chani very busy in the kitchen today." Miri didn't answer, and Shmuely helped himself to some cookies from the freezer. "Would you like a tea?" he asked his wife. "I'm fine," she muttered. "Gotta finish here."

Miri filled the last tray with chicken, dressed it and put it in the freezer. She sat down next to her husband who, oblivious to her distress, was happily munching his goodies, and broke her vow of silence.

"Fraidy Goldman called."

"Mmmm?" Shmuely responded. "These cookies are good. Am I allowed another one?"

"Shmuely, I am trying to tell you something important, and all you think about is cake?"

"Oh, I didn't realize. Excuse me." Shmuely sat himself up in his chair and straightened his tie. He pushed his glasses up on his nose and crossed his hands over the table. He then cleared his throat and turned towards his wife, affecting a look of interest. "What did Mrs. Goldman have to say?" he asked in his best professorial tone.

"Shmuely, seriously! She's coming for coffee tomorrow and she has some news about Ahuva that she wants to share." Miri's tone was frantic, but completely lost on Shmuely, who responded, "Really, that's nice."

"What, exactly, is nice about that?" Miri wanted to know.

"Why shouldn't it be nice? Ahuva stayed in her house last time she came for Shabbos, didn't she? I am sure she wants to tell you what a wonderful daughter-in-law we're getting."

"She doesn't. She sounded really nervous on the phone, and I am sure she doesn't have good news to share. She really didn't want to tell me why she was coming at all, but I made her. And then she was like, 'Sorry for saying anything, I'll talk to you tomorrow.'"

"You *made* her tell you? Miri, we've discussed this before," Shmuely's tone was serious. "She didn't want to say anything, and you forced it out of her. Now you got *her* upset for saying something when she clearly didn't want to, and *you're* here, sitting on *shpilkes* and biting your nails, when in all probability she was going to say something really innocuous like… like, I don't know, Ahuva inadvertently broke her shower when she stayed there and it is really expensive to fix."

"Very funny," Miri said tiredly. Shmuely looked at his wife who was hanging her head. They *had* talked about this before, and Miri had made countless commitments to curb her curiosity.

"I really wouldn't worry," Shmuely continued. "There is nothing you can do right now anyway, so why work yourself into such agitation?"

"But what if something really *is* wrong?" Miri couldn't help but ask. She was a woman, after all, and there is a reason *woman* and *worry* start with the same letter.

"Then you'll find out tomorrow and you'll have plenty of time to worry then. Why lose sleep tonight?"

Miri accepted the logic in Shmuely's words, but could not sleep anyway.

*   *   *

"Whatever happened with that mother you were telling me about?" Rachel asked.

Ian laughed at the memory. "I saw her again today. You can't imagine the look on her face when she saw me. But then, I guess I didn't look so happy either."

They were sitting in a pizza shop in West Long Branch and regaling each other with summer intern work stories.

"She looks at me, and she's shooting daggers, muttering under her breath something about wanting a real doctor to look at her precious Jimmy, not a student like me. So I said, 'Let me see if I can free up Dr. Tawil. He's busy with another patient, but I'm sure he'll want to take care of you and Jimmy.' Mind you, Rachel, that Jimmy, or whatever his name is, had a cold. It did not turn into an ear infection, despite the fact that his mama brought him to the office three days in a row. I told my dad that if this is what his patients were like, I better not join his practice!"

Rachel laughed. "My friend Alison had one of those mothers. She worked in a day camp one summer, and there was one mother who wouldn't take home her kid's project if it wasn't perfect because '*my* Tyler colors inside the lines.' And the kid was three!" Rachel shook her head. "Those are the children who are going to end up in therapy, you know. The ones whose parents stifle them with their expectations."

Ian nodded. "What else is going on? Anything on the twin front? I haven't heard about that in a while."

Rachel took a sip of Diet Coke. "Nothing happening. She sent the petition so we'll find out soon enough if we're really twins or not. She's busy with her fiancé and stuff and she doesn't really seem to care to go beyond this, so I guess I'm happy."

"You guess?"

"Well, this has sort of whet my curiosity, and now I'm wondering if I want to meet the lawyer."

Ian nodded again. "No problem. If that's what you want."

"I'm not really sure what I want. I'm back and forth every day. Why can't I be like Ahuva and just be happy to have found a sister?"

"Well, she didn't go through what you went through to find your mom, did she? She just gets a picture and meets a new sister."

"This is going to sound pathetic, I know," Rachel told him, "But I am jealous of her security."

"What does that mean?" Ian wanted to know.

Rachel swirled the straw in her cup and was silent as she tried to formulate her words. Finally, she looked up and spoke earnestly "I mean, here I am going crazy about finding my birth mother and wondering who I really am, and she is this happy girl who is getting married." Rachel bit her tongue. *Rachel Bergmann, what is wrong with you?* This was not the first time she had blurted 'marriage' to Ian, but now she had really gone a bit too far. *It's one thing to let down your guard in front of a man, but to ask him to marry you?*

But, the voice of reason was back, *that's exactly what you want. If he would ask you to marry him, you would be ready to throw your birth mother — and sister — to the wind. She only surfaced in the first place because of your breakup with Brad.*

"That is ridiculous," Ian softened his tone with a smile. "How do you know how secure she really is, deep down? How do you know she isn't moving forward with that urge of hers to show this

Michelle Stern that she is a happy, secure young woman on the verge of marriage?

"Nobody looking at you thinks that you are insecure. Right? Even I don't think so," he grinned. "So maybe she really is insecure too, only good at hiding it. She's Orthodox, right? So her marriage was arranged. How secure would you feel if your parents informed you of who you were going to marry?"

"I told you," Rachel sounded exasperated, "The marriage is not arranged."

"That's what she told you," Ian retorted. "How do you know it's true?"

Rachel didn't answer. How could she know if it was true or not? Except that hearing it from Ahuva, and seeing the happiness on her face as she talked about her fiancé made her believe that it *was* true. *I'll ask Sarah,* she decided, and then said it aloud. "I'll ask Sarah Kessler. She is practically Orthodox by now. Did you know she is in Israel this summer? I think she is staying for a year. I'll ask her how they get married."

Ian smiled, happy to have successfully diverted Rachel's thoughts. "So, how'd you like to meet my parents?"

Rachel looked up, surprise and pleasure written all over her face. "I'd love to," she said simply.

"About time, huh?" Ian grinned. "Maybe you won't have to go Orthodox to get married, after all."

Chapter 34

"YOU NEVER TOLD ME about the meeting with your sister, you know, Ahuva," Michal said over the phone one night. "It was a while ago, wasn't it?"

"Yeah, it was. I haven't really had a chance to talk with you, with your brother-in-law's wedding and *sheva berachos* and stuff in Toronto. How was it by the way?"

"Very nice, but don't change the subject. We were talking about you. How was that meeting?"

"It was good. I'm happy we met," Ahuva answered. "We're twins, apparently, Rachel and I, and she's also adopted."

"Well, that makes sense I guess."

"What does?"

"That she's also adopted," Michal responded. "If you're twins then it makes sense that she's adopted. It's unlikely one twin would be given up and the other would be kept."

"I guess."

"You don't sound very pleased," Michal noted.

"It's not a thing you're pleased about, or not." Ahuva's voice was curt.

"What's the matter?"

"Nothing," Ahuva answered. "It's just — Rachel was busy looking for her mother the whole year. She has her mother's name and found out about her and everything. She gave me the info."

"Okay."

"So I also sent back a petition. I want to confirm everything. That we really are sisters and whatever."

"Sounds good to me," Michal said. "What's the matter?"

"Nothing. Just it will take 6-8 weeks to process and I'll be married by then."

"Hmm." Michal was not really sure where this was going.

"Exactly. And I'm not going to be focusing on this when I am married for two weeks. I'll have more important things to worry about, I hope."

"Right," Michal said laughing. "Like what five-course meal to prepare for supper. Don't bother with those, Ahuva. Just make chicken and rice."

"Who cares what I make for supper?" Ahuva retorted. "That's not the point! The point is that it will be too late by then."

"What will be too late? I'm missing something here, I think."

"It's pathetic, really. But I just got this bug into my head that I wanted her to see me get married. I don't know why I care. I never even *thought* about her before. And now I won't know who she is until it's too late."

"I thought you said Rachel told you who she is?" Michal asked.

"She did, but I want to confirm. She could be wrong."

"Don't be ridiculous. You guys are completely identical; you were both born in Chicago and share a birthday. What are the odds you don't share a mother?"

"Well, if you're going to be like that, what are the odds that you find an identical twin you knew nothing about?"

"Ahuva, come on! Don't be like that. Fine, it's not something that happens every day, but it's not impossible." Michal laughed suddenly. "Chalk it up to *kallah* nerves. I thought you promised you wouldn't be like that."

"This has nothing to do with being a *kallah*, Michal! I do *not* have *kallah* nerves. I am so normal."

"Well, a normal *kallah* has *kallah* nerves," Michal responded. "Besides, you're as bad as they come! Where were you at Yehuda's bar mitzvah?"

"I was there!" Ahuva protested.

"Really? I didn't see you. Come to think of it, no one saw you — except Moshe, I guess. And what about the time we went shopping together for Sarala? I seem to recall having a hard time pulling you away from housewares and into the baby clothes section where I needed your advice. You were coming to help *me*, if I remember correctly."

Ahuva laughed. "Don't be mean, Michal. Or I'll tell you about a certain *kallah* I knew who spent an *hour* sweeping the floor after a *seudah* on Shabbos."

"No you won't," Michal answered. "That was the discussion at the bar mitzvah, by the way. We were deciding who was worse, you, me or Shevy."

"I hope you said Shevy. She was the absolute worst. She could hardly remember her name!" Ahuva giggled. "Remember that? We went to camp that Shabbos to visit you and someone asked her who she was, and she said 'Avraham Gelbstein' because she thought they asked who she was engaged to!"

Michal laughed, "I totally forgot about that! I must remind her. Yup, she was bad."

"And you couldn't go fifteen minutes without mentioning Yaakov, Michal. I am the best," Ahuva concluded.

"If you say so," Michal conceded. "I can't wait till you finally get here. We'll have so much fun in Lakewood."

"You better be nice to me, Michal. I know what it's going to be like. You and Shevy are never going to come shopping with me because it's going to be too hard to get out with your kids and Shevy is as bad a mother as she was a *kallah,* and her life revolves around Dovy. 'Oh, I'm sorry, Ahuva, Dovy sneezed. I'm just running him to the doctor to make sure he doesn't have an ear infection, but either way, I don't think he should go out now.'"

"Ahuva, stop!" Michal gasped. "My sides are killing me, and I am in the middle of drinking!"

"Anyway, I need to go, I'm getting a click..." Ahuva ended on a singsong, and laughing, Michal said goodbye.

*   *   *

Miri woke in the morning with a pit in her stomach, but she could not remember why it was there. Was it the dentist? Did her cakes for the *aufruf* flop yesterday? Did it have to do with Leah and Chaim's grandfather?

Suddenly, it hit her like a ton of bricks. *Fraidy Goldman!* Miri thought she would rather stay in bed than face the day that loomed ominously before her. *What would Fraidy Goldman say? What was wrong with Ahuva?*

Miri brushed her teeth slowly, tooth by tooth, in preparation for her appointment. She wished she could fast forward the day, at least until after her meeting with Fraidy. Then what? Miri was having a hard time planning her day.

Don't think, she commanded herself. And then she answered, *Oh, you sound just like Shmuely!*

Somehow she made it to the dentist and back. She sent Chani to do some grocery shopping and cleaned the house in anticipation of Fraidy's visit. *Whatever she will say, it won't be that my house was dirty.*

Finally, the dreaded hour arrived, and with it Fraidy's knock on the door. Miri opened the door wide and planted a smile on her face, "Come in, make yourself at home," she invited.

Chapter 35

FRAIDY CAME IN AND sat down in the living room. Miri went to the kitchen to bring some coffee. This was a coffee meeting, wasn't it? Either way, the coffee would help her get through whatever was going to take place.

Miri walked into the living room bearing two mugs. She handed one to Fraidy and sat down opposite her. "What's going on?" Miri tried to take the businesslike tone out of her voice, but her nerves were making it quite impossible. She had no interest in small talk. *What did Fraidy know about Ahuva?*

Fraidy seems pretty nervous herself, Miri noted. She shifted in her seat and made a *berachah* on the steaming drink. "It's like this," Fraidy began. "I really liked the *kallah* when she stayed with me the Shabbos that she was here. She made a really good impression on me, and… I…" The words seemed to be stuck in Fraidy's throat, and she breathed in the steam of the hot liquid, as though to steady her nerves.

Say it. Say it, Miri demanded silently. The suspense was almost too much to bear.

"Well, I really wouldn't say anything, you know. I liked the *kallah* a lot. She seems like a really nice girl… but something happened, and we discussed it — my husband and I — with the Rav..." Fraidy broke off again.

If it's that shower curtain, I'll scream, Miri thought. What else could she have done that only Fraidy knew about and that required speaking to a Rav? She nodded, willing Fraidy to continue already.

"Well," Fraidy tried a different tactic. "You know I do Pathways, right? So they send out this newsletter, you probably got it also, but I don't know if you looked so closely. It was actually my Tzippy who pointed it out to me." Fraidy stopped again, and looked at Miri pleadingly, her dismay at being the one who was required to tell *lashon ha'ra l'toeles* written all over her face.

Realization, coupled with relief, began to dawn on Miri, but she said nothing, wanting to hear Fraidy out.

Fraidy took a gulp of coffee and put her mug down on the end table beside the couch. She reached into her purse and pulled out the Journeys/Pathways promotional magazine. Miri recognized it; she had thrown it out last week when it arrived in the mail, without looking at it.

Fraidy turned the pages until she found what she was looking for. The article was about the various seminars that Journeys sponsors, and there were pictures taken of previous weekends. There, displayed prominently in the middle of the page was a picture of four girls around a piano. The girl sitting on the bench was undoubtedly the *kallah*. Or her twin.

I'm surprised they would have used this picture, Miri thought. *Rabbi Lazarus knows what happened the last time this picture was used.* She looked up and laughed.

Fraidy turned to Miri, obviously surprised. "I guess you know?" she sounded uncertain.

"Fraidy, if you knew how nervous I was since you called!" Miri sputtered between her laughter. "I had no idea what to think!"

Fraidy didn't react, and Miri calmed down and explained. "We were at the seminar with this girl. My husband spoke. We had already met Ahuva, and I have to tell you, I was as horrified as you were. I also thought she was Ahuva. But she's not."

Fraidy looked thoroughly baffled, and Miri continued. "You might not know this, but Ahuva is adopted. So is this girl. I think her name is Rebecca, or something like that."

"Oh." Fraidy was stunned.

"Yes, as a matter of fact, if not for this girl, Moshe and Ahuva would probably have been married already!" Miri told the whole story to her younger friend, and they both had a good laugh. "I'm sure you realize this is confidential," Miri said as she finished her narration.

"I'm so happy!" Fraidy said. "I really, really like Ahuva. Did I tell you that she brought a game for my kids, and even played it with them? Besides giving me that beautiful candy dish? The kids love her and Tzippy looks up to her like I don't know what! Did I tell you she gave Tzippy a personal invitation to the wedding? She was on cloud nine for days afterward!"

Miri glowed. If Fraidy had said all those wonderful things about *her*, Miri could not have been happier.

After she escorted Fraidy to the door, Miri ran to find the phone. This could not wait until Shmuely came home. He'd say "I told you so," sure, but it was worth it. Life was perfect.

*   *   *

Ahuva dropped the invitation in the mailbox and instantly felt lighter. It might not accomplish a thing; it might go to the wrong address. For all she knew, she might even have sent it to the wrong person, but she had thought long and hard about it and came to the conclusion that unless she did this — sent the invitation — she would never be at ease.

There was no return card in the envelope, and that too was the result of many hours of thought. But Ahuva didn't want a response. It didn't matter to her whether or not the recipient of her invitation would actually be at her wedding. All Ahuva wanted was that she know this wedding was taking place. That she know that her daughter, Ahuva, was living a wonderful, *normal* life even though she had been given away at birth. The envelope had no return addresses either; Ahuva had eschewed the envelope that came with the invitation for a plain white one whose only distinction was that it was the correct size. She did not want to be easily traced. If the recipient wanted to find her, she'd have to do some investigating.

Ahuva turned from the mailbox and breathed more easily. *Whatever happens happens. I've done what I needed to do. Now let me focus on something happier.*

*　　*　　*

"Beth, did I tell you that I'm going to meet Ian's parents?" Rachel demanded.

"Uh, only about six or seven times. In the last minute. And ten or eleven last night. You're starting to sound like a broken record, Rach. I think I am going to put a new one in."

"Okay, I'll calm down. It's just that I'm so…"

"Excited. I know. You've been bitten by this marriage bug ever since your meeting with Ahuva. It doesn't have to mean anything, you know. I met Daren's parents a while ago, and do you see me sporting a ring?" Beth sounded bitter.

But she doesn't know what else he said to me, Rachel thought. "*Maybe you won't have to go Orthodox to get married, after all?*" Rachel had memorized this sentence and replayed every nuance in her mind. But she kept quiet. *"Not everything has to be shared."* Her mother had taught her that when she was ten years old, and the lesson came unbidden to her mind. But Rachel didn't need the reminder; she heard the cynical note in Beth's voice, and did not want her best friend to resent her happiness. Besides, what Beth said was true.

"Did I tell you I got her invitation today?" Rachel tried to move the conversation to more neutral territory.

"Really, when is it? You are going, right? Are you bringing Ian?"

"I don't know. He wasn't invited, and I am not sure what the proper protocol is. He can't crash, but on the other hand, I won't know a soul and it's not like the bride herself is going to run around introducing me to people."

"So ask her if you can invite him."

"I guess," Rachel was not sure.

The conversation turned to wedding dresses and Orthodox customs, and goodwill was restored between the friends.

Chapter 36

"ANY REPLIES TODAY?" DOVID asked after the family settled around the supper table. It had become the refrain in the past few weeks as preparations for Ahuva's wedding went into full swing.

"Not so many today. Who did we get, Ahuva? Bubby and Michal and the Brachmans. I think that's it, no?" Rivky answered.

"And Rachel."

"Oh right."

"Rachel who?" Dovid asked, confused. "Oh, you mean your... Bergmann?" Dovid could not bring himself to refer to Rachel as his daughter's twin. He was happy for Ahuva that she had found Rachel, but preferred to leave the latter outside of his family unit. Rachel was a Bergmann, not his daughter's twin.

"Yep," Ahuva answered. "I guess I'll need to call her and tell her what to wear. The last thing I need is for her to show up in some sleeveless dress. And she looks exactly like me!" Ahuva shuddered, remembering.

"I don't think anyone will confuse you this time. You will be the *kallah*, you know. All decked in white," Rivky smiled at the thought. "But it is a good idea."

"Maybe tell her what time to come," Dovid suggested. "Outside our circles, people usually come on time. You don't want her there for the *kabbalas panim,* sitting around with nothing to do."

"Yeah."

"And maybe tell her to bring a friend. Then she'll have someone to sit with and to talk to. It'll make her more comfortable."

"Good idea," Rivky approved. "I still have not forgotten Kramer's wedding in Chicago…"

"Right, you went right after you got married and you didn't know a soul," Ahuva finished her mother's thought. She had heard the story at least a thousand times in her twenty-two years. "That's what made me think of it."

Rivky smiled and continued the story where Ahuva left off. "I was so bored. If not for that lady whose husband was a friend of the *shver,* I would have cried of boredom." She turned to her husband, "You didn't even look for me!" The wedding had taken place about six weeks after the Steinhardts' own — almost forty years before — and Rivky repeated the same complaint each time she retold the tale.

"As I am sure you know, I was *davening,*" Dovid defended himself for the umpteenth time. He turned to Ahuva, "Remind me to tell the story to Moshe. I'd rather he hear it from *me*. And I'll need to warn him not to *daven* at *chasunahs,*" Dovid said dryly.

"*Chas v'shalom!*" Rivky exclaimed. "Only, if he drags his wife to Chicago for a wedding six weeks after his own, he should look out for her and make sure she feels taken care of!"

"Ahem," Dovid made a show of choking on his chicken. "If I recall correctly, it was you who pushed us to go."

"Because they paid for our train tickets! Obviously they wanted you! I was so excited to be the wife of someone who was needed at a wedding."

"And it was your first train ride. Don't forget that. Besides, I thought we got over this a while ago. I must have apologized about a million times." He turned to Ahuva with a grin. "Tip for marriage: Don't do this to Moshe."

Rivky opened her mouth to protest, but Dovid cut her off. "So," he said, changing the subject, "Are you going to Lakewood tomorrow to set up the apartment?"

"We were planning to," Rivky answered. "But if the furniture is coming this week, we'll wait until it comes."

As soon she had gotten engaged, Ahuva had pored over Steinhardt Design furniture catalogs with her father and had ordered what she needed to set up her new home. She was somewhat limited by the size of her apartment, but still the furniture she had chosen reflected her upbringing and the fact that she was the owner's daughter.

"I think it's coming next week, so I guess you won't be going tomorrow."

"I'd rather not postpone," Ahuva said quickly. "If the furniture won't be there tomorrow we can still do kitchen things. Anyway, I need to meet with the principal of Bnos Leah tomorrow. She wants to see my lesson plans to make sure they fit in with how the school does things. Once I'm married I won't be available to meet with her until just before school starts.

"Oh, I forgot about that. I was planning on stopping in to see Dina while you meet with the principal," Rivky said referring to her sister. "So we'll leave it as is."

Dovid motioned to Ahuva, who got up and began to clear the supper dishes.

"Thank you," Rivky said. "I guess I'll have to get used to doing everything myself once you're married!"

Chapter 37

"HELLO."

"Hi, Rachel?"

"Yeah. Is this Ahuva?"

"Yeah. How are you?" Without waiting for an answer, Ahuva continued, "I just wanted to tell you, I got your return card yesterday. I am so happy you will be coming. There are a couple of things that you should know..."

"Yeah, I know, I'll wear black," Rachel interrupted.

"Black?" Ahuva repeated, puzzled.

"Aren't you supposed to wear black?" Rachel asked.

"Supposed to wear black? What are you talking about?"

"The Orthodox wear black. Everyone knows that."

Ahuva laughed. "No, you can wear whatever color you want. There is no mitzvah to wear black. People wear it because it is slenderizing. And it matches everything. But there *is* a dress code. Try to wear a long skirt and long sleeves, and a high-ish neckline, if you can. That's all."

"Okay." So that was the reason for the choked-up neckline. It was part of a dress code. *But Ahuva had looked pretty good in hers,* Rachel thought, *so claustrophobia aside, I guess I won't look so bad.*

"Also," Ahuva continued, "You should probably bring a friend with you. You won't know anyone there and this way you'll have someone to talk with. Let me know who will be coming and I'll make sure to sit you together."

"Great. Thanks for the invite. I'll bring my boyfriend, Ian." Rachel answered quickly, and it sounded like she had been waiting for the extra invitation.

"Uh, your boyfriend?" *This is not happening.*

"Is there a problem with that?" Rachel was genuinely puzzled. "Is there a dress code for men as well?"

"Um, no. I mean… Well, I think it would be a good idea to bring a girl along. We sit separately at weddings and stuff, and you wouldn't really be with him, so…" she trailed off.

"Oh." Rachel was taken aback. "You sit separately? What does that mean?"

Ahuva gave Rachel a quick rundown of what she could expect at the wedding, and Rachel took it in, suspending judgment.

"I've only been to two weddings in my life — two cousins, and it was very different. This will certainly be an experience!" Rachel tried to look at the bright side. "Well, thanks for letting me know. I'll text you once I know who is coming with me."

*   *   *

"Steven, grab the mail, will you? I'll look at it on the plane," Michelle asked her husband as she finished zipping up her suitcase.

"I thought you had the Post Office hold it?" he responded.

"Starting tomorrow. We're still home today, and I need something to do on the plane."

"You're funny, Michelle. Aren't you going to be working on Lewis?"

"Steven, it's a six-hour flight. Just get the mail, please," she sounded exasperated.

He did, and then they both promptly forgot about it until about an hour into the flight. Michelle turned to Steven, "Where's the mail?"

Steven reached into his briefcase and pulled out the stack for his wife. She went through it absently; really, what kind of mail was she expecting? Michelle separated the credit card offers, bills and magazines. She was glad about the latter. They would help her pass the time.

"Oh, here's something else," Steven said, handing his wife a large envelope. "It must be junkmail, though, since there is no return address."

"Let me see. Thanks." Michelle took the envelope and turned it over in her hand. It did look like junk, but the envelope was hand addressed. Curious, she opened it and pulled out the invitation inside. "Huh?" she muttered. She recognized the letters as Hebrew even though she was unable to decipher them.

"What is it?" Steven asked.

"I'm not sure. It's in Hebrew."

"Open it, silly."

"Oh, I didn't see that it opens." The card opened right to left, and she needed to turn it around. The first thing she saw when it was open was a note written on the blank side of the card.

I'd love you to see me walk down the aisle
— Ahuva

Michelle felt chills running down her spine. She looked at the opposite page and saw that she was holding an invitation to the wedding of Ahuva Steinhardt and Moshe Friedman.

"This must be for you," she told her husband. "I don't know who they are.

Steven took the invitation from her and read through it. "Not me. Never heard of these people." He handed the invitation back to his wife.

"So it must be the wrong address." She picked up the envelope on her lap and looked at it. It was addressed to Dr. and Mrs. Steven Brown. That was Steven and her. Who could have sent it?

Steven looked at the inscription again. *I'd love you to see me walk down the aisle.* "Shelly, I wonder if it's…" he stopped at the look on his wife's face.

"Don't be ridiculous," Michelle snapped. "Just because I'm obsessed does not mean that my daughter would send me an invitation to her wedding." Michelle's denial was swift and forceful.

"We'll see," Steven murmured. Michelle did have a point, but something about the wording of the message made Steven think that the "obsession" went both ways.

They were about two hours into the flight when Michelle brought it up again. "Besides," she said to her husband without preamble, "She'd only be twenty-two years old. Have you ever heard of a girl getting married at that age?"

"Only one way to find out," Steven answered, smiling. "We'll go to this wedding."

Michelle suddenly felt constricted. "No we won't. No, we *won't*. I never heard of these people, and I never heard of Monsey, New York. We'll get lost going there. I'm sure it's hours from Boston and I don't think I'll be up to traveling."

"We'll see," Steven promised. "But I'm not ruling it out. We might just end up there."

"No, we won't. We *won't*."

*   *   *

"But, Shmuely," Miri said, "now what? How many people have seen that picture and know Ahuva, and know she is marrying Moshe? I am sure they all came to the same conclusion as the Goldmans, but they are too nice to say anything."

After Miri's initial excitement over Fraidy's mistake, and her phone call to her husband, she thought the matter over and came to the conclusion that her relief had been premature.

"Don't say that," Shmuely replied. "The Goldmans were very nice to come over. They wanted to make sure we went into this with our eyes open, that we were not blinded by the name Steinhardt and that if there is a problem we should know about it before it is too late. I think that was very nice and took a lot of courage."

"You know what I mean," Miri dismissed Shmuely's words with a wave of her hand. "What are we supposed to do? We can't exactly walk around with a sign that says 'It is not Ahuva,' can we?"

Shmuely did not respond. For once, his wife had a point. He thought for a minute and said, "We'll just have to trust that people are *dan l'kaf zechus* and not worry so much about what 'everyone' will say or think. There is not much else we can do. We know that we are doing the right thing, and that's what really matters."

Miri had to be satisfied with that. After all, she could not really walk around with a sign, could she? And did she really want to?

Shmuely was not finished. "It's the same with Avigail, Miri," he started to say, and Miri cut him off.

"I know what you are going to say," she informed him impatiently. "We've gone through it before, and I know, Moshe is getting married despite Baruch, and so, *im yirtzeh Hashem,* will Chani."

"No, Miri, that's not what I was going to say. I was going to say that we should learn from our daughter. She made a hard decision, but she made the right one, despite what others would say about her husband joining the workforce." *Despite what her own mother had to say about her husband joining the workforce,* were the words Shmuely wanted to say but couldn't. He willed Miri to understand what he meant.

Miri nodded her head slowly and wouldn't meet her husband's eyes. She couldn't deny that Avigail was much calmer than she used to be and that her house was more relaxed. Neither could she pretend that Baruch had any part, good or bad, in the outcome of Moshe's *shidduch.* But she didn't want to believe that Avigail's story and Ahuva's story had any similarities. On the one hand, there was a young woman who looked exactly like the Friedman's new daughter-in-law, and whose picture was probably in every *frum* home. *Everyone* got those Journeys brochures! And the Friedmans were forced to smile and take it in stride, saying nothing. The information was not theirs to share; it was a Steinhardt concern.

On the other hand there was Avigail and her decision to have her husband leave *kollel.* Whether or not it was a really hard decision for her daughter to make, or it had been resolved with ease, Miri couldn't say for sure. When she had spoken about it with Avigail, her daughter had clearly been on the defensive, justifying all the reasons why it made sense and was the right thing for their family. And Avigail was living happily and relieved with her decision.

No, there might be similarities in the two cases, but they were really quite different from each other, Miri concluded. She patted herself on the back and gave herself points for being mature about the situation. *We are doing the right thing. We can't worry about everyone else.* Miri felt a certain sort of smug satisfaction in that. She walked around with a gleam in her eye.

*   *   *

The trip to Boston was successful in the sense that Dr. Lieberman accepted them for treatment. But Michelle and Steven spent the first week arguing almost nonstop.

As soon as they were settled into the hotel, Steven whipped out his laptop and looked up the name Dovid Steinhardt.

Did you mean David Steinhardt? Google asked him. There was a link to a furniture design company called Steinhardt Design. A look at the blurb told him that Mr. Steinhardt had one daughter, who, Steven knew, was Ahuva.

Steven went back to the Google search page and found a couple of blogs with Dovid Steinhardt's name.

Almost everyone had nice things to say about him. He was the owner of a successful company and seemed to use his money wisely — at least in the eyes of the bloggers. In many of the posts, Dovid was described as a *ba'al chesed* or a *ba'al tzedakah*. Steven had no idea what those words meant, but the Hebrew fit in with the invitation.

So this girl's father was a successful businessman and, from all accounts, a fine, upstanding citizen. But why was it important to Ahuva Steinhardt that Michelle and he watch her walk down the aisle?

He had his suspicions, but still he could not be sure.

Eventually he came to a post that read:

> Don't know why you all are blinded by this man Dovid Steinhardt.
> I never came across a bigger scoundrel.

The poster continued to complain that Dovid had cheated the writer when furniture was delivered that did not live up to Steinhardt Design's name, and the company refused to allow the writer to return it. *Finally, he sounds human!* Steven laughed to himself.

Many posts followed this, replete with words like *lashon ha'ra, motzi shem ra, Chafetz Chaim* and others that Steven could not read, much less understand.

And finally, he found what he was looking for: Isn't his daughter adopted?

The answer: Yes, and what does that have to do with the price of tea in China?

Steven stopped reading. He had what he needed.

Chapter 38

"WE ARE *NOT* GOING!" was Michelle's refrain. Steven had looked up the location of the wedding and found it was only a four-hour trip from where they were in Boston. The wedding would be held two days before they were due to fly back to Los Angeles and Steven felt that whatever the outcome of treatment with Dr. Lieberman over the next few months, going to the wedding would be a balm for Michelle. He thought it would bring that painful chapter of her life to an end and allow her to move forward in whatever direction their life together took them.

"I don't deserve to be there," Michelle told her husband.

"Why ever not?"

"Did I ever even think of the children I gave away? I can't even be sure they are girls."

"I thought you told me you heard the nurse say they were girls when they were born."

"Yes, but maybe I heard wrong. Maybe I don't remember. It wasn't exactly my happiest moment. I was quite distraught and I could have distorted the information," Michelle found comfort in her logic. She was acting immaturely and she knew it. What she was saying went against all her lawyerly instincts, but these were emotions. You can't fight emotions, logic or not.

Steven was exasperated and said no more on the subject until later that night.

"I have never expressed any interest in those children," Michelle told her husband when he brought up the subject again. "I wouldn't have even thought about them in the last few years, if…" she stopped, too choked up to continue. Michelle swallowed and started over. "I would have been happy to continue with my life with my own young children, and I wouldn't have wanted to be reminded of them. I am *not* going to this girl's wedding.

"What right do I have to march into someone's life and take my place as mother when I have completely ignored them for two decades? You keep saying that if this doesn't work we'll adopt. Would *you* want your child's life upset like that?"

"She *invited* you, for Heaven's sake!" Steven practically yelled. "She *wants* you there!"

"She didn't invite me to her wedding," Michelle answered peevishly.

"Now what is that supposed to mean?" Steven demanded.

"Did you see any response card? Was there a number to RSVP? There wasn't even an address to write back! Where's the invitation in that?"

"Well," Steven countered, "Did you see any mention of a reception afterward? Any dinner being served, or cocktails and dessert? There was no reason to RSVP."

"Exactly. She doesn't want me celebrating with her on the most important day of her life."

"The invitation was in Hebrew," Steven said. "They obviously do things differently than we do. Maybe their weddings are a solemn affair and all there is to it is the actual marriage ceremony?"

"Maybe. Too bad we won't find out."

*   *   *

"Whoa, Beth, total rehaul," Rachel said to her friend who had come to spend the weekend at the Bergmann summer home.

"What?" Beth asked, curious.

"First of all, black is *slenderizing*," she said, overemphasis on the last word. "But the sleeves and pants thing is real. They don't wear them."

"Oh, you're talking about the wedding again? Seriously, Rach, if that's all you're going to talk about, I'm outta here."

"Want to come? She invited you."

"Huh, you're not bringing Ian?"

"Nope. Ahuva said that I wouldn't see him at all during the wedding. She said men and women sit separately and dance separately and I don't know what else. She told me to bring a girl-friend."

"Whoa. Yeah, I'm coming! This I got to see for myself!"

*   *   *

"I have nothing to wear. Neither do you." Michelle insisted on being difficult. As Steven brought up the matter yet again, she understood she would end up going to Ahuva Steinhardt's wedding, and as much as the prospect frightened her, it also excited her. But she would put up a good fight.

"When did that ever stop you, Shelly?" Steven's voice was softer and his tone comforting. If Michelle was talking about clothes, he reasoned, she was reconciled to going. In that case, he wanted to make the path as smooth as possible for her. "We'll go tonight and get you a nice dress and I'll add another suit to my wardrobe though goodness knows I don't need a new one any more than you do."

Chapter 39

THE WEDDING WAS BEAUTIFUL. Ahuva looked radiant in her stark white gown, and if Miri was disappointed that the *kallah* had chosen iced mocha as the color scheme she didn't complain. In her wildest dreams Miri could not have imagined she would be the mother-of-the-groom at a wedding such as this one. The entire world was there, it seemed. Dovid and Rivky Steinhardt both came from large families and their friends seemed to number in the thousands.

Could it really be that she, Miri Friedman, was the *machateniste* accepting *mazal tovs* in front of an eleven-piece band? Were those flowers real? As she walked back into the ladies' side after breaking the plate, Miri pinched herself. *This had better not be a dream!*

*   *   *

Rachel and Beth stood on one side of the room, fascinated by the scene. So many people! And all, it seemed, in black. "What's with all this black?" Rachel whispered to Beth. "Ahuva told me we could wear color… but it looks like we're the only ones not in black! Hasn't anyone here heard of summer before?"

"Come on," Beth responded with a grin, "Haven't you heard? 'Black is 'slenderizing.'"

They followed the crowd of women and girls heading towards the bride, who appeared to be seated on a throne. Rachel's first thought when she saw Ahuva was that she would wear her hair like that at her own wedding. If it looked that good on Ahuva it would look good on her too, right? And the bride was wearing white. At least there was something normal at this Orthodox wedding.

They reached the bridal chair, and the bride jumped up and enveloped her sister in a hug. "I'm *so* glad you're here," Ahuva cried. "Oh, I'm so happy!"

Rachel smiled, "Didn't I tell you we'd come?" she asked.

"Yes, but I don't know, you could have decided not to. Oh, I'm so happy! It really means a lot to me." She turned to Rachel's companion, "You must be Beth," Beth smiled and murmured her congratulations.

"We're not really sure what the proper protocol is, and what we're supposed to say now," Rachel said. "But you look beautiful, Ahuva. We wish you lots of joy and happiness." Beth nodded in agreement.

Ahuva laughed. "The rules aren't so rigid. You said just the right things. I hope you enjoy yourselves. I'm *really* glad you came," Ahuva said again. There were others waiting to offer their congratulations, so they moved back to stand again at the side of the room.

Ahuva watched them go, and it was a minute before she gathered herself sufficiently to greet the next woman in line. She really was happy, she reflected. Rachel was her only blood relative at this most important time of her life. Unless… unless Michelle Brown would come. Ahuva had received the answer to her petition just a week before, and she was happy she had sent the invitation earlier.

Would Michelle (there was no way Ahuva could think of her as anything else) come? Ahuva wasn't really sure she wanted her to. Yesterday she had prayed that her birth mother would come and introduce herself. But now, wearing white, in the midst of the crowds, the music, the smorgasbord at her wedding — at *her own wedding* — she wasn't so sure Michelle Brown was welcome. *Well, she can come,* Ahuva thought, *and she can watch me walk down the aisle, but introduce herself?* — there was no time to think things through. Ahuva greeted a group of giggling students. She sent a special smile to Mindy Glassman and Faigy Baum and caught her mother's eye as the latter came back into the room after "breaking the plate."

Rivky watched with a tender smile as her daughter greeted her guests. Her manner was gracious and warm; Ahuva had that special gift that made each guest feel welcome and wanted. Rivky seated herself next to Ahuva, who pulled her close and motioned towards a tall girl standing with a friend at the side of the room. Both were dressed modestly, but somehow it was clear that they were not really sure of how things were done.

"That's her," Ahuva whispered. Rivky looked again. "She really does look like you! Seeing her in person makes me understand why your mother-in-law did what she did all those months ago." She squeezed Ahuva's hand, and as if on cue, the band began playing the music that would call Moshe to claim Ahuva as his rightful bride.

*   *   *

They had arrived quite some time ago; it seemed that the ceremony was running late. Steven was uneasy, worried that Michelle might take it in her mind to turn and run. They took up a spot in the back of the hall near the band. Michelle was wearing a conservative black summer suit, but noticed right away that the other guests in the hall seemed to be dressed for winter.

They heard lively music coming from somewhere in the hall,

and Michelle turned to her husband, "So this is *not* a solemn affair, after all. And all we were invited to was to see her walk down the aisle, not to partake in the festivities."

"What do you want, Shelly?" Steven asked, exasperated and seeming to forget that he was on a mission of comfort tonight. "An emotional reunion in the middle of a wedding?"

"Steven," she whispered, as the guests surged into the hall. "The men and women are sitting separately. Should we move?"

"Do you want to?"

"No!" the answer came swiftly. "Stay here!"

They waited for what seemed an eternity. "Look," Steven pointed to a young girl dressed in gold.

"The bride?" Michelle asked in confusion. The girl could have been Michelle twenty years ago. "Why isn't she in white?" She watched as the girl found a seat in the audience. "That isn't the bride," she told her husband scornfully. "She's sitting down."

"Who else do you think it could be?" Steven responded meaningfully.

Michelle held her breath and didn't answer. Could it be? She had not dared hope her daughters would know each other. *Dared hope?* she asked herself with contempt. *You haven't so much as thought about your children to wonder what became of them, let alone to hope.*

The music started and the groom walked down the aisle flanked by his parents. Michelle kept her eye on the girl in gold and watched her tap someone on the shoulder. She felt a sudden burning desire to hear her daughter's voice, to know what she was saying, and she slipped from her husband's side and walked up the side of the aisle.

Rachel tapped a girl in front of her and asked her to explain what was happening. Ahuva had given her a crash course to prepare her, but she wanted a hands-on explanation. The girl turned around to answer, but when she looked at Rachel her mouth fell open in shock. "What's the matter?" Rachel asked. "Nothing," was the stammered reply, "But you look exactly like Ahuva."

Rachel smiled but said nothing. "Can you explain to me what's going on here? I'm not really familiar with Orthodox weddings."

"Sure," the girl moved closer to Rachel and Beth. Michelle moved closer as well, making sure to keep herself hidden. She did *not* want to meet this daughter of hers. Ahuva had made contact with her; who knows if her twin even knew of her existence?

So they didn't grow up together, Michelle thought. *I wonder how they met.* She didn't know the identity of the girl her daughter was questioning, but from the girl's reaction it was obvious they had never seen each other before. *What difference does it make,* she thought, irritated at herself. Why was she taking all this so seriously?

After the groom reached the canopy someone sang a short song. The girl explained to Rachel and Beth that the song was a special welcome for the groom, and there would be the same for the bride. "Why did everyone stand?" Beth asked. "You are supposed to stand for someone who is on the way to fulfill a *mitzvah,*" the girl explained. "Getting married is a mitzvah." Rachel felt her heart quicken. *I want people to stand at my wedding, too,* she thought.

The music started again, another slow, moving tune, and Michelle felt tears come to her eyes. She turned to see the bride, Ahuva, walk down the aisle with her parents. Michelle leaned forward for a closer glimpse, and saw the bride's twin do the same.

Rachel, as befit Marc Bergmann's daughter, was usually cynical about all things Orthodox. There was no place for spirituality in her concept of Judaism. Yet that was the only way she could describe her feelings while watching this ceremony. Everything seemed… beautiful wasn't quite the word, but it captured her emotions. There was quiet in the room as the bride circled the groom. Then, the officiating rabbi recited two blessings while holding a cup of wine.

She was standing too far away to clearly see what was going on under the canopy, but Ahuva's friend filled her in. "He's giving her the ring now."

"What's he saying?" Beth asked. "Is that the equivalent of 'I do'?"

The friend laughed. "I guess you could say that. The words translate as, 'With this ring you are sanctified to me,' which basically means they are married."

Different men, all very distinguished looking, were called upon to bless the bride and groom under the canopy. They each held a cup of wine as they recited the blessings. Rachel was too caught up in the radiance of the scene to register the fact that no woman had been called up to give a blessing. She would normally have had much to say about the obvious male chauvinism. Instead, she turned to her informant and asked, "When does she give him his ring?"

"What?" came the startled reply. And then, "Oh, she doesn't. Orthodox men don't wear rings."

Michelle moved back down the aisle to her husband's side. As she watched the rest of ceremony, she could not contain the flow of tears. The atmosphere felt holy and Michelle found herself praying as she had never done in the past. *Please G-d, help me.*

She watched as the groom stepped on something, very forcefully — and suddenly the solemn atmosphere turned festive. The band began to play a lively, happy tune and a crowd of men surged up to the canopy and began to dance. Had she still been standing near her daughter she would have heard her ask Ahuva's friend what was going on.

*   *   *

"The glass is broken to commemorate the destruction of the Temple. Our joy can't be complete until it is rebuilt."

"And what happened to, 'You may now kiss the bride?'" Beth asked.

"Oh, we don't show that kind of affection in public," came the answer. It was swift and satisfied.

"Even at a wedding?"

"Even at a wedding."

"So what happens now?" Rachel did not want to dwell on what was missing — nothing seemed to be missing; the service had been complete in its own way, and anything extra would have cheapened it, she thought. *I want this at my wedding,* the force of her conviction surprising her, and she thought of what her parents would say, and of Ian's feelings. *But I do. I really do. This is the real thing.* She wasn't sure how she knew it was true, but she did know it.

"Now the bride and groom go into *yichud,* a private room. This is the first time they will be alone together."

"Wow," Beth breathed. "Very different, but I kind of like it."

*   *   *

"Let's go," Michelle whispered vehemently. "Let's go!"

Steven seemed mesmerized by the proceedings and did not hear his wife until she had repeated her request two more times. "Why?" he asked. "Don't you want to stay and see what will happen? And what about our gift?" He didn't want to go, and it no longer had anything to do with Michelle or her daughters. He wanted to see what this Orthodox wedding was all about. The ceremony had been moving, and he wanted to stay for the rest. That there were festivities was obvious and, invited or not, Steven wanted to see this through.

"We weren't invited," Michelle seemed to read his thoughts. "We watched her walk down the aisle and that is what she wanted."

"Shelly," he begged, "We're here. Let's at least…"

"No!" Michelle's voice was louder than she had intended, and she was thankful that they were standing close to the band and that the music was even louder than her voice. "You forced me to come and see this and I did. Steven," she implored, "this was hard enough, don't make it worse. We have to drive back to Boston tonight to see Dr. Lieberman tomorrow, and I don't want to get to the hotel too late. Besides," she added, throwing Steven's words back at him, "What do you want, an emotional reunion at her wedding?" *Don't listen to me,* she pleaded silently. *Make us stay!* She had a sudden desire to stay amidst the celebratory crowd and watch her daughters — both of them — rejoice in Ahuva's marriage. She wanted to prove to herself that giving them up had been the right decision, that by giving them up she had afforded them a chance of happiness in a way they could not have had had she raised them as a young single mother without prospects.

"You're right," Steven conceded. "Let's just find someone to give this gift to."

Michelle felt suddenly defeated; she had wanted to graciously acquiesce to his desire to stay. His concession to her now compelled her to leave.

The crown thinned out somewhat, it seemed as though the guests were all going to a different room of the banquet hall. Michelle saw the girl that the bride's twin had spoken to during the ceremony. She waylaid her with an impulsive hand on her arm.

"Please," she said, and was amazed that her voice did not sound at all out of the ordinary. "Do you know where I can leave a gift for the bride and groom?"

"No, I'm sorry, I don't," the girl answered, and was shocked into silence as she took a closer look at the woman with whom she was speaking.

Michelle could read her thoughts: *You look so much like Ahuva, and the girl to whom I was speaking before!*

"We have to leave now. Do you think you could point out one of the wedding party to me?"

"Oh, anyone in a mocha gown." She paused, and then in answer to Michelle's silent prayer, offered to take the envelope from her and hand it over.

"Thank you, thank you so much!" Michelle smiled and, as the girl walked in the direction of the mocha-clad women, ran from the room and out into the night. Tears streamed unchecked down her face. But they were tears of happiness this time, for although she was reluctant to admit it, the glimpse of her daughters had provided that closure Steven had assured her it would.

It wasn't only closure. She was surprised at the degree of comfort she took from having witnessed her daughter's wedding. Her daughter's Jewish wedding. With surprising clarity she brought up the memories she had buried for the past twenty-two years. While dealing with the adoption agency throughout her pregnancy, she had been insistent that her daughters be sent to Jewish homes. Even at their birth, through her fear and panic, she'd had the presence of mind to ensure this would be the case. *I didn't simply give them up,* Michelle thought proudly. *I paved the way for them to have a beautiful life. And I was right for doing so. I was without support; I would not have been able to bring them to where they are now. I certainly would not have been able to offer them such a meaningful marriage ceremony.*

She smiled contentedly. She had not lived the kind of life her daughter Ahuva did, but she was inexplicably pleased that Ahuva lived that life. And she was satisfied that it was due to her insistence that her children were raised Jewish.

Michelle turned to her husband. "Thank you."

*   *   *

Rachel walked back from the ceremony with Beth at her side. Beth was animatedly discussing what they had just witnessed, but Rachel did not hear a word. She was trying to process what she had seen, but the only coherent thought she had was the same she had had while watching her sister marry. With a sincerity that surprised her, Rachel prayed, *Please G-d, I want to get married also. And I want to have such a wedding.*

*   *   *

Miri was in her element after the *chuppah*. She had requested that the photographer take a picture of Rivky and herself with the rest of their old Bais Yaakov class. Miri had tracked down every girl — including Shiffy Schneider whom no one had ever had anything to do with — and invited them all. She was excited to be hostess at this upscale reunion. Well, semi-hostess, but she did not give that another thought.

*   *   *

Rachel and Beth followed the crowd to where the wedding dinner was served, and were pleasantly surprised to find they were seated at the table of the girl they'd spoken to at the ceremony. They looked around, marveling at everything — the barrier between the men and ladies, the dinner music which was so unlike what they were used to, the way everyone was dressed, and the fact that there so many children at the wedding. In time, the music started up again and, suspending all judgment, they eagerly turned to see what would happen next. They watched as the women formed two lines, waving decorative arches in the air. The music stopped, then started again, and the doors opened to allow Ahuva to fly through the arches into the waiting arms of her mother.

Feet tapping to the beat, Rachel watched fascinated as the women crowded around Ahuva. She stood up to get a better view as the bride danced with her guests. It was so *different* than what she was used to. She had danced at many parties — bar and bat mitzvahs when she was younger, proms and graduation parties, even a couple of weddings — but this kind of dancing was totally out of her experience. She thought about how she would feel, dancing with a crowd of women at her own wedding, and she wasn't sure. Yet the women here seemed so happy. They didn't seem to be missing anything. On the contrary, they danced unselfconsciously, seemingly wanting nothing but to rejoice with the bride.

Rachel was shaken out of her reverie by a tap on the shoulder. Irritated at the interruption, she turned to find Ahuva's mother standing next to her. "This is really beautiful. I'm so glad I came," she said. "Come, Rachel," Mrs. Steinhardt invited, holding out her hand, "Ahuva would like to dance with you." Surprised and flattered, Rachel followed Ahuva's mother.

Miri watched as Ahuva smiled to her mother and took Rachel Bergmann's hand. As they slowly turned round and round, Miri stared in shock, a bitter taste in her mouth. *We can't exactly walk around with a sign that says 'It is not Ahuva,' can we?* The words echoed in her head, mocking. *Guess we can,* she thought grimly. And then, *The important thing is that you know you are doing the right thing,* Shmuely's voice rang in her mind. *You can't worry about what other people think.* It would be a lesson well-taken, even if learned from her daughter-in-law. *I was going to say that we should learn from our own daughter. She had a difficult decision to make, but she made the right choice, despite what others would say about her husband joining the workforce.* Shmuely's words echoed in her mind. Miri watched as Ahuva signaled to the photographer, and then she turned resolutely and gathered Avigail to dance.

Ahuva and Rachel turned slowly round in a circle. "Thank you so much for coming," the bride said. "It really means a lot to me. You know you're my only blood relative in the room."

"Thank you for inviting me. And for reaching out to me. You look beautiful. You should always be this happy."

The twins smiled, and Ahuva turned to signal the photographer. "Let me give you a *berachah*," Ahuva said after their picture was taken. Rachel looked at her, unsure of what that was. "Don't worry, it's a good thing," Ahuva laughed, and she leaned close so only Rachel could hear her words. "You should have lots of *berachah* and *hatzlachah* and we should share in *simchahs* together." Rachel understood just about every other word, but the sincerity in Ahuva's voice and the pressure of her hands brought tears to Rachel's eyes.

Ahuva gave her a hug, and touched and a bit overwhelmed, Rachel moved out of the circle of happy dancers and back towards her table where she would sit and watch.

*   *   *

"She's gonna forget," Mindy told Faigy cynically.

"Why do you think so? When did she ever forget about me or you?"

"Yeah, but this is her *wedding*. You should hear how my sisters talk about their weddings. They say they don't remember a thing."

"Well, I won't let her forget. You'll see."

They needn't have worried. As the tenth grade class gathered in a circle around Ahuva, she signaled to Mindy and Faigy and pulled them into the middle. "Thanks for coming," she told the girls whose faces were flushed with excitement. Ahuva danced with other students too, but the duo had had the unique status of being *first.*

*   *   *

Baila Cohen arrived at the hall, breathless. She was not able to stay for the whole wedding, but there was no way she was going to miss giving a personal *mazal tov* to the girl she felt was her savior. She ran into the circle of dancers and saw that she had arrived just in time, for the group of girls from her *kallah* class was dancing together with Ahuva. She pushed her way into the middle and Ahuva grabbed her hands. "Pretty soon this will be you," Ahuva said.

"Give me a *berachah*," Baila answered. "I need some good ones so I can practice giving them myself."

"Well, you should be as happy as I am. And your life should be filled with *berachah*. And of course, a big *refuah sheleimah* to your brother."

Baila's eyes filled with tears. They were tears of happiness, for Ahuva and for herself who would be standing under the *chuppah* in just a few weeks — with her trousseau intact. And they were tears of appreciation; she should have known that Ahuva would not forget about her and her predicaments. No doubt Ahuva was behind that "raffle" she and her mother and sisters had won for free custom gowns. Finally, they were tears of *tefillah*; that she should always be this happy, and that Chaim Meir should indeed merit a *refuah sheleimah.*

*   *   *

Rachel couldn't pull herself away from the wedding, and though Beth had gotten bored a short time after the meal, she refused to leave. "No, I want to see everything." They watched as Ahuva danced with what seemed to be hundreds of women. She never tired, and those around her never tired. At one point, Rachel was pulled into the circle by a guest, and rather than resisting, Rachel took Beth's hand and the two of them joined the dancers. The music and this form of dancing were strange, but the joy felt natural. It was real, and it was contagious.

Rachel felt another tug on her hands, and found herself in the middle with Ahuva once more, this time together with Beth. "I'm so glad you're still here," the bride said. "I take it you're enjoying yourself?"

"Oh, yes!" Rachel responded, and Beth, still not sure she approved of Rachel's continued pleasure in so foreign a scene, just smiled.

"Can I meet the groom?" Rachel asked. "Is that allowed?"

Ahuva looked startled, and Rachel knew she had made a faux pas. Obviously, meeting the groom was not done. But Ahuva regained her composure and said to her sister, "Sure. After this dance there'll be *bentching,* that is, Grace after Meals. Come up to the head table then, and I'll introduce you."

Ahuva's new sisters-in-law formed a circle around her and she gracefully disengaged herself from Rachel and Beth and joined them. Rachel and Beth moved back to the crowd.

Rachel was curious about the Grace after Meals and stayed until the end. She didn't go up to the head table, though. There would be time enough to meet Ahuva's new husband. Her relationship with her sister was only just beginning.

Epilogue

THE LAST DAY OF *sheva berachos* was drawing to a close, and Moshe and Ahuva were in their apartment looking at the wedding pictures Michal had already developed. They were seated at the dining room table Dovid Steinhardt had specially made for his only daughter. Ahuva could not focus on the pictures. She felt she needed to pinch herself awake. The whole past week, starting with her wedding, seemed like a dream. Was that really her in a *shaitel*? Was she the *kallah* being praised at *sheva berachos?* One of Moshe's *rabbe'im* had tried to wish her *mazal tov* last night; he addressed her as "Mrs. Friedman" and Ahuva had not turned around to acknowledge his *berachos*. She had hardly heard him, the way one does not respond to someone else's name. Ahuva smiled at the memory. She had practiced the sound of her new name many times. Her new *siddur* had it embossed in gold lettering, but she knew it would be a while until she truly thought of herself as Ahuva Friedman. In the meantime, she pinched herself again. *It's indecent to be so happy,* she thought.

Ahuva snapped out of her reverie as she heard Moshe's voice. "I never saw this picture before!" he exclaimed. "She really does look like you, you know."

Ahuva took the picture from her husband and saw herself standing next to her twin sister, twin smiles on their faces. "I guess. She was supposed to meet you, I told you. She asked me if I could introduce her, but she left early."

"I hear. But you'll invite her over sometime. I'm sure I'll meet her."

They were interrupted by a knock. Ahuva opened the door to find her new sister-in-law Avigail, standing on the threshold, with tantalizing aromas escaping from the steaming container in her hands.

"Thank you, Avigail!" Ahuva said. Moshe came to the door as well, "Do you want to come in and see the pictures?" he asked his sister.

Avigail shook her head. "I'd love to, but the kids are in the car." She turned to leave. Oh," Avigail remembered suddenly, "Here are some envelopes from the *chasunah* that I forgot to give you."

As Ahuva set the table for the first supper she and her new husband would be sharing alone, Moshe opened the envelopes and called out the names of their benefactors. "Keep them in the envelopes, okay, Moshe?" she called to him. "I want to make sure I have everything organized for the thank-you notes."

"Come here, Ahuva. Look at this one." He sounded awestruck.

Ahuva walked over to where he was standing and looked over his shoulder. He showed her the card as a check fluttered to the floor, unheeded. "Take a look," he whispered. It was a conventional Hallmark card wishing them joy as they began their life together. And underneath the printed words was a handwritten message:

You looked beautiful, Ahuva.
Thank you for sharing your happiness with me.
Michelle

Made in the USA
Middletown, DE
09 May 2022

65277123R00158